TERRAFORMING MARS

Mankind is on the brink of achieving a second planet to live on: Mars.

Vast corporations spend fortunes to compete to transform the Red Planet into an environment where humanity can thrive. The potential rewards are enormous, the risks colossal.

As the biosphere becomes habitable, immigration from Earth increases, and social and political pressures stress the already fierce corporate rivalry. While scientific advances are daily miracles, not everyone is working toward the same future.

In a savage place like Mars, the smallest error can be lethal.

T0064956

BY THE SAME AUTHOR

FREELANCER
Traitor's Code
Prince's Mission
Assassin

PERCEIVERS
Mind Secrets
Mind Control
Mind Evolution
Mind Power

THE MAGICAL COMEDIES (as Lucy Shea)
If Wishes Were Husbands
Fairy Nuff
Women in a Spin

NON-FICTION
The Making of Judge Dredd (with David Chute and Charles M Lippincott)
Stasis Leaked: The Unofficial Behind the Scenes Guide to Red Dwarf
Babylon 5: Season by Season One
Babylon 5: Season by Season Two
Babylon 5: Season by Season Three
Babylon 5: Season by Season Four
Babylon 5: Season by Season Five

IN THE SHADOW OF DEIMOS

JANE KILLICK

First published by Aconyte Books in 2021

ISBN 978 1 83908 086 9

Ebook ISBN 978 1 83908 087 6

Cover art by René Aigner

Distributed in North America by Simon & Schuster Inc, New York, USA

Printed in the United States of America

9 8 7 6 5 4 3 2 1

ACONYTE BOOKS

An imprint of Asmodee Entertainment Ltd

Mercury House, Shipstones Business Centre

North Gate, Nottingham NG7 7FN, UK

aconytebooks.com // twitter.com/aconytebooks

CHAPTER ONE

Martian dirt crunched under Luka's boot as he took his first step onto the planet that was to be his new home. After another step, he was finally free of the landing vehicle and paused a moment to feel the solidity of Mars beneath his feet. It was good to be heavy again. The gravity was not much more than a third of Earth's, but after six months floating in the near weightlessness of a spacecraft its presence was reassuring.

Turning away from the landing vehicle, Luka looked out across the vast, majestic landscape of the untamed planet. The rusty, red dirt stretched as far as the horizon to meet a sky tinged with pink by the dust in the thin, unbreathable atmosphere. In the distance to his left, the triple mountain peaks of Tharsis Montes reached up to touch the small, bright, white disc of the sun, while what felt like less than a kilometer to his right the ground fell away into the canyons of Noctis Labyrinthus. The enormity of the expanse ahead of him was almost frightening after the confines of his journey, and the quickness of his breath echoed inside his helmet.

Because Mars was not only beautiful, it was also dangerous. Without his rad-suit, Luka would freeze in average temperatures of minus thirty, suffocate in air with almost zero percent oxygen, and eventually succumb to the effects of cosmic and solar radiation.

Luka walked further from the ladder and almost stumbled in gravity he wasn't used to as the next migrant descended from the landing vehicle. Luka, like the other forty-nine people who had left Earth with him, had turned his back on the planet where he was born to seek out a new life. Most of them believed the advertising which hailed the migrants as pioneers taking the chance to grasp exciting opportunities in the new frontier. Even if it meant the only way to afford their passage was to sign up as indentured labor for the ThorGate corporation. But for Luka, it was the chance to leave behind the pain of his life on Earth. The overpopulated, polluted, blue-green planet was the place where his family died and turning his back on that was the only way he felt he could survive.

"Welcome to Mars!" came a woman's voice over the speaker inside his helmet.

He looked around and, from the way the other migrants were doing the same, he knew that she was broadcasting to them all on their team channel.

"My name is Anita Andreassen," came the voice again, in a Norwegian accent. "You can see me over here with the flags."

Standing a little apart from Luka's fellow confused travelers, all in identical white rad-suits, was a suited figure waving two triangle flags like someone guiding an aircraft into land. Each flag was printed with a lightning symbol flashing through a blue and red depiction of a doorway with sliding doors which were the elements of the ThorGate logo.

"One of the things you'll learn on Mars is that everyone looks the same in a rad-suit," she continued, lowering the flags as all the migrants seemed to have worked out where the voice was coming from. "We'll get you settled in to your habitat soon, but I know that you'll be keen to have a look around and stretch your legs after the journey. Please go slow. It takes a while to get used to the gravity and the closeness of the horizon. Also, make an effort to look at where you're walking. You might not realize how restrictive the view is out of your helmet until you kick a rock you didn't see and fall over. We've all done it, so if it happens to you don't be embarrassed.

"Anyway, I'm sure you've heard all the safety briefings so many times on the journey that you can recite them in your sleep. So, take a few minutes to look around – it's a view you'll get used to, but never get tired of – then we'll board the bus to your habitat where a special welcome meal is waiting for you."

Anita pointed to her left where the "bus" was waiting. It was more like a military vehicle than the sort of bus Luka used to take to school when he was a child in Cologne. It had six, fat, off-road wheels, high sides dusted with particles of red Martian soil and windshields at the front and the rear.

"What's that?" A male voice came over Luka's helmet speaker. It took him a moment to realize that Anders, one of the other migrants, had turned on his communicator to broadcast to them all. He pointed up into the sky.

Luka raised his head and saw, against the pink backdrop, a pinprick of light as bright as the sun.

"That must be the asteroid," said Anita. "A little bit earlier than I thought, but don't worry, the guidance system will bring it down at a safe distance. Although, asteroid crashes are best viewed from inside, so let's get you all on the bus."

The migrants around him didn't move. They were mesmerized by the light as it became larger and brighter. The ball of fire streaked through the sky with a plume of gas trailing behind it. The more Luka stared, the more the fiery missile seemed to have two tails. Luka blinked to clear his vision and, when he looked again, he was sure there were two objects hurtling through the atmosphere.

"It's coming towards us!" shouted Anders, over the comms.

With terror, Luka realized his fellow migrant was right. There were two fireballs. One sailing overhead like a shooting star, the other cutting a blazing path towards them.

"On the bus so we can get to the habitat," said Anita, with a hint of concern in her voice.

Some of the migrants stumbled towards the bus, but others were still mesmerized by the falling asteroid. More had turned on their comms to broadcast generally, and the sounds of panic in several different languages reached Luka's ears. His beating heart was telling him to run, but in the rad-suit and the unfamiliar Martian gravity he feared he wouldn't be quick enough and might fall. The migrant next to him dropped to the ground like a soldier taking cover under enemy fire. Luka took one last look at the flaming asteroid – now so large that it blotted out the rest of the sky – and ducked down to do the same. Instinct caused his knees to buckle, and he landed on all fours.

Dust blew up all around him as the space rock shot past. Heat from the fire passed over him and the breeze from the asteroid's wake unsettled the thin Martian atmosphere. Puffs of vapor from Luka's fast, relieved breath briefly formed on the inside of his visor before they were cleared by the ventilation system of his suit.

The asteroid disappeared less than a kilometer away and fell into the nearest canyon of Noctis Labyrinthus. Luka didn't see it crash, but he felt the tremor ripple through the ground and tensed his muscles to steady himself. Above him, a white contrail hung in the sky, like a witness to the rock's trajectory, pointing into the chasm where a cloud of red dust had been thrown up by the crash.

Anita's voice called out across the cacophony of amazed, scared, and confused voices clogging up the team's comms. "The asteroid was supposed to crash a long way from here. I don't know what happened. Stay here while I go check what damage has been done."

She ran to the bus, using the half-hopping method that people who live on Mars had developed, and dropped her flags at the hatchway. Climbing on board, she promised to return.

But, as Luka watched the bus leave with its fat wheels kicking up dust, he had the horrible feeling that they had been abandoned.

CHAPTER TWO

Julie stood at the window of her office and watched the cloud of dust rise up against the horizon as the asteroid slammed itself into the bedrock of Mars. The kinetic energy of such an impact would be enough to heat the ground and cause it to radiate warmth for many centuries. It was a crude but effective method of terraforming that, one day, would play its small role in making the globe habitable by humans.

Even so, she cursed the maverick chief executive of CrediCor corporation for the flamboyant way he did things. Multibillionaire Bard Hunter was so full of himself that he liked to hurl asteroids at the planet in full view of all human settlers, rather than away from the equator or on the other side of Mars. The Terraforming Committee, so eager to encourage him to contribute his own fortune to the enterprise, entertained his whims without question. Just thinking about it made Julie's hands clench into fists.

It would never have happened when she was in charge. But that was all taken away from her in 2315 when the World Government invited corporations to play an official part in terraforming Mars and lured them into the project with universal tax funding. That was the moment that she, as the head of the United Nations Mars Initiative, found she had to fight for resources alongside all the other organizations on the planet. Officially, UNMI's projects had favored status when they put their terraforming proposals forward for approval. In reality, UNMI's status didn't make up for the business acumen and investment the other corporations had to offer.

So, she cursed Bard Hunter and all he represented in the knowledge that today's asteroid crash would be tomorrow's dust accumulation: on their solar panel arrays, the city's roof, and the dirt tracks which were the closest thing they had to roads on Mars.

The sound of rapid knocking on her office door caused Julie to turn from the view. Kareem, without waiting for a response, barged in. Her deputy appeared flustered. He had swept back his jet-black hair so many times that the grease from his palm made it sheen and his bare chin, where he had recently shaved off his beard, seemed to exacerbate his worried expression.

"Have you seen the asteroid?" His usual quiet and reserved English accent made his concern sound even more alarming.

"I saw it." Julie glanced back at the window where the crash site was a haze of dust.

"You're not watching ICN?" Kareem said.

"I'm perfectly capable of watching an asteroid crash without some idiot commentator at Interplanetary Cinematics telling me what I'm seeing."

"Then you *didn't* see it!" said Kareem. After all their time working closely together, he'd seemed to have gotten used to Julie's particular brand of sarcasm. He looked over at the view of Mars. "Window, switch to ICN."

The image on Julie's window, which was actually a live stream from a camera on the outside of Tharsis City, switched to a different Martian landscape. This view had the subtle logo of Interplanetary Cinematics News in the top right-hand corner and the words asteroid crash emblazoned across the bottom. The feed was from a camera looking at a different part of Mars which Julie recognized as out towards Noctis Labyrinthus. The familiar vista appeared as it always did, with the red dirt stretching out across the Tharsis upland and the mountains rising in the distance. But in the middle of the image, was the white wisp of a contrail and the haze of dust slowly dispersing into the sky like a trail of smoke from a campfire.

The sound of an excited commentator burbled out of the speakers: "…no idea what, if any, damage has been done. We're also still waiting for any word from CrediCor…"

"Window, sound off!" Julie ordered and the commentator abruptly shut up. She frowned at her colleague. "Kareem, what's going on? I saw the asteroid crash. It came down exactly where it was supposed to."

"The main piece did, but it must have splintered on entry because a piece broke off and came down over there." He pointed at the image on the window.

"Isn't that near ThorGate's new construction site?" asked Julie.

"Yeah," said Kareem, rubbing the point of his chin. He grinned at her. "Want to take a look?"

She knew they shouldn't, it really wasn't any of UNMI's business. But Kareem's curiosity was infectious.

"Let's take a rover," she said.

The asteroid was so large and had struck the canyon with such force that it acted like a missile, creating a path of devastation through the deep valley. Most of the space rock had shattered into rubble on impact, but several large pieces had survived to lodge themselves at the base of the five kilometer deep channel. It was still possible to see where the pieces had been blackened by the heat of its searing descent through Mars' carbon dioxide atmosphere and where they had broken. The light gray material of the inner asteroid contrasted against the red of the planet.

Julie watched it all on one of the screens of ThorGate's mobile monitoring stations, which had been brought within a few meters of the canyon. An observation robot had been sent down the slope and was relaying pictures to a cluster of people in rad-suits. Kareem watched by Julie's side, occasionally stepping from left to right to see past the helmets of people who had more right to be there than they did.

"Is that a piece of metal?" he said over their private comms channel as he pointed at the screen.

Jutting out of the rubble, Julie could see a twisted piece of something silvery which could be steel but was most likely magnesium. Strong, light, and abundant on Mars, magnesium was cheap and efficient to find on the planet and didn't risk oxidization. She stared, dreading what that small scrap of debris meant.

"It must be from ThorGate's research station," she said, stating the fact without allowing emotion to seep into her voice. "The one which caused all that controversy when they proposed building it last year, remember? All the other corporations lobbied against allowing ThorGate to set it up in such a prime location."

"Were people stationed there?" asked Kareem in concern.

She nodded, recalling the uncomfortable statistics she'd once read in a report. "An initial team was supposed to go in to set up, as far as I remember. After that, it was due to accommodate twenty, maybe thirty scientists."

He swore.

Julie looked closer and she saw more evidence of human habitation crushed beneath the rubble. If the asteroid had made a direct hit, the station would have been completely obliterated by the force of its missile-like strike, but it appeared to have been on the edge of the impact zone. Some remnants of the building might have survived, but anyone inside would almost instantly have been killed. They might have experienced a moment of terror before they were either crushed by the asteroid or made to suffocate and freeze to death if they were exposed to the unforgiving Martian atmosphere.

She turned from the image on the screen and tried to push the unpleasant thought from her mind.

Further down the ridge, a news crew from Interplanetary

Cinematics with the yellow, red and black logo of their corporation emblazoned on the back of their rad-suits, was capturing footage from every angle possible on that side of the canyon. Back at Tharsis City, Julie was used to seeing a single operator remotely controlling several HoverCams in a room, but out on the Martian surface the thin air meant flying something even as light as a camera required helicopter blades more than a meter wide which could be dangerous, especially if the required personnel for safety backup and maintenance wasn't on scene yet, so each camera had to be handheld by an individual person. Personally, Julie thought it was the practice of ICN to make reporting more personal for viewers.

Others without a corporation logo on their backs milled around the canyon like confused tourists, some of them perilously close to the edge and leaning over to get a closer look. From what she could tell, they were the migrants who were due to build the nearby city and had landed shortly before the asteroid crash. One woman, who seemed to know what she was doing, went down the line telling everyone across the general comms channel to move back. By the sound of her accent, it was likely she was part of the ThorGate corporation which proudly maintained its Nordic roots. As she turned, Julie caught a glimpse of her face through the bubble of her helmet and recognized her as Anita Andreassen, the corporation's Head of Martian Projects.

"I think we should go," said Kareem over their private comm channel. "Before they find any bodies. That's not an image I want to have in my memory."

"You're probably right." She was about to head back to the rover when the news crew began running over to where another rover was driving up to the throng of parked vehicles.

"What's going on?" Julie asked.

"No idea," said Kareem as they watched the camera operators gather around the rover's hatchway.

The hatch slid sideways, creating an opening in the body of the rover revealing a rad-suited figure.

"Rufus, can I get your reaction?" said an eager voice over the general comms.

Immediately, Julie knew who it was who had attracted the news crew's attention. Rufus Oladepo was the Chair of the Terraforming Committee and, therefore, the closest thing Mars had to a head of state.

"When I've had a chance to look around," came Rufus's recognizable booming voice in response. He had what many termed an "international" accent with hints of American, South African, and Nigerian reflecting the cross-cultural world of politics in which he operated.

Rufus stepped out of the rover and strode purposefully across the plain. Two camera operators chased after him and two others ran backwards out in front, pointing their cameras towards him and trying not to fall over. Julie realized he was heading directly to the part of the ridge which she and Kareem had selected as an appropriate vantage point. Deciding she needed to leave before they got caught up in the media circus, she began to step away. But Rufus had already spotted her.

"Julie Outerbridge!" he declared as he closed in on her position. "What interest has UNMI in this crash?"

Julie accessed the controls on the arm of her rad-suit so she, like him, was broadcasting on the general channel. "Just seeing if we can help," she said, aware that everyone around her, including the news crew, was listening. "UNMI has been operating on Mars for longer than most corporations and we have a great deal of expertise."

"Commendable," said Rufus, but his expression through the bubble of his helmet, hidden from the cameras, revealed he remained suspicious.

Just as Julie remained suspicious of him.

The attention of everyone out on the ridge was drawn to Rufus and they swarmed around his position, meaning Julie could no longer get away without it being obvious. She shot a look across at Kareem who shook his head to suggest they would have to stay.

Rufus peered over the edge to where the person on the safety line had successfully negotiated the slope of the canyon to reach the bottom. He maintained a safe distance and turned to the cameras so he stood tall within the dramatic landscape of Mars.

"Like everyone," he began, "I was horrified to hear of the asteroid disaster which occurred this morning. It was especially disturbing to learn that the fragment crashed here at the site of ThorGate's new project to build Noctis City. By some miracle, no one was stationed at the research unit at the bottom of this canyon when the asteroid hit. If they had been, the tragedy could have been much worse."

Julie's own sense of relief was echoed in the audible sigh of those around her who were still broadcasting over the general comms.

"But, nevertheless," Rufus continued. "This is something which should never have happened. It is my intention–"

"I've found something!" yelled a young, male voice, cutting across Rufus's speech. It was one member of the team who had remained clustered around the screen, which showed the observer robot's camera stream, while everyone else was listening to the Chair of the Terraforming Committee.

"What is it?" came Anita's voice. She hurried over with bounding strides.

"I think I can see something... human," said the man with quiet concern.

A sick feeling welled up in Julie's stomach as she thought about the horrific death the person must have suffered.

"Are you sure?" said Rufus, pushing his way past the onlookers to stand directly in front of the screen. "I have it on good authority that no one was there."

"I'm afraid I am certain," said the man. "It's an arm. I think it's wearing a WristTab."

"Can you access it remotely?" said Rufus. "Does your robot have that capability?"

"If the WristTab's not completely smashed," the young man replied.

The tension increased as they waited and watched the screen to find out. Or, perhaps, it was only in Julie's imagination that everyone around her was nervous. Cocooned in her rad-suit with only a few people broadcasting across the general comms channel, there really wasn't any way to tell. The observational robot pivoted and zeroed in on the flickering WristTab, but not enough to see anything. The young man concentrated his efforts on the screen's mechanics to see what information the WristTab could offer.

"OK," said the man. "There's some residual power. Not enough to pull any data, but it's still possible to read the identifying tag. The WristTab belongs to Giovanni Lupo."

A female scream ripped across the comms and Anita clasped her gloved hands to the bubble of her helmet. She staggered sideways with the weight of the news and someone standing next to her had to grab her arm to stop her from falling. "Gianni? No!" Her grief-stricken cries echoed terrifyingly through every helmet in the vicinity before they were cut off as she switched her comms away.

The same rad-suited figure who had taken her arm led her away from the canyon. A shocked silence, punctuated by the occasional hiss of static, filled their helmets.

Rufus turned from the scene of devastation and seemed to become taller as he raised his chest in a defiant pose. The camera operators from the news crew knew what this meant and two of them scuttled back to focus on him, while their colleagues maintained their sights on Anita's private moment.

"It is with great sadness that we learn of the death of Giovanni Lupo," said Rufus. "His loss will be felt deeply by every Martian who knew him and worked with him, and also by friends and family back on Earth. This is a tragedy that should not have happened, and I want to assure you that this incident will be fully investigated and lessons learned so we never have to experience such an awful event again."

"Who's going to investigate?" asked someone from the news crew.

"That is a good question," said Rufus. He paused as he apparently considered his answer. "It is my belief that we need someone independent of the Terraforming Committee. And clearly independent of ThorGate who experienced the tragedy and CrediCor whose asteroid is at the heart of this disaster. It also needs to be someone who has the confidence of the whole of Mars. Which is why–"

Rufus turned to his side and took slow and careful steps in Julie's direction. Her stomach twisted as she feared what was about to happen.

"–someone from the United Nations Mars Initiative is the obvious choice," he continued. "Someone known and trusted by both Mars and Earth. I am humbled to announce that Julie Outerbridge has accepted that role."

Rufus slapped his arm across Julie's shoulders above her air tank and her whole body shuddered. ICN cameras swiveled to focus on her, and she found herself staring down the lenses of multiple recording devices. She forced a smile, knowing the clear bubble of her helmet offered no protection from their prying gaze.

Inside, she was absolutely furious.

CHAPTER THREE

The day after the asteroid crash, Luka stood on the ridge
of Noctis Labyrinthus and looked down into the deep
canyon where a team of ThorGate workers and robots were
clearing away rubble to recover what was left of Giovanni
Lupo's body. They were so far away at the bottom of the
valley that all he could really see was a cloud of dust, but
it made him reflect on how lucky he was not to have been
one of the asteroid's victims. If it had descended just a few
meters lower, if he and his fellow migrant workers had been
standing closer to Noctis Labyrinthus, the asteroid would
have struck them like a bowling ball, running them down as
if they were a collection of helpless skittles.

"Hey you! Whatsyourname!"

Luka turned to see the workforce supervisor, a surly man
named Alvar Vertanen, was standing right next to him,
glaring so hard through the bubble of his helmet that the
contortions of his face made his moustache bristle.

"Luka Schäfer," said Luka. It was going to take him a while

to get used to not hearing people creep up on him when they were wearing rad-suits on the Martian surface.

"We didn't bring you here to be a tourist. Stop admiring the view and get on with your work."

Al Vertanen walked off to where a team of other migrants were assembling a collection of building materials on the ridge, taking his bristling moustache with him.

The migrants had been engaged by ThorGate to build a great city at the most coveted part of Noctis Labyrinthus. The network of canyons, as long as the River Rhine and formed by volcanic activity in the planet's ancient past, were a valuable part of Mars' real estate. Water ice would often form as frost in the shadows of its deep valleys, and the canyons provided ease of access to underground sources of water and geothermal power. The building, to be called Noctis City, would have unique access to Valles Marineris, a deeper and more extensive system of ravines which stretched across a fifth of the Martian equator. One day, when humans had terraformed the planet, those ravines would be filled with liquid water to create a majestic system of oceans teaming with aquatic life. Noctis City would stand in prime position at the head of the waters, more strategic than even the Suez Canal which had brought nations to the brink of war on Earth more than three hundred and fifty years before.

Luka had repeatedly seen the visualizations of what the area would look like in the future and, for once, he didn't think they were an exaggeration. When Noctis City was finished, it would be a magnificent landmark on the Martian surface. Although, from where he stood at the edge of the canyon, the reality in 2316 was a collection of building materials and confused laborers trying to get to grips with their work at the same time as adjusting to conditions on Mars.

Luka joined them as they assisted colleagues in building a series of platforms at strategic places down the long steep slope of the canyon. At five kilometers, it was an unfathomable distance for someone who had grown up on Earth to imagine. If the route to the bottom had been a flat road back home, it would have taken up to an hour to walk that distance. In Noctis Labyrinthus, where there was no road and the terrain was at a forty-five degree angle, it was a longer and more difficult journey. So, the platforms would be used as bases from where the laborers could work. In the initial phase of construction, they would drill thousands of magnesium poles into the side to form the first foundations of the city. Nestled into the slope, it would have a degree of protection from the extreme conditions on Mars.

Peering over the dizzying edge, he could see ten rad-suited figures standing precariously on the slope some twenty meters down looking like mountain climbers in harnesses attached to safety lines on the top of the ridge. They had made an excellent start, with a semi-constructed platform jutting out from the side like a balcony on a tall building and dozens of poles drilled into the rock to be the beginnings of scaffolding. Very soon, they would run out of poles, and that was the reason Luka was there.

He selected to broadcast over the team's comms. "This is Luka on the top of the ridge. I'm ready to accept the first delivery of materials."

"Understood," said one of Luka's colleagues, a man he had traveled with called Mike Cheng. "We'll load them up."

A pile of magnesium poles was waiting next to a mobile crane. The crane itself was a robust and versatile machine which could be programmed to carry out repetitive tasks automatically, but on this occasion was controlled by a human operator who sat in an open cab.

Mike and another rad-suited figure produced a piece of fine woven netting as large as a bedsheet which they lay on the ground next to the poles and loaded with the metal struts until there was a small pile. The four corners of the netting were then attached to a steel chain hanging from a crane to form a sling.

"Everyone clear!" said Mike while he and his colleague stepped back from the netted parcel. "Ready to lift."

The jib of the crane raised the sling into the air. Luka imagined the sound of the metal poles clinking together as they shifted their position within the netting. He had to imagine it because the thin Martian atmosphere carried virtually no sound.

With the sling swinging slightly, the crane made its way to where Luka stood. He supervised as the crane lowered the poles to the ground. He detached the netting from the hook at the end of the crane and, with the help of three others, they unloaded the magnesium before sending the crane and the netting back to collect some more.

It was unexpectedly cumbersome working in the rad-suit. His field of vision was restricted in the helmet, and he sweated more than he thought he would in the enclosed, regulated environment. Wearing it was simply more difficult than he had imagined and was certainly more awkward than he had experienced during his initial training. Not that he had received much training on Earth before taking the lunar shuttle and departing the Moon for Mars. ThorGate had been in an inordinate rush to recruit and dispatch its construction workforce to meet the launch window after the World Government made its terraforming announcement, and it was fair to say, a few corners had been cut.

Either way, it was exactly the kind of work Luka wanted. It kept his mind from thinking about what he'd lost back on Earth.

With the next delivery of poles, Luka saw an opportunity to speed up the process for the workers in the canyon and switched to broadcast over the general comms channel. "This is Luka up on the ridge. Is the team on the slope ready to accept some more poles down where you're working?"

"Uh, yeah," said a man with a strong French accent who Luka recognized as Paul Remy, a migrant who had come to Mars later in life than many and who brought with him a wealth of construction experience from Earth. "We were going to winch them down as we needed them. What are you suggesting?"

"We could get the crane to drop the next batch directly to you. You're not that far down, I think it could just about reach."

"Yeah, that's a good idea. Rebecca, what do you think?"

Luka waited while the Frenchman privately discussed the idea with colleagues across his own team channel and came back to Luka for the go-ahead.

So, when the crane returned with a second net, it

maneuvered closer to the edge and Luka supervised as the jib arm jutted out over the drop and increased the length of the chain to slowly lower the collection of poles into the canyon. About two thirds of the way to where it needed to be, the net touched the rock face and Luka told the crane operator to stop. From there, Paul and the rest of the team were able to release the net and drag it to their semi-constructed platform where they unloaded the poles ready for use.

During the final few moments of unloading, the alarms on their suits warned that their oxygen was running low, and they needed to return to replenish their tanks. Luka was relieved, as he was exhausted and this signaled it was almost time for a break for all of them. The team hooked the empty net back onto the chain and the crane operator returned it to the top of the ridge. She then hopped out from the cab while Luka detached the net from where it dangled at head height.

About half the laborers joined the operator to take a break in the pressurized enclosure of the vehicle which had brought them from the habitat. Luka and a selection of the workers remained to secure the site and assist the team on the slope to return. Once that was done, they would follow to join the others in the habitat vehicle for a rest.

As the last person made it to the top of the ridge and removed the safety line from their harness, something darted across Luka's field of vision.

He turned and saw the crane swinging to the right with its chain dangling precariously from the jib. It cast a swift moving shadow like a bird swooping low. He thought, for a moment, that someone was playing a trick on him from inside the cab, but when he looked through the front windshield, he saw it was still empty.

The crane swung back again. Luka ducked on instinct as the chain lashed out above his head. Standing up straight again, he realized how close it had come to hitting him.

Someone, who was broadcasting over the general comms when they shouldn't, swore in a Scandinavian language Luka didn't understand. He spun to watch the crane seem to change direction, making any trajectory for the chain impossible to track.

"Look out! Look out!" cried another in English.

Rad-suited figures scattered, running awkwardly in the Martian gravity to get away from the crazed machine.

"Is someone operating it remotely?"

"Stop! Whoever's doing this – stop!"

The jib arm swung back again, flicking the chain out like a whip which struck out at one of the workers from the canyon. He went to duck, but his reaction was a moment too late. The tip of the chain smashed into his helmet.

Luka caught the brief glimpse of Paul's terrified face through the clear visor of his helmet as he was knocked backwards, slipped at the edge of the canyon, and tumbled down its rocky slope. Luka watched in horror as Paul's head bashed against one of the magnesium poles jutting out of the rock and he was only saved by landing onto the platform and grabbing onto the edge to stop him falling further. But he had a crack in his helmet and, as he rolled himself back to lay on the center of the platform, the white mist of oxygen-rich gas leaked out of the fissure. He slapped at its surface with the palms of his gloved hands in the hope of stemming the flow as his cries became thin and increasingly panicked in the escaping air.

"Hold on, Paul! We're coming, we're coming," Luka cried.

Several of his colleagues scrabbled down the canyon towards Paul, without wasting time to attach themselves to safety lines. Luka watched them – desperate to help but knowing they had far more expertise than him – as he feared he could be witnessing the second death on Mars in as many days.

It might have been three deaths if someone standing nearby hadn't grabbed his arm and pulled him from the path of the swinging chain which had returned to take another swipe at him. Its tip barely missed him, and he stood, breathing hard, as the crazed machine kept thrashing in front of him like a horse trying to throw its rider. It had to be stopped. Luka looked around, but the person who had pulled him out of the way was no longer there. He might not have the experience to save Paul, but he knew he had something else to offer that would help.

He realized if he didn't do something, nobody would.

Luka crouched low and scurried underneath the reach of the jib arm towards the empty cab. Hauling himself up into it, he sat in the operator's seat and stared at the unfamiliar controls. Two joy sticks were moving themselves on either side of a dusty computer screen filled with data. He quickly took in the information on power reserves, coordinates, and a whole other collection of graphs and numbers he didn't understand and knew he had no time to figure out. Beneath the screen, a row of dials and buttons probably did something very important, but he didn't understand what they did either and none of them were an obvious "off" switch.

He could figure it out though. He just had to rely on his old skills – those he'd left behind on Earth.

He tapped at the computer screen, preparing to troubleshoot. Nothing happened. It was only a display, not a touchscreen. He cursed himself for his Earth-based thinking. The particles in Mars dust were known to cling with static to any machinery around them and that meant touchscreens couldn't be used on the exposed surface. If he couldn't access the crane's systems through the computer screen, he would have to go to the heart of the controls.

Under the dashboard there should have been a shield to protect the electronics, but it was missing. The wires and circuit boards were covered in a film of Martian dust. He bent down to get a better look, but his helmet was too big to fit in the gap and it banged against the dashboard. Machine maintenance was supposed to be carried out in a pressurized environment, not out on the planet surface. He slipped off the operator's chair and maneuvered his body into the space as much as he possibly could and felt his way around the circuitry. Encumbered by the thickness of his gloves, he couldn't feel very much and yanked at anything he could get hold of. On his fifth attempt, he must have found the power cable as he pulled out a wire and the jib arm shuddered to a stop.

"It's stopped! It's stopped!" came a cry over the comms.

Luka relaxed back with a sigh of relief and clonked his helmet against the seat of the chair behind him. The controls were half hanging off from where he had pulled at them, and he decided to finish the job. He reached to pull the whole thing out from under the dashboard so it could be examined later.

He emerged out of the cab clutching the offending collection of electronics as three people climbed out of the canyon onto the ridge. In the center, relying on the other two either side of him to walk, was Paul with a strip of gray patch tape stuck across the front of his helmet. Behind him, one of his rescuers carried an emergency air canister attached to a line from his suit.

If it hadn't been for their quick thinking and expertise out on the unfamiliar Martian surface, it could have been very different. It was a stark reminder, as if Luka needed it, of how close they lived to death every single day and how they relied on each other for survival. The somber thought continued to ruminate in his mind as he followed them to the vehicle which would take them back to the habitat and to safety.

CHAPTER FOUR

Julie watched herself on ICN and wished someone had warned her that the news crew had been waiting for her outside UNMI headquarters. They caught that startled look in her eyes as she stepped into the street and was confronted by two HoverCams and a smiling reporter. Her hair, which she had recently shortened so her light brown strands streaked with blonde finished at the bottom of her ears, hadn't been brushed carefully in her rush that morning. Her skin was exceptionally pale and there were shadows under her eyes created by the overhead lighting. She looked, she had to admit, tired and stressed.

She remembered the reporter asking what she hoped to find in her investigation into the asteroid disaster and how she'd tried to respond in a noncommittal way which would fail to excite anyone watching. Looking at the footage on the window in front of her, she had at least achieved that. "It's early days yet," she watched herself say. "I have to speak to Rufus about the scale of the investigation first."

Indeed, she was watching the news feed while she sat outside of Rufus's office before having exactly that conversation. It had been a short walk from the UNMI offices on Main Street in Tharsis City down to the Terraforming Committee headquarters, where an officious woman had told her to sit in the reception area where the window was set to display ICN. She sat alone among the collection of low, upright armchairs upholstered in red, green, and brown fabric. Only occasionally did one of the Terraforming Committee staff walk by, glance over in her direction, and pretend not to be staring as they recognized her as the head of UNMI.

Julie ran her fingers through her hair in an attempt to brush it neater ahead of her meeting with Rufus. Meanwhile, the news report continued. It had, thankfully, moved away from pictures of Julie, and the reporter was speaking over footage of the downed asteroid. "Many commentators have expressed relief that more people weren't killed," he said. "Just one technician was at the research center at the time of the crash and none of the scientists who many people feared might have been stationed there. We caught up with Doctor David Kobayashi, one of those very scientists, and got his reaction."

The images on the window changed to show the outside of some sort of sports center. Julie didn't recognize it and assumed it was somewhere in Thor City, the complex ThorGate had built for its personnel. A man in white martial arts attire, who had that same startled look Julie had seen in herself, was stopped by the news crew as he approached the entrance.

"It's awful, absolutely awful," he told the ICN camera in a southwestern American accent, distinct from Julie's own Baltimore one. He was a handsome man, in his early thirties, with a fringe of black hair which he swept across his forehead. Although, under the attention of the news camera and after what must have been a stressful day, he looked completely washed out. "It could have been us. It could have been all of us."

"But you're still here for your martial arts class?" suggested the voice of the reporter, off camera.

"What else is there?" said Doctor Kobayashi. "The only thing you can do when you escape death is continue to live."

He turned away and walked into the sports center. The report continued to speculate on all the unanswered questions posed by the disaster, but Julie was still thinking about what the scientist had said. She found it chillingly profound.

Rufus emerged from his office and stood in the doorway, with the sense of calm authority he always seemed to carry. His tall, lithe body virtually filled the doorframe and his smooth dark skin seemed to glisten with health under the lights. Despite the weaker Martian gravity which didn't require people to be muscular, it was obvious he worked hard in the gym to maintain his strength.

"Sorry to keep you waiting, Julie," he said. "I had some urgent messages to send off to Earth. Please, come in."

Julie gave him a sideways glance as he stepped back to allow her inside. "I've just been watching myself bat away questions on the ICN feed," she said, allowing her anger to show in her voice.

"There's a lot of concern about the asteroid disaster, quite naturally." Rufus strode over to his desk, which lay at one end of the spacious room, and reclined into the padded fabric of his substantial office chair.

"But they're asking me about it, thanks to your stunt at the crash site."

"Are you referring to me asking you to lead the investigation?"

"Asking me wouldn't have been a problem. Deciding that I would agree and announcing it on the news without talking to me first is the problem."

She paced around Rufus's spacious office. It was an ostentatious room designed to reflect the status of the Chair of the Terraforming Committee, with a desk large enough to be a dining table and an informal area where two sofas gathered around a coffee table. Rufus lorded over it like a medieval king who was comfortable in his palace.

"Julie, why don't you sit down?"

"Because I'm too angry, that's why!"

Rufus sat upright in his chair and rested his elbows casually on the desk to give her his full attention. "If you didn't want to be involved in discovering what happened with the asteroid, why did you go to the crash site?"

"What sort of a question is that?" she replied, feeling like he was trying to manipulate her.

"A reasonable one," he retorted. "You have to accept that you're no longer in charge here. The Terraforming Committee was democratically elected and that gives me the right to make certain decisions without consultation. What I said to the ICN crew out at Noctis Labyrinthus is the truth: we need someone trusted and independent to carry out the investigation. I can think of no one better than you. You should take that as a compliment."

"You may not have needed to consult with the rest of the Committee, but you could have at least consulted with me."

"You're right. I apologize."

"And that's supposed me make me feel better?"

"That was my intention, yes," said Rufus. "Look, are you going to sit down and have a reasonable discussion or are you going to continue to pace around and make me feel dizzy?"

Julie grabbed the visitor's chair on the near side of the desk and dropped into it.

"Much better. Perhaps I can offer you a drink? I may have some coffee left from the last shipment from Earth."

"Is that supposed to be a bribe?"

"It's supposed to be an offer of coffee."

Julie sighed and sagged a little in her chair to calm herself. "You have to understand, Rufus, I have UNMI to run. You can't just give me another job to do at the same time. Our greenhouse gas emissions are behind schedule, the atmospheric pressure on Mars has barely increased since the terraforming announcement, and we need to be in a good position to put our proposals to the Terraforming Committee on the next funding round."

Rufus leaned even further over his desk. "I understand the pressures of your job, Julie, I do. But this has to be an independent investigation by someone without reproach. I apologize for thinking on my feet, but I saw you there and I knew you were the right person. I can't do it, I'm a Kelvinist.

Everyone knows our position on warming the planet first means we support CrediCor's asteroid program. No offense to your greenhouse gas operation, but it could be hundreds of years before a thicker atmosphere is able to hold onto enough heat to make Mars habitable. Even with those super things you're so keen on... the fluro whatsitsnames."

"Perfluorocarbons," said Julie. "Super greenhouse gases."

"Even with those things. The point is, I wouldn't be seen as impartial in an investigation. If we had a police force on Mars, maybe things would be different. I could merely hand everything over to them. But our security services are only personnel in uniform, they're not investigators. We need to find out what went wrong and why. Only then can we stop a similar disaster happening again. You may have been a spontaneous choice, Julie, but you were the right choice."

"What you're saying is, I can't say no."

"Your opportunity for that was at the crash site. You've effectively already said yes."

Julie thought about it for a moment. "Fine. I'll do it. But next time, I'd appreciate it if you speak to me before you broadcast it all over the solar system."

"Duly noted." He smiled and leaned back in his chair again. "You have my full support in this investigation."

Julie stood. "I'll hold you to that, Rufus."

Rufus grinned. "I'm sure you will."

CHAPTER FIVE

Luka scraped the final bit of his beef steak around the plate to scoop up the last of the gravy, brought it to his mouth and chewed on the tender protein. Less than a year ago, he would have thought his meal bland and unappetizing but, after six months on a spacecraft eating pre-packaged meals, he could appreciate what little taste it had. Not that the brown, artificially grown protein slice had been anywhere near a cow, but at least it made an effort.

He had managed to procure himself a table on his own in the communal space of the construction habitat which doubled as a recreation area and dining hall depending on the time of day. With almost all the fifty migrants in there at the same time, it was full of the chattering voices of colleagues. The whole habitat felt spacious after their journey to Mars in a cramped spaceship. He even had a private room, with his own bed, rather than having to get whatever sleep he could in a sling floating in the weightlessness of space.

The habitat had been constructed largely out of the Martian soil by robots programmed to build the structure to precise specifications. It would be their home for several years as they worked to construct and fit out Noctis City. There had been no room for them at ThorGate's main operational base, Thor City, which was in any case a considerable journey by rover or bus from the site.

With his prescribed calories consumed, Luka glanced at his WristTab which was showing a safety alert about the dangers of extreme radiation events. "In the event of a major solar flare," the message declared, "Mars will be subject to lockdown. All personnel must stay inside or return to–". He dismissed the message and made a mental note to delve into the settings at some point and shut the thing off.

Luka found the connector he had been looking for on the side of the WristTab and reached across the table to where he had left the hunk of electronics pulled from the crane. He dragged it closer to him, leaving behind a trail of Martian dust despite having made an effort to clean the thing in the airlock. Under the lights of the habitat, and without his rad-suit getting in the way, Luka was able to identify most of the disconnected wires and cables. He hesitated, knowing he should pull Alvar away from damage control to give him the electronic hunk, but his curiosity got the better of him. He plugged the data cable into his WristTab and downloaded all the surviving information to review. If something had gone wrong with its programming, he might be able to figure out what it was.

The sound of voices around him lessened and Luka looked up to see that Al Vertanen had entered and was heading for the center of the room. Without his helmet or the additional bulk of a rad-suit, he seemed a smaller man, but stocky, with the sort of build and demeanor which suggested he was not the type of person to pick a fight with.

"I just want to let you know–" he addressed the room, raising his voice until the last of the chatter subsided, "–that I've just come back from seeing Paul. He's fine. A little shook up, obviously, with some impressive bruises which are going to hurt for a while, but nothing broken. The medics can't find any sign of serious oxygen deprivation, so the breach in his helmet looks to have been relatively minor. But it could have been much worse if it hadn't been for the quick actions of Anders, Robert, and Morten…"

Applause rose up from the tables. Luka joined in as he saw everyone's gaze had shifted to a corner near the door where the faces of the three heroes of the hour were flushed with embarrassment.

"Some of you have asked me what went wrong with the crane," continued Al, "and my honest answer is that I don't know – *yet*. I promise you that it is being looked into. I know that, after today, I don't have to tell you to be careful out on the construction site. But I'm going to tell you anyway: watch out for yourselves and your colleagues. And remember Mars has more ways to kill you than Earth, OK?"

Murmurs and nods of agreement disseminated around the room, followed by the gradual return of chatter as Al left his position in the center of the floor and headed towards Luka.

"I believe you are owed a thank you as well," he said, grabbing hold of a chair and sitting opposite him at the table.

Luka, embarrassed, shrugged off the compliment and avoided Al's gaze. "I only cut the power to the crane."

"You did more than that, it seems." Al looked across at the dusty collection of electronics on the table. "Is there a reason you didn't give this to me right away?"

Luka expected the admonishment and tried to explain. "I'm sorry, I didn't know how to turn it off. I thought I would take a look at the code to see if there are any obvious errors, but I understand you need it." He offered it across the table, and Al slowly took it.

"I only came over to commend you for stepping in to do something. But also to say that Anita Andreassen would like to thank you in person – perhaps you can take this dusty collection of junk to her and explain what happened. There'll be transport waiting for you in the morning."

"Transport?" asked Luka.

Al chuckled. "You're not expected to walk all the way to Thor Town."

"I meant, she wants me to visit her?"

"Of course! Consider it an opportunity for a nice day out. Come and get this before you leave, OK?"

Luka approached Thor City across the Martian plain, peering past the head of his driver to see the view through the windshield. "Thor Town", as it was affectionately known, only accommodated up to around five hundred people. Like the migrant habitat, it was built from compacted Martian soil bricks which provided adequate shielding, but unlike the habitat, which was relatively small and unremarkable, it appeared to rise out of the ground like a series of red mountains on the horizon. Surrounding it were banks of a solar array which swiveled to track the sun as it moved through the sky, while the panels glinted like worshippers at the foot of the building.

Stepping out of the rover into the pressurized vehicle station, Luka smelled Thor Town's clinically clean air. Like everywhere he had been since he had left the spacecraft, he was breathing an artificial mix of oxygen and nitrogen extracted from nitrates in the soil and oxidized rock which was pumped into the environmental system. Filters removed extraneous carbon dioxide and trace elements so the hints of human odor, the smell of food, and the grease of machinery were taken away until the atmosphere was devoid of anything other than the gases needed to sustain human life.

The driver led Luka out into the main street that ran through the heart of the complex. It was almost like a little bit of humanity's ancestral home had been transplanted to the new frontier. Even the lighting had a yellow tint to mimic the color of sunlight on Earth. Lining the street were rows of buildings that reminded Luka of the apartments, offices, and shops that he might have walked past in one of the suburbs of Cologne. The designer had even gone to the lengths of putting windows in the façades of the buildings, despite them only opening out to another version of inside. There was no such thing as letting in some fresh air in Martian cities: only letting in some exactly-the-same air.

There was a person in a salon having their hair cut,

customers collecting pain medication from a pharmacy, and a shop selling luxury food. Luka found himself staring at a woman who was, in turn, staring at a single exquisite portion of cake made from soft, golden sponge which was displayed in the shop. It was small enough to fit into the palm of her hand. She was contemplating, no doubt, whether the experience of eating it would justify what was likely to be an exorbitant price. She was, Luka estimated, in her thirties, about the same age as him, but that was not the case for everyone he passed. A child no older than ten almost ran into him as an older boy – possibly his brother – chased after him. A man who had to be at least in his seventies caught Luka's eye as they passed each other and smiled a silent hello. Luka was so surprised, he only thought to return the smile at the last minute.

It was a short walk to Anita's office, located inside a giant structure at the end of the street. The building spread as high and as wide as the city enclosure itself and had a central door twice as large as was necessary for a person to walk through with the familiar ThorGate logo above.

The driver took Luka inside, squared everything with security and took him up two flights of stairs to Anita's office where he made his excuses and left.

Anita stood from her desk. "Luka Schäfer," she said and reached out a hand for him to shake. "I'm glad you could come."

It was the first time Luka had seen Anita Andreassen without her rad-suit. She was shorter and younger than him with light brown skin that gave her face a healthy color while her deep brown eyes suggested an assured intelligence.

"Is that the offending component from the homicidal crane?" she asked, looking down at where Luka was holding the computer hardware he had yanked from the machine.

He placed it on the desk. "Al said you might want to examine it."

"Why don't you sit down and we can talk about that."

Luka sat in the only other chair in the room and took the chance to have a proper look at the office. It was a sparse space dominated by Anita's desk where, interspersed between three computer screens, were a half-drunk glass of water, a stray fork, and a plate with the crumbs of something left on it. The room had no view out onto the street and instead used a computerized window opposite the door which displayed an as-live image of an Earth landscape, as if her office had been built overlooking one of the last rainforests.

Anita glanced down at the computer screen to her left before looking back across the desk at Luka. "Your file says you had a successful career on Earth programming industrial robots."

"That's right," said Luka.

"I thought you could tell me what might have gone wrong with the crane." She nodded down to where Luka had placed the crane's computer hardware. "Al said you exhibited an interest in understanding the reason behind the malfunction."

"I haven't had a chance to take a detailed look at it."

"But you've had an initial look?" Anita suggested.

"I downloaded the code into my WristTab if that's what

you mean," Luka said, feeling somewhat guilty for his actions. "If you're asking me to take a professional guess, then I would say it was a hard disk failure which caused a subroutine to crash."

"Could it have been sabotage?"

"Sabotage?" said Luka.

"There was a lot of anger when ThorGate won the contract to build Noctis City. Some of the other corporations think we wield too much influence on Mars."

"ThorGate has more resources than any other corporation. It makes sense for it to be in charge of some of the major projects."

"Not everybody thinks so. Some would even like it if we failed."

"You think someone could have caused the crane to malfunction on purpose?"

"Could they?" said Anita.

Luka shrugged. "Sure, it's possible. The shield plate was removed from around the computer component, so I suppose someone could have tampered with it and not had time to put it back. But equally, it could be shoddy maintenance. It doesn't take much for Mars dust to get in there and do some damage."

Anita thought for a moment. "So, you think cockup rather than conspiracy?"

"Without any evidence to the contrary, that would be my preferred explanation."

She frowned. "Looks like I'm going to be speaking to my maintenance team."

"That's only my initial assessment. You should get

someone else to make a proper evaluation." Luka pushed the component across the desk towards her.

"That's only part of the reason I asked you here."

"Oh?"

"You heard about Giovanni Lupo, I assume?"

"Yes," said Luka. "My condolences. I understand you two were close."

The rumor was they were more than close. Talk in the migrant habitat was they were lovers. Her scream across the comms channel when she heard he'd died seemed to confirm the rumors were true.

The sentiment appeared to catch Anita off guard, and she dropped her gaze as she took a moment to compose herself. When she spoke again, it was with a noticeably dry throat. "Gianni was one of our main programmers here at ThorGate. His passing leaves an unexpected hole in my staff. A man with your skills could fill that position."

"No." Luka shook his head. "I signed up to be part of the construction crew. I came to Mars to do a physical job. I don't want to be sat looking at computer screens all day."

"And yet you downloaded the crane's control code to look at on your WristTab. A computer man is always a computer man, no matter how much he might think he wants to walk away from it."

"The answer's still no. I know you must be dealing with a lot at the moment, I understand what it means to lose people you love in tragic circumstances, but I left my old job for a reason."

"So I see from your file," said Anita, glancing back down at her computer screen. "I understand that you want a clean break from your past, but I want an experienced programmer on my team. We can't both have what we want."

Luka thought for a moment as he sensed the helplessness of being backed into a corner. He realized what she was getting at. "The contract I signed means ThorGate virtually owns me, so I suppose I have no choice."

"You do have a choice, Luka. I won't compel if you really want to spend the next few years of your life helping to put an endless supply of red Martian bricks on top of other red Martian bricks. But don't turn me down just yet." She smiled warmly at him. "Let me show you something first."

Anita drove Luka the short distance from Thor Town to the worshipping panels of the solar array which surrounded the city. Although they had looked close to the building when approaching in the rover, in reality they lay further out from the complex than was advisable to walk. He realized why as the white disk of the sun began its descent into the afternoon and caused the shadow of Thor Town to grow longer. The distance of the solar panels was precisely calculated to avoid the shade cast by the building they served.

With a final check of their rad-suits completed, Anita and Luka stepped out of the rover to view the array in person. There were rows upon rows of panels, each filled with blue tessellating photovoltaic cells which shimmered like water to form an electronic moat of power to keep the city alive.

"This is what ThorGate is known for," said Anita over the comms.

"Power generation," observed Luka.

"Which makes what I'm going to show you a little embarrassing."

They stepped closer and Luka could see that many of the panels were already collecting a dusting of Martian soil particles. On the panel directly in front of them, a small robot which looked like a toy tank with a large gun turret in the center, fired a jet of air across the cells and blew away the dust. Clinging onto the side of the panel, the robot tracked its way further up towards the top to blow another blast of air to disperse the debris.

"We're quite proud of these things," said Anita. "We used to have to clear all the solar panels by hand at least once a day. Brushing the dust off can cause minor abrasions so we used compressors to take air from the atmosphere, hold it until enough pressure is built up, and then release it to blast away the dust. It's a bit like the leaf blower our neighbors used to use at home. We had a lot of trees where we lived in Oslo. They looked beautiful, but in the autumn when the leaves fell… Anyway, using valuable employees to spend all day walking up and down the solar array with modified leaf blowers was not efficient."

"Which is why you have the robots," said Luka. "I heard about them. Simple, but effective."

"Yes and no," said Anita, as the robot they had been watching finished the panel it was on and trundled along a connecting cable to the next one. "They're great until they fall off. Which they do too often."

Anita walked between the row of solar panels until she stopped at another one of the robots which was on the ground at her feet. She picked it up, brushed the dust from it and set it back on the array. The machine gripped onto the side, waited a moment as if adjusting to its new position, then blew a cloud of dust away from the cells.

"I appreciate the tour, but what has this to do with me?" said Luka.

"Gianni was working on a way to fix the problem of them falling off. At least, he was supposed to be. He seemed... a little distracted before he died."

Luka looked out across the array and, once he saw past its shimmering beauty, he could see the black blobs of little robots working away on the edge of many of the panels. A couple of the rows seemed not to have their own robot, and that's when he spotted two of the small black machines languishing on the ground like lone pebbles on a sandy beach.

The robot which Anita had replaced continued with its work and puffed another cloud of dust away from the photovoltaic cells. When it reached the bottom corner, it wobbled before making the turn onto the lower edge. Luka took a step forward and watched more intently as the robot stopped, drew in air from around it and puffed it out of the cannon. The force of the blast, although not much greater than a child blowing out their birthday candles, caused the robot to wobble again. But the plucky machine managed to hang onto the track, negotiate the corner and move up the other side where it had less trouble maintaining its grip.

"That's your weak point," said Luka, pointing at the base of the panel. "The planet's gravity is pulling at the robot. I know the gravity is less on Mars, but it's still a significant force or we'd all be floating off into space. When it blasts air up across the panel, it acts like a jet engine creating thrust in the opposite direction. Whereas at the top of the panel, and to some extent at the sides, the direction of the thrust is different to that of gravity and the robot is able to hold on more easily. Negotiating the bottom corners also looks like it could be a problem. There must be some variable which means the robot sometimes falls off and sometimes it doesn't. It's probably something as simple as there being dust on the track."

"That was our assessment too."

Luka, getting carried away with the thrill of problem solving, formed the beginnings of a possible solution in his mind. "I imagine the robot could be programmed so it doesn't travel along the bottom of the panel at all. Maybe it can clear the dust just by going along the top and sides. If it could also blow air at its own track to keep it free of debris, that might help."

Through the bubble of Anita's helmet, he could see she was smiling. "So, you'll take the job?"

Luka felt outmaneuvered. In his own enthusiasm, he had fallen into her trap. "I didn't say that."

"I think you did."

"This is just as much an engineering problem as a programming one," he insisted. But his protestations did no good.

"If you understand that, then you are the person I need," said Anita. "I'll make the arrangements for you to join ThorGate's technical team today. Someone can bring over your things from the construction habitat and you can get settled into a new room at Thor Town. You'll find the facilities here are much better."

Before Luka had the chance to reply, Anita had turned from him and begun the walk back to the rover. Luka took one last look at the little robot as it negotiated the connecting track to move onto the next solar panel and followed.

CHAPTER SIX

Mah Chynna swiveled round on her chair and her long, black hair flicked back behind her. She sat in front of an array of screens, each showing a different aspect of asteroid data. Most were lists of technical detail, but the central screen displayed close up footage of a dark, gray, knobbly rock in the asteroid belt between Mars and Jupiter. On the far right, she had one of the screens tuned to the Interplanetary Cinematics reality channel with the volume turned down low, so whatever trivia the participants were talking about it was merely a burble within the gentle hubbub of CrediCor's communal office.

"Mah Chynna?" asked Julie. She had been directed to the woman's desk by one of the other employees who had pointed rather vaguely towards the back of the room. If the woman's station hadn't been the biggest in the office, Julie would still be wandering around asking other people where to find it.

"I'm so sorry, I didn't realize the time," said the long-haired woman who, it appeared, was indeed Mah Chynna. "You're Julie Outerbridge. I recognize you from the news."

Julie felt self-conscious. She would never get used to meeting strangers who knew who she was because they had seen her face on TV. "Is there somewhere we can talk?"

"Yes, of course. We can go into my boss's office. It's all arranged. Just one moment."

Mah Chynna turned off all the screens on her desk and led the way past the other employees who pretended to busy themselves with work while they watched the two women out of the corners of their eyes.

"I hope you don't mind me asking," said Julie. "But is Chynna your given name and Mah your surname? I don't want to get it the wrong way round."

"That's right," said Chynna. "I'd much rather people ask me than make assumptions. You wouldn't believe the number of ignorant people who call me 'Mah'. Except they usually pronounce it 'May', like the month in English. I know now why so many Chinese say it's easier to switch your name around. But I think, why should I change to the Western way of doing things? China has put a lot of money into the World Government and space exploration – it's everyone else who should be changing *their* names round."

Chynna led Julie into a modest sized office just off the communal area. It was clearly designed for one person with a single desk and a chair behind. It had a window which stretched along the whole of the back wall showing a live view of Mars out towards the impressive volcanic shield of

Olympus Mons. On the near side of the room, away from the desk, were two low, soft armchairs upholstered in red fabric and placed around a small table. Chynna sat on one of them and offered Julie the other.

"Before we start," said Chynna. "I want to say that I feel terrible about what happened. Everyone at CrediCor does. It makes no sense. I know people think we just grab the nearest asteroid and hurl it at Mars, but that's not the case. Every aspect of each mission is carefully calculated and checked at every stage. It couldn't have gone wrong."

"Except it did," said Julie.

"I've looked over the data and I don't understand why."

"I'll get to that later, but let's start at the beginning. You're the Asteroid Controller for CrediCor here on Mars, is that right?"

"Yes, I coordinate the whole project from here, liaise with CrediCor teams in the asteroid belt, and monitor all operations from asteroid selection, through flight trajectory, mass and velocity calculations, crash site assessment – right up until the moment of impact."

"What happened with this asteroid?"

"What they're saying on the news is right. It fractured during entry – a piece splintered off and diverted from the planned trajectory. But it shouldn't have happened. Each asteroid is carefully chosen and deep scanned to make sure it has the structural integrity to withstand the stresses of entry through the Martian atmosphere. That asteroid was as structurally sound as the other five we've brought down this year. It shouldn't have broken apart."

"Perhaps you missed something," suggested Julie.

"I didn't miss anything," insisted Chynna.

"Then one of your colleagues missed something. Or there was a variable you didn't allow for."

"There was not."

"You can sit there all day and claim you didn't make any mistakes, but it won't change the fact that a fragment of the asteroid went off course and killed a man. You're lucky the number of casualties wasn't higher."

"I already said I'm sorry about that, but I'm not taking the blame for something which wasn't my fault." Her accent became stronger as she became more offended.

"I'm not seeking to blame you, I'm seeking the truth," said Julie. "I will need to review all your data on the asteroid and its journey to Mars."

"I'd like to help you, but that's privileged information which belongs to CrediCor. I'm not allowed to let it go outside of the corporation."

"I'm conducting an official investigation on behalf of the Chair of the Terraforming Committee," Julie stated.

"I don't mean to be rude, but you're also the head of a rival corporation. Do you know how much trouble I would be in if I gave it to you?"

"I'm going to need that information to conduct my investigation. Until we understand what went wrong and how to make sure it doesn't happen again, the Terraforming Committee won't allow any more asteroid crashes."

"But that's CrediCor's main business here. We've got asteroids lined up ready to go. If we don't bring them down on schedule, we'll be behind on our program. The terraforming Mars project itself will be behind."

"Then the sooner I can have the data, the sooner my investigation will be over and we can all get back to doing what we'd much rather be doing. I can put in an official request via your boss if you're concerned it might reflect badly on you. I'm entirely prepared to take my request all the way to Bard Hunter on Earth – one corporation head to another – if I really have to."

"No need," said Chynna after a moment. "I'll get the necessary permission to pass on the data. We have nothing to hide."

Julie nodded. She couldn't expect anything more from an indentured employee. "I'd appreciate it if you could get that done as soon as possible."

"Of course."

Julie stood and made her way out of the office, causing the heads of a dozen CrediCor employees to turn as she entered the communal area. Almost as quickly, they turned away again and pretended to be engrossed in their work.

Chynna followed, but stopped when she reached her own desk. "By the way," she called out to Julie across the office. "You won't be able to get hold of Bard Hunter. He's on a yoga retreat."

Julie stopped and turned, not quite sure she had heard properly above the background hubbub. "A yoga retreat?"

"Yeah," said Chynna. "No one's been able to contact him for months. I suppose you can go off and do crazy things like that when you're that rich."

"I suppose so," said Julie.

As she turned to leave, she began thinking about all the crazy things she would love to go off and do if her salary equaled Bard Hunter's. There were many, many exciting things, but none of them involved yoga.

Julie sat at her desk staring at the data sent over by CrediCor the day after her request and saw only what Chynna said she would see: an asteroid profile perfect for crashing onto Mars. Scans showed it to be of chondrite formation, made of clay and silicate rocks without fissures which could have led to fracturing. There were lists of calculations which determined mass, velocity, fuel requirements, flight trajectory options based on different points in Mars' orbit, gravitational effects of other celestial bodies… and so it continued.

She rubbed her eyes, but when she took her hands away her vision seemed more blurred, not less so. She had a basic understanding of astrophysics, but the minutiae of calculations required to bring an asteroid from the belt and crash it into Mars were more than she could handle. She was a terraforming expert. What she knew about methods for extracting carbon dioxide from the soil and its effect on warming the planet could bore the pants off guests at any dinner party, but the intricacies of the CrediCor data were lost on her.

Admitting defeat, Julie leaned back in her chair and swung out her arms behind her to stretch her hunched up shoulders. She would pass all the data to others in UNMI to look at, but she suspected there was nothing to find. CrediCor almost certainly had, as Chynna said, nothing to hide. Or if they did, it had probably been surgically removed from the data before it left the corporation.

A quiet knock on Julie's office door caused her to look up.

Kareem entered holding a dusty, lumpy rock the size of a large, odd-shaped bowling ball. By the way he was carrying it, it was just as heavy.

"Ah, Kareem. Just the person," said Julie. "How good are you at advanced math and astrophysics?"

He gave her a quizzical look. "I have a Masters in Applied Mathematics with a specialism in Climatology, as you know. Why?"

Julie didn't get a chance to answer before he placed the thing he carried on her desk with a thud that made the whole structure vibrate. A puff of Martian dust particles fell off the rock and surrounded it with a sprinkle of rusty red.

"You seem to have brought me a dirty rock," she said.

"It's part of the downed asteroid," said Kareem.

"How kind of you!" said Julie sarcastically. "It's not even my birthday."

Kareem rolled his eyes as he brushed his hands on his shirt, sending more particles of dust flying up into the room. "You don't see it, do you?"

"It's a dark gray dusty rock which has made a mess of my desk. Is there something else I'm supposed to see?"

"It's *dark* gray. Exactly!" Kareem seemed very excited about the concept.

Julie, however, remained nonplussed. "I've spent the last two hours staring at mass spectrum analyses and velocity calculations. I'm trying not to resort to raiding the shipment of coffee Dad sent to me last year. And it's getting really late. Why don't you be kind to me and explain it slowly? From the beginning."

Kareem pulled up a chair and sat perching on the edge

to lean forward so his face was close to the rock. "Do you remember when we were at the Noctis crash site and saw what was left of the asteroid fragment?"

"I remember."

"Do you remember what color it was?"

"Most of it was rubble and the larger pieces were black on the outside from carbonization."

"But where the larger pieces had sheared off from the bulk of the asteroid, you could see the color of the rock."

Julie finally made the connection. "Which was a *lighter* gray."

Kareem grinned.

"You can't be suggesting it's not the same asteroid."

"I was skeptical at first," said Kareem. "I thought maybe I had misremembered or it only appeared to be a different color because of the angle where we were standing or the low light levels at Noctis. But I watched back the news footage and I'm not mistaken."

Julie looked up at her window which was showing a star-filled Martian night sky. "Window, play ICN footage of Noctis asteroid fragment. Sound off."

The window relayed the same pictures taken by the observation robot on the day of the crash which revealed several large, light gray pieces lodged at the base of the canyon.

"That," said Kareem, pointing at the window, "looks to me like either an M-type asteroid or a W-type. Nickel-iron composition, maybe with some stony material and silicates."

The neurons in Julie's tired brain fired faster as Kareem's words clashed with what she had been reading. She checked the CrediCor data on her screen. "The one which was brought from the asteroid belt was supposedly of 'chondrite formation' – that's a C-type, right?"

"Yeah."

Julie stared at the dark, dusty rock on her desk with renewed interest. "Which is what this has to be. From what I understand, C-types are darker because of the amount of carbon in them."

"I'd have to have it analyzed to be sure, but that's what it looks like to me."

Julie tapped the top of the asteroid. "You're sure this is from the main crash site?"

"When a team when out to survey the area, I got them to bring me back a piece."

"Good thinking," said Julie. "Although, you couldn't have got them to brush the dust off first? The wretched stuff gets everywhere as it is."

"They were doing me a favor." Kareem seemed exasperated with her.

Julie looked up again at the footage playing on the window as it focused in on the remains of a dusty, white human-made object sticking out from the rubble. "The ICN recordings aren't evidence enough to prove anything. We need a sample from the Noctis site to analyze and compare."

"That's what I was thinking," said Kareem.

"Why am I not surprised," said Julie. "I'll arrange it."

"Don't arrange it. We should collect it ourselves, and we can take another look at where it crashed while we're there."

Julie suddenly had the feeling that this was where Kareem had been steering the conversation all along. "Sometimes I wonder who's in charge here," she said. "You or me."

"You, Julie, obviously," said Kareem, all exasperation wiped away. "I'll book out the rover so it's ready for us to set out at first light. Which I think is at 8:33 tomorrow."

"You seem to have it all thought out. I suppose I will see you at the rover depot at 8:33."

"Great!" Kareem stood and headed for the door.

"Kareem!" Julie called after him. "You forgot your dirty rock."

"It'll be fine there overnight," Kareem called back. "I'll pick it up tomorrow."

Julie sighed as he rushed out. "Window off," she commanded, and the ICN footage faded to black.

She lifted her arm, set an alarm for the following day on her WristTab and grayed out her diary for the morning. "Yeah, *I'm* the one in charge," she said to herself.

Not that she minded that much. She was more interested in taking the short walk out of the office to her apartment where the bliss of sleep awaited her.

CHAPTER SEVEN

Luka thought that if a child were asked to describe a typical Swedish man, then they would have described Erik Bergman. He was tall and thin with a mop of bright blond hair which sprouted untidily from the top of his head into a shaggy fringe at the front and an abrupt wedge cut into his neck at the back. Many white people on Mars appeared pale through the lack of exposure to UV light from the sun, but Erik was paler. It was like the melanin in his skin, which had barely bothered to show itself in the long dark winters of his native Nordic country, had finally given up when it got to Mars and withdrawn completely.

Ironic all around, Luka thought, as there was more UV on Mars due to the lack of ozone. While indispensable, perhaps the rad-suits were a bit *too* effective.

Erik led Luka along the corridor of the accommodation block and stopped at one of the identical doors that led off it. "This used to be Gianni's room," he said and put his

WristTab up to a reader beside it. The red indicator light turned to green, there was a click, and the door slid open.

Luka stepped into a basic room with all its personality stripped away. The bed was a frame and a mattress with a pile of clean, neatly folded bedclothes on top. The doors to the wardrobe had been left open to show it contained nothing but a couple of wire hangers. The set of drawers and a couple of chairs were generic and looked as if they had come directly from the storeroom. A second closed door led into the bathroom. There was a window set into the wall opposite the bed, but it had been turned off so it displayed a black screen. With no other computers in the room, it almost certainly doubled as the main access to the town network.

"It's better than you had at the construction habitat, I'm sure," Erik said.

"Yes," said Luka, even though it was more or less the same. A little bit bigger, perhaps.

"With luck, your stuff will arrive tomorrow and you can make it a bit more cozy. It's er…" Erik checked his WristTab, "…a couple of hours until dinner, but you're welcome to join me and some of the guys over food later. We can tell you all the gossip."

"Thank you," said Luka. "I'd like that."

"There's some formal stuff to go through, but we can do all that tomorrow. It feels bizarre for me to be showing you the ropes because if you're replacing Gianni, you're sort of my boss."

"I'm not replacing anyone," said Luka. "I'll just be one of the tech crew. Like you."

"Sure thing!" said Erik in a bright and breezy manner. "If you're still up for dinner in a couple of hours, come find us in the dining hall."

Erik waved goodbye and stepped out of the door.

Luka touched the control on the inside and the door slid shut again. He touched it a second time to lock it.

He sat on the bare mattress of the unmade bed and sighed. This was not what he had come to Mars to do. The demands of construction on a planet not yet made for humans would have given him little time or energy to think. Work hard, play hard with colleagues afterwards, and collapse into bed exhausted so sleep would pull him into an unconsciousness without dreams. That was what he had planned for the next few years of his life. Computers and programming robots, although it was what he trained to do and what he was good at, involved his mind and that allowed unwelcome thoughts to invade.

However, he was where he was. In a room with no traces of its former occupant, staring at the black of a window.

"Window on," he commanded.

The screen brightened to show an animated ThorGate logo. The central blue polygon faded in from a gray background, two red sliding doors traveled in from either side and the familiar white lighting flashed through the center, while the word "ThorGate" appeared beneath.

"Welcome to Thor City," said a pleasant female voice. "To use this window, please set up your profile."

Luka sagged as soon as he realized he had barely accepted the job before he was having to deal with computers. He would have rather spent the two hours before dinner getting used to the idea that life on Mars was going to be different than he had imagined, but instead, it felt like he was getting straight to work. Setting up a profile was supposed to be easy, but it always took longer than it should, even for someone like Luka who knew what he was doing.

He connected his WristTab, went through the authorization process and watched the screen in the hope his profile would be smoothly transferred. Except, nothing happened and the ThorGate logo continued to animate in front of him.

"There has been an error," said the pleasant female voice.

"What do you mean there's been an error?" Luka answered back.

"There has been an error," it repeated.

"Window, describe the error."

"The setting up of personal profiles on this window is blocked."

Luka frowned. The whole point of windows in workers' rooms was to set up personal profiles. There was no reason to block them.

"Do I have the authority to remove the block?" he asked the window.

"The block is a hardware problem."

"A hardware problem? What do you mean, a hardware problem?"

"I have no more information."

"Yeah, I bet you don't. Why do systems programmers always make their operating systems so annoying?"

"I have no information," replied the window.

"That was supposed to be a rhetorical question, you stupid machine." He sighed again. "Window off."

There was very little that could go wrong with a window because it was a sealed unit, with most of the computing power existing in the town's main servers which it connected to via a cable. The early Mars settlers had, from what he understood, abandoned the idea of using wireless other than for WristTabs and full-sized Tabs because of the amount of radiation shielding they had to put in.

Luka looked around his sparse room. He had nothing to unpack and the only other thing that he could do to occupy himself before dinner was to make the bed. That made fixing the hardware problem suddenly much more interesting. But he needed a tool to take the window out of its mounting before he could even begin investigating.

His gaze settled upon the wire hangers in the wardrobe. It took a bit of manipulating, but he was able to bend the hook of one of the hangers into just the right angle to slip into the gap between the window and the wall. He jostled it loose on one side, then on the other, until he could prize it out from the bottom. The window came away from its mount with such an unexpected "pop" that he almost dropped it. But he was able to steady his grip before laying it face down on top of the chest of drawers.

The window was, as he expected, a sealed unit consisting of a black cover with a network cable sticking out of the back and disappearing into the wall. He tried prizing the back off using the wire hanger, but it was nothing like as manipulative as the specialist tool he should be using and so he had a second look around to see if there was something more suitable. He was about to see if the clasp of his WristTab was capable of the task when he noticed a black, thumb-sized slab sticking out from beneath the network cable where it was attached to the window. He hadn't seen it at first because it was the same color as the cover, but the angle from his position sitting on the bed allowed it to catch the light.

Luka reached round and pulled it free. It was a small data stick. The technology was rare because all data was usually shared over the network. It was unusual to see one, especially stashed behind the back of a window.

He turned the stick over in his palm and, on the back, saw that someone had scratched the words, *nel caso in cui.* Someone's name, perhaps?

Curious, but wary that data sticks could be used to infest a system with malware if an unwitting person gave it access, he double-checked his WristTab personal profile was backed up, isolated it from the Mars network, and plugged the stick into the WristTab connector. A video began to play on the small screen. It was of a man talking to the camera which appeared to be some sort of report or diary entry. Luka didn't pay much attention to what he was saying while he completed a quick scan and confirmed the stick contained no malware and only videos. Dismissing it as not very interesting, he stopped it playing.

Luka jostled with the network cable at the back of the window again, to ensure it was securely plugged in, and the screen automatically loaded his profile. He placed it back into its slot on the wall and brought up a map of Thor Town to get a better idea of his bearings. He found details of where he would be working quite easily, and also memorized the short walk to the communal dining hall where he was due to meet Erik and "some of the guys."

But the existence of the stick bothered him. The whole room had been stripped of every last remnant of anyone who had ever lived there. Like a hotel room, it had been scrubbed, cleaned, and made fresh for the next occupant. Except for the data stick. Almost as if it had been hidden deliberately. But hidden in such a way that a new occupant was bound to find it when they tried to set up their profile on the window.

Now he was curious. Luka sat back on the bed and streamed the contents of the data stick to the screen.

The video began to play again. The man talking to the camera was a little younger than Luka, probably in his late twenties. He was a white man with short dark hair, a neatly trimmed beard and wide, dark eyes. He appeared to be in the exact same room as Luka, except that he was sitting on a chair pulled up close enough to the camera so his face filled the frame. Hints of the room behind showed what it might look like when someone had been living there for some time. The bedclothes were ruffled, an item of clothing which might be a jacket was slung over the back of the man's chair, and there was some sort of calendar, or works diary, pinned up on the wall behind him.

"The new boss started today," said the man, in an accent Luka identified immediately as Italian. He had traveled extensively in Europe when he had worked on various robot projects. "She is… not what I expected."

The man smiled and lowered his eyes away from the camera as if a little embarrassed. "She is feisty and dynamic, not intimidated at all by coming into an established team. She is Norwegian, obviously, because you can't work for ThorGate without being managed by someone from Norway at some point down the line, but she didn't act like she had a divine right to be in charge. Not like Lars used to be. Anita Andreassen came in like she was one of the team, doing everything she could to put us at ease. She even greeted me in Italian: 'Piacere di conoscerti, Giovanni,' she said. Her pronunciation was terrible, but it broke the ice."

Luka realized he was looking at the face of Giovanni – or "Gianni" – Lupo, the man who was killed by the asteroid. The man whose job he had taken. The man whose room he was sitting in. He watched with greater intensity.

"There was something else about Anita." Gianni dropped his eyes in embarrassment again. "I probably shouldn't say this… but it's my diary, so I can say what I like. I'm only talking to myself, after all. My first reaction when she came in was how beautiful she looked. When Anita laughs, it's like she's not just joining in with the joke, she's spreading joy to everyone. Or maybe she was only spreading joy to me. Is it taboo to say that you fancy your boss? I think it is, so I won't say it. I won't even admit it to myself. I will be a good worker and carry out the tasks she asks of me to the best of my ability. Especially if she asks me to dinner."

Gianni blushed as he looked away from the camera. "I've said too much for one day. Even to myself. Video recording off."

There were more diary entries, but Luka didn't watch any more.

Up until that point, Gianni had been just a name. His death had been a terrible tragedy, and it was awful to see how it affected other people, but it didn't mean anything to Luka.

Not really. Now, confronted by the ghost of the man, Gianni became a real person to him. A man who had a personal life, who had a work life, and who had very human emotions. All of which made his death seem more real and his loss more poignant. Luka had watched the asteroid which had killed him blaze through the atmosphere and crash only meters ahead of where he and the other migrants had crouched in fear. What had been merely terrifying at the time suddenly held a greater significance.

He hadn't expected to feel sadness at the death of someone he had never known. But sitting there, in the same room where Gianni had sat and confessed to having a crush on his new boss, he felt they had a connection. The following day, Luka would be starting the same job the young Italian had left behind and he would, effectively, be stepping into a dead man's shoes.

It was an uncomfortable thought.

CHAPTER EIGHT

Julie stood on the Tharsis uplands overlooking Noctis Labyrinthus in almost exactly the same spot as she had done on the day of the asteroid disaster. With no news crews or confused and worried workers wandering around, the place had a serene calm. Even the construction crew working on Noctis City further down the canyon were merely rad-suited dots quietly going about their business.

Kareem came out of the rover to join her, carrying a monitoring device, which was effectively a screen and a joystick with a short-range transmitter and receiver boosted via the more powerful equipment in the rover. The technology was used out on the planet surface to connect to remote cameras where it was impractical to take a fully equipped mobile monitoring station. "I was right," he said over the comms. "ThorGate left their observational robot down there and it's still working."

Julie looked over his shoulder at the screen and saw

the image relayed from the base of the canyon. It had been mostly cleared of rubble, although there was still the occasional small rock in the camera's field of vision. "That robot's an expensive piece of kit to simply have been left," she said. "I think the official term you're looking for is that they stationed it there." She winked.

"I imagine they *stationed* it there in case they needed to examine the crash site further," Kareem said. "If you have to take it down there and bring it back up every time you want to do that, you're going to lose two hours out of your working day."

"Handy for us."

"Yeah," said Kareem. "If we can find a suitable piece of asteroid debris to bring back up to examine, we can use the coordinates of the observation robot to guide our sample collector to the right spot."

Julie was finding it difficult to make out anything specific on the screen, as the whole site had been dusted with a fresh accumulation of Martian dirt and it had all started to blend into the red landscape.

"Let me have a better look," she said, taking the device out of Kareem's hands.

"I told you, it would be easier to do this from inside the rover."

"And I told *you* that we've made the effort to drive out here, we might as well get out and have a look around."

"It's Mars," Kareem said, sarcastically. "It looks red and rocky, like any other part of Mars."

Julie gave him a sideways glance. "One of these days I'm going to send you on winter assignment to one the polar regions so you can appreciate the white of the carbon dioxide ice caps."

"No, you won't. You need me too much."

"Mmm," said Julie, knowing he was right, but not giving him the satisfaction of acknowledging it.

She concentrated on the image in front of her. With her hand off the joystick, the observation robot had stopped and was showing her an image across the base of the canyon. It looked like ThorGate had cleared away much of the rubble, most likely when they had removed what was left of Giovanni Lupo's body, but the large remnants of the asteroid were still there. Julie swiveled the robot left and right to get a good view of the terrain and was able to make out three shards languishing in the place where they had fallen.

"You keep looking for a suitable sample to bring up and I'll get the sample collector out of the rover," said Kareem, as he turned away.

"Yeah," said Julie, uncertainly. With the whole site sprinkled with red dust, it was difficult to see what rock was native to Mars and what rock had come from the asteroid belt.

Nevertheless, she endeavored to look. Steering the robot to around the back of the nearest shard, which was so tall it towered above the little machine's field of vision, something caught her eye and she let go of the joystick. It was only small and at the edge of the image, but it looked like a piece of mangled metal. There had been metal objects inside ThorGate's research station, of course, but this looked like something altogether different.

"Kareem!" she called over the comms.

"What?"

"Come look at this."

"Just let me get this robot out of the rover."

"Forget the sample robot, just come back!"

She heard him grumble over the comms, but she didn't care because she needed his opinion.

Julie adjusted the joystick and closed in on the object. It was definitely metal and, even though there was an accumulation of dust on top, it was possible to see scorch marks where it had been subject to intense heat.

Kareem returned to her side. "What?" he said.

"What do you think that is?"

He peered at the image. "Part of ThorGate's squashed research station, I imagine."

"Do you think it could be part of the asteroid guidance system?"

"I doubt it," said Kareem.

She handed him the device so he could see the screen more clearly. Then she watched his dismissive expression turn into something more thoughtful.

"Maybe…" he said.

"Part of the engine, perhaps, designed to withstand high temperatures. Look at the scorch marks!"

Kareem let out a long breath, which sounded loud coming out of the speaker at Julie's ear. "What do you want to do about it?"

"Go get it," said Julie, with excitement.

Kareem looked unimpressed. "It's trapped under what's left of the asteroid, you can't expect the sample robot to pick it up. You'd need specialist equipment to move the rock or cut it out or something. We can call out a UNMI team, but by the time they get out here we won't have enough of the day left."

"I've got a better idea." Julie turned to look further down the canyon to where the construction crew was working to build Noctis City. "Why don't we ask the people over there to do us a favor?"

CHAPTER NINE

ThorGate wanted to automate the construction of Noctis City as much as possible. Many of the tasks, such as taking materials to the bottom of the canyon, were labor-intensive and repetitive. Ideal for robots. The machines had been commissioned already, but their basic programming could only take them so far. Adapting them to specific conditions was Luka's specialty. He had programmed construction robots from Cologne to Copenhagen, and making the transition to Mars was relatively easy. So, only a few days after his departure for Thor Town, he was back at the construction site for a meeting with Al Vertanen.

Luka made sure to get there early and take the opportunity to take a look around at what progress had been made.

It was impressive. There were literally hundreds of magnesium poles jutting out from the side of the slope and the team had built five platforms spaced about every hundred meters down the side of the canyon. The slope itself was dotted with up to thirty laborers all working away, the furthest of them like tiny white specks against the red vastness of the rock face.

They had also started work on a series of industrial elevators to make it easier to move materials and people down the slope from platform to platform. The flat base of the first elevator was already sitting at the top of the ridge on a pair of tracks and was ready to be tested with a significant weight. One worker, who Luka recognized as Morten Nilsen, had evidently decided that he – rather than a load of ballast –was going to be the first one to take a ride on it and stepped onto the elevator.

"Send me down!" Morten said over the comms. Luka chuckled at his enthusiasm.

The base jolted beneath Morten, and he staggered half a step sideways.

"Sit down, Morty!" came another voice. "Al will kill me if you fall off."

Morten swiftly moved to a sitting position as the elevator moved down the tracks with the base safely remaining horizontal. "I wouldn't be too happy about falling off either," he admitted.

As the top of Morten's helmet disappeared from view, another rad-suited figure emerged from a rover which had just arrived on site. Luka tried to work out if it was Al Vertanen, although he couldn't tell until he got close enough to see his mustached face through the bubble of his helmet.

Luka switched his comms to broadcast on the workforce supervisor's private channel. "Morning, Al!" he said.

"Congratulations on your promotion," the supervisor replied.

"I'm not sure that's what it is," said Luka. "But thank you."

"I'm told you're the top man for the job, which is just as well," said Al. "I want to start work at the bottom of the canyon, so I'm going to need those robots ready to go soon or I'm going to fall behind schedule."

"Shouldn't be a problem. I need to know how much you want to be automated and how much you want to be under the control of a human operator. The more you automate, the quicker construction can proceed, but the human element will always give you more flexibility, no matter how clever the robot or its programming."

They talked technical details and options for some time. It was all familiar stuff to Luka as most of the variables which made Mars construction different to Earth construction were already accounted for in the robots' core programming.

Some movement among the other workers caught Luka's eye and he turned to see they had broken into a round of applause. Small clouds of dust rose from their gloves as they clapped them together, but there was no sound. He felt like he'd suddenly been struck deaf. Then he saw that Morten was returning on the elevator which had almost resumed its position at the top of the canyon. Morten stood and raised his arms above his head in a victory salute – almost falling over as the base juddered to a halt.

"What is he doing?" Al growled. Inside his helmet, his moustache bristled. "Excuse me."

The workforce supervisor switched to broadcast on the team channel and strode through the gathering of applauding people to where Morten was stepping off the elevator. "What are you doing riding that thing before we've installed a safety rail?" Al demanded.

"I was careful," Morten insisted.

"That's not the point," Al went on. "There are safety protocols for a reason. What if you'd fallen over the edge and killed yourself?"

"It needed to be tested. I tested it. It works. If we'd waited to set up a safety rail, we'd still be doing it into tomorrow..."

Luka mentally tuned out the health and safety squabble, although it continued to be relayed in his helmet as he saw another rover approaching. He thought, for a moment, it was Anita come to check up on him or to view the working elevator for herself. Then he realized the rover had come from the opposite direction to Thor Town.

The vehicle drove straight past the designated parking spot for rovers and stopped much closer to the ridge in a cloud of thrown up dust. A figure stepped out almost straight away, without the time it would normally take to operate an airlock, which meant they had probably been traveling fully suited up without bothering to pressurize the cabin. Usually, people only did that if there was a malfunction of the rover's environmental controls or they were traveling such a short distance that it wasn't worth making the cabin habitable.

Most of the other workers were still enjoying the spectator sport of Al and Morten's argument, so when the rad-suited person emerged from the rover, none of the others turned to look. Only Luka was watching, which meant they naturally headed towards him, waving at him as they approached.

Luka had only been listening on the team comms and had

to use the controls on the arm of his rad-suit to access the general channel.

"…hello?" said a woman in an American accent.

"Hello." Luka waved back.

"Ah, you can hear me. Good," said the American woman, walking up to him. "I wonder if you could do me a bit of a favor. I'm investigating the asteroid crash site a little way along the canyon."

As she got closer, Luka saw enough of her face to recognize her. "You're Julie Outerbridge," he said.

She stopped. An amused smile played on her lips. "Yes, that's right."

Slightly taken aback at seeing a vaguely famous face, he offered a gloved hand and they shook, somewhat awkwardly through the bulky material. "I'm Luka Schäfer."

"We've found something under what's left of the asteroid," she said. "Well, think we've found something. But we can't get it out with the equipment we've brought with us. I thought you might be able to help? I know it's a bit of an imposition, but…"

Luka didn't even allow her to finish the sentence. After watching Gianni's video diary and getting a sense of the man whose life was taken away far too young, he wasn't one to refuse. "It's not an imposition. Many people at ThorGate knew Gianni Lupo. I'm sure they would be happy to help the investigation into how he died."

Luka had seen Julie on the news back in the days when he had little interest in Mars. She was one of those public figures he had vague awareness of, who burbled away in the background of his life, saying things he considered to be of little consequence. By the time he started to think about leaving Earth, she had been sidelined and didn't appear on the news so much. He had seen her again a few times on the ICN feed, but he had been too wound up in his own issues to pay much attention. Despite that, it was a strange feeling to be standing next to her. Like a fictional character had stepped out of his TV into real life.

The *real* Julie Outerbridge was somewhat different to her screen image. Her voice was the same – a soft American – and her facial features were the same too, but the officious woman who had delivered statements to the media appeared more human in person. Her skin, from what he could see through the bubble of her helmet, was unadorned by makeup and, like most of the white people he'd met on Mars, she had taken on a light, unhealthy pallor. Very much like Luka's own skin, he realized, after months in a spacecraft away from Earth's warming sunshine.

Al, once he had finished berating Morten for ignoring health and safety rules, was more than happy to provide assistance "to our UNMI friends," as he put it. He had known Gianni, if not as a friend then as a colleague, and wanted to help in the investigation in any way he could. He gathered up a handful of workers, who in turn gathered up their equipment, and followed Julie in a couple of ThorGate construction vehicles to the asteroid crash site.

Luka volunteered to join them and stayed at the top of the ridge to liaise with the two people from UNMI while the rest of the team made the long journey to the bottom of the canyon. He met Julie's deputy, an Englishman called Kareem, and spent some time talking to him about the challenges of construction projects on Mars before borrowing his monitoring device to take an advance look at the area of the crash site where Al and the others would be working.

Al, once he arrived at the bottom, found the observation robot, smiled, and waved into its camera. He set up a comms booster to ensure they were in constant contact with those on the ridge.

"I've found your squashed piece of metal," he said over the general channel. "Looks like it might have been exposed when they cleared all the rubble to remove Gianni's body."

"Can you get it out?" asked Kareem.

"Getting it out's not the problem," said Al. "Making sure it doesn't destabilize the chunk of asteroid it's attached to is the problem. But we can do it, absolutely. That's why you called in the experts, right?"

Kareem chuckled over the comms. "Right."

Al discussed with his team how best to proceed, keeping their conversation on the general channel so Luka and the couple from UNMI could listen in. There was some concern about how best to cut into the rock and how embedded it actually was in the base of the canyon. Without scanning equipment to determine how much of it had gouged itself into the bedrock and how much of it was just sitting on the top of loose soil, it was largely guesswork. They decided to proceed with caution and took their time to install supports and to set up a seismic monitor to alert them to any movement beneath their feet.

Julie, who had been waiting in the rover, came over to join

her colleague. "Are you happy they know what we need?" she asked Kareem.

"You do know that they can hear you," he said. "You're still broadcasting on the general channel."

"I know," said Julie.

"Yeah, I'm happy," he confirmed. "Al's team will get out as much of the guidance system as they can – if that's really what it is – plus a sample of the rock. Didn't you hear all this discussion over the comms?"

"I did, but I wanted to make sure I'd understood," said Julie. "Why don't you take a break in the rover while the ThorGate team are working? You could take the opportunity to top up your air tank."

"I'd rather stay," said Kareem. "I don't want to miss anything."

At that point, Al interrupted their conversation. "Look, we're going to be a while setting up before we even start cutting into the rock down here. If I were you, I'd go while you can."

"You heard the man," said Julie.

With both of them ganging up on him, Kareem had no choice but to do as he was told.

Luka smiled to himself and suddenly remembered how his wife, Sabine, would tell their children to "go while you can" before they embarked on a long trip. Lena, their daughter, was very good at doing what she was told and dutifully went to the toilet before leaving the house. But their youngest, Oskar, would always think he knew better than his mom, then beg them to stop for a break as soon as they were ten minutes down the road.

Al's team worked quickly, but it still took them an hour to get the work done, and more than another hour to make their way back up the slope. So, when the workers finally returned with the specimen, there was some pent-up excitement on the ridge. Kareem and Julie moved in to take a closer look while Luka hung back at a polite distance. As far as he could tell, Al had retrieved a mangled piece of metal which had been subjected to intense heat and fused to the rock. It was so squashed there was no telling what it was, but the couple from UNMI seemed delighted.

"Thank you so much!" said Julie over the comms.

"My pleasure," said Al, his moustache moving on his upper lip as he broke into a smile. "We'll get this into your rover for you, then we need to return to the construction site."

As Luka watched them, he noticed a haze of dust rising from the planet's surface out over the plain. At first, he thought it might be a dust storm, but he soon realized it was an approaching rover.

"Al, this is Luka. I think we're going to have company."

"Are they from UNMI?" said Al.

"We didn't tell anyone we were coming," said Julie.

Kareem groaned. "Don't say it's an ICN crew."

The person at the end of the safety line indicated they were ready to come up and Luka drew in the winch while they climbed up the slope. Simultaneously, the rover emerged from its dust trail and slowed enough to indicate it was about to park alongside the other vehicles.

"Al, did you say Anita was coming to the construction site today?" said Luka.

"You're not suggesting she's coming here?" came his reply.

"If she went to the site and asked where you were..."

"Terrific!" said Al, in a way which suggested "terrific" was the exact opposite of what he meant. "Send the line back, I'm coming up next."

Julie and Kareem, between them, managed to carry the specimen of rock and mangled metal into their rover. They offered to stay and explain everything, but Al assured them it would be better if they were out of the way when she got there. So, as the hatch to the rover opened and Anita stepped out onto the dusty ridge, Julie and Kareem were already making a quick getaway.

"Luka Schäfer! Is that you?" came Anita's angry voice through the speaker in his helmet. "What are you doing out here?"

He didn't have time to explain before Al reached the ridge and, mercifully, became Anita's sole focus of attention.

"Alvar, do you want to explain what's going on?" Anita demanded.

Al frowned and his moustache bristled as he released himself from the safety line. "Anita, my apologies. I was called away to help the UNMI investigators."

"Called away by *UNMI*? They're a rival organization."

"I'm aware of that, but they're investigating Gianni's death. You want to know more about how Gianni died, don't you?"

"Of course I support the investigation. Gianni was my friend. But you're employed to build Noctis City, not go around behaving like you're part of a good neighbor program."

"Anita," said Al, taking a conciliatory tone. "They needed

help. We had the expertise and the equipment. It made sense to lend a hand. It's only taken a couple of hours."

"A couple of hours we've now lost on the construction."

Luka kept his head down and kept operating the safety line. The rest of Al's team said nothing and, one by one, quietly emerged onto the top of the ridge. Like him, they knew that it was best not to get involved.

"We can make up the time," suggested Al.

"You better," snapped Anita.

"Let me get my team and our equipment back to site and then we can discuss progress. We've got the elevator working – I can show you."

"Not if you're going to be making up the hours you've squandered out here, you can't. You haven't got time for pointless demonstrations and, quite frankly, neither have I. You have a week to get back on schedule."

"I'm sure we can do it in a week."

"I'm glad to hear it," said Anita. "We can't afford to let the schedule slip, Alvar. That's why I put you in charge. You understand that, don't you?"

"Yes, Anita," he said.

She turned her back on him and walked across to the rover. As she disappeared inside, Luka and the rest of the ThorGate workers stood and waited for Al to say something. But there was no telling if Anita was still listening across the channel, so all he asked was for them to pack up their equipment and go.

CHAPTER TEN

No one cooked in Thor Town. Providing cooking facilities for everyone in every accommodation block was a waste of resources and space. Not that there was a great deal of food to cook anyway. Fresh produce from one of the few farms established on Mars was combined with artificially grown protein and limited supplies from Earth to feed the population on a diet that was strictly rationed. There were a few restaurants where people could buy specially prepared meals using disposable income saved up from whatever work they did, but mostly people ate in communal food halls.

As he carried his tray over to a table where Erik was sitting, Luka couldn't help but compare it to what they ate on the shuttle leaving Earth. A meal prepared by mass caterers and dished out to a population with nowhere else to go who were typically offered a choice of three options each mealtime. Refusing those options without the means to pay for an alternative – which was the case for most indentured workers most of the time – meant going hungry. Going hungry was not only unpleasant for the individual, it was frowned upon by the corporations who knew malnourished workers made for inefficient workers. Mars, as a fledgling civilization, had no room for unproductive members of society.

"Hey, Luka!" Erik waved him over. Not that his bright blond hair was difficult to find in a crowded room. He tapped at a spare place next to him at the table.

Luka sat, joining a table of most of the core tech crew from the Thor Town office. Other than Erik, there were two women, Myra and Inger and another man, Roman. Luka had only been introduced to the three of them a few days before and didn't know them very well at all. It was the most he could do to remember their names.

"So, I hear you met with that Outerbridge woman today," said Erik, eagerly. "How's her investigation into the asteroid going?"

Luka glanced up from his meal of sausages, potatoes and a small pile of peas which was more of a garnish than a portion. "She didn't say."

"Didn't say?" said Erik. "Didn't you ask her?"

"It didn't seem appropriate."

"Luka! I was relying on you for all the gossip."

"Is that why you invited me over? For the gossip?"

"I may be shallow and unsubtle, but at least I'm honest," said Erik with a grin.

Inger rolled her eyes, like she had been working with the man for too many years to be impressed with his idea of humor. "Don't mind him, Luka," she said. "You could put a hundred signs around a pile of stinking excrement telling people to watch where they step and Erik would still put his foot in it."

"Eww, Inger!" said Erik, wrinkling his nose. "Do you mind? I'm eating."

"Ah, eating," said Myra, poking at her tray of food with her fork like she was trying to tell if it was still alive or not. "So, that's what we're doing. I wonder sometimes."

Luka shoveled in a mouthful of potato mashed into a meaty gravy and savored its warm, granular texture infused with salt umami. "I actually think it tastes quite nice. It's better than I had on the journey out here."

"The new migrants always say that," said Erik. "I sometimes think they lock people away in a spaceship for months on end just so they're grateful when they get to Mars."

"How else are they going to get here?" said Inger. "Teleport?"

"I don't see why not," said Erik.

"The laws of physics would be one good reason," quipped Myra.

Luka thought that was funny and laughed before he had finished his last mouthful of food. A piece of potato almost went down his airway and he broke into a fit of coughing. Roman, who continued to say nothing, put a cup of water in Luka's hand. Grateful, Luka sipped at it between coughs and snatched breaths.

When it was obvious Luka wasn't going to die at the table, Erik waved across the crowded room at another one of their colleagues. Pete, an affable American, was quite young, in his twenties, and had one of the better technical minds on the team.

"Hey, Pete!"

Pete broke into a grin at Erik's elaborate waving and brought his tray to join the table. There wasn't a spare seat for him, so they all shuffled up and he found a chair from somewhere to bring over. Pete slung the rather large bag he was carrying across the back of the chair and delved into his food with the eagerness of a starving man with somewhere else to be.

"How was the power plant?" asked Erik.

"Running at almost full capacity," said Pete between mouthfuls. The power plant was apparently where he had been during the day. "They keep bringing more people to Mars without remembering every person requires power to live here and supply is limited until they build another plant. No offense, Luka."

"None taken," said Luka.

"But I did come back with…" Pete reached round for his bag which he rested on his lap while he unzipped the top. Reaching in with both hands, he pulled out something white and round. "…a soccer ball!"

Erik squinted across the table at it. "You mean, a football."

"Whatever," said Pete, bouncing it on the floor so it came back up to his waiting hands. "It's a ball you play games with."

He bounced it again. Although it moved relatively slowly in Martian gravity, it otherwise behaved like a ball would on Earth. If Luka remembered his physics lessons correctly, that was because of the conservation of energy. When the ball landed, it exerted the amount of force needed to bounce back to almost the same place that it had left. Within the pressurized environment of the dining hall, even the resistance of the air was the same as on Earth.

"Odd thing to bring back from a power plant," Luka remarked.

"Not if you made an arrangement before you left with a guy who works there," said Pete. "He had it shipped out flat from Earth, then pumped it up with air when it got here. He said I could borrow it for a small fee."

"Let's have a go," said Erik. Pete handed him the ball which he dropped to the floor and kicked gently against the wall. The ball bounced back obediently to his foot. Erik grinned. He kicked it again.

"Isn't there a sports facility in Thor Town where they have footballs?" said Luka. "I'm sure I saw it on the map."

Pete had just taken another mouthful of his dinner and so Myra answered for him. "Yeah, but you have to book up, you need to arrange a team and there's a waiting list." She got up off her chair. "Kick it over here!"

Erik tapped the ball with the side of his foot, and it trundled along the floor towards her. She laughed as she tapped it back. Others sitting at tables close to them turned round to look as their tentative kickabout became more confident. Erik struck the ball a little harder with the toe of his shoe and it flew up in the air towards one of the other tables where it struck the back of a woman's chair.

"Watch it!"

"Sorry!"

She seemed to accept Erik's apology but, within minutes, she and the others at her table packed up to leave as the impromptu game of soccer continued.

Inger and Roman stood up to join in.

"Are you coming, Pete?" said Inger. "It's your ball."

Pete, who had almost finished his food, set aside his knife and fork as the ball rolled towards him. He kicked it back gently.

One of the people sitting at another table came up to them and Luka thought he was going to be angry. But, instead, he explained that he and his friends had finished their dinner, were just about to leave and thought they would offer to bring over their chairs to act as goalposts. Erik and the others accepted their kind offer and suddenly there was a facsimile of a soccer pitch at one end of the dining hall. Curious faces from other diners turned to watch as Luka's five colleagues sorted themselves into teams.

"Don't just sit there, Luka, get up!" Erik called over.

Luka shook his head. "No, I'm fine, thanks."

"Without you, it's two against three. Come and make up the numbers – you can be on Pete's team."

Succumbing to the inevitable, Luka pushed his tray away and walked over to join in the game.

"Remember," said Erik. "You won't need to kick the ball as hard as you would on Earth. The same force will send it higher and further. Try to use more direct and lower shots without relying on the effect of gravity."

"That's if I can remember how to kick it at all," said Luka. It had been years since he had played soccer.

But, as the ball came towards him, he found his skills were still there and he easily caught it at the side of his foot. He testily pushed the ball along the floor, and it moved obediently, if a little faster than he had anticipated. Walking rather than trying to jog in the Martian gravity, he dribbled it along the floor, adjusting his technique, tapping it left and right. Erik came towards him to challenge for the ball, but Luka swerved left, stumbled a little as his muscle memory tried to make him run, managed to recover in time and caught the ball on his right foot. Maneuvering in front of the goal, he remembered Erik's advice to aim low and direct and kicked the ball between the two chairs.

"Goal!" cried Luka as the euphoria of his small victory tingled through his body. Like he was thirteen again and out on the grass playing with his mates.

"You're too good," said Erik. "I should have had you on my team."

"I was in FC Cologne Under Sixteens," said Luka.

"Seriously?" said Erik, appearing genuinely impressed. "You played professional football?"

"Soccer," corrected Pete.

"Whatever," said Erik. "You didn't tell me you were a professional."

"Under sixteens," Luka emphasized. "It's not like I played in the World Cup or anything."

Erik didn't seem to care about the distinction. "We should get you on the ThorGate team."

"ThorGate has a team?" asked Luka.

"All the corporations have a football team," said Erik. "There's a Mars tournament every year and we absolutely have to stop Ecoline winning again."

"I wasn't *that* good when I was a kid," Luka insisted. "They put me in defense, but I concentrated too much on my schoolwork, and they dropped me after a year."

"Believe me, compared to the rubbish team we have at ThorGate, you're good."

The others had continued knocking the ball between them while the two men had been talking and, suddenly, a misjudged kick sent the ball sailing in the air towards them. Instinctively, Luka jumped up to intercept it on his chest. He absorbed the blow so it didn't bounce right back, and allowed it to slowly drop towards the ground where he caught it with the bridge of his foot. It was so much easier in Martian gravity. He kicked it back up and transferred it to the other foot. Then higher to bounce on the top of each thigh. He laughed as he remembered the hours of practice it had taken him to master "keepie uppie" as a child. If only he had learnt to play soccer on Mars, he would have aced it in a matter of days!

Nevertheless, his demonstration was enough to entertain the crowd in the dining hall and he heard the surrounding conversation revert to a hush as more people turned to watch. On the next bounce, he added just enough energy for the ball to go a little higher and he leant forward to catch it on his neck. But he was out of practice, completely misjudged how slowly the ball would fall, it bounced off the top of his spine and dropped to the floor.

The crowd applauded anyway. Luka felt himself go red as he reached under a dining chair to retrieve the ball. When he stood up again, he saw Anita standing a few meters away from him, saying nothing, but glaring at him with her meal tray in her hands. Luka looked away, embarrassed.

Pete relieved him of the ball. "Let's make arrangements for us to play another time, yeah?"

"Yeah," said Luka.

Pete stuffed the ball back in his bag and the onlookers went back to their meals and their conversations. Luka glanced back at where Anita had been standing, but she had disappeared into the crowd.

Luka lay back on the bed in his room and found himself smiling.

Maybe coming to Mars was going to be OK.

Mucking about and playing soccer with the others was such a *normal* thing to do. He felt warm inside as he remembered people applauding. It gave him a sense of what life on Mars, at a personal level, could be like.

Anita's disapproving expression also lingered in his mind. Both in the dining hall and out at Noctis Labyrinthus. The way she berated Al made her seem angry and bitter, not like the woman Gianni had described being attracted to in his diary.

Luka delved into the drawer where he had hidden the data stick and stared at it for a moment. If Gianni had continued to talk about Anita in his diaries, then the key to understanding her better could lie within those videos. But part of him felt it would be intruding on Gianni's privacy to watch the secret thoughts he had recorded in the solitude of his room.

Luka had never seen the point of recording a diary himself. Life was too busy, his mind too jumbled, and he was too embarrassed to think that his ramblings would be discovered and watched by other people if he ever videoed them. Apart from people who decided to share their life with the world in pursuit of fame and fortune, he didn't really understand why anyone would want to keep a record of their innermost thoughts. Whatever the reason, he didn't think it was for a stranger to pry into. And yet, the way that Gianni had hidden the stick in his room – as if expecting a stranger to find it – suggested the opposite.

Luka was torn. He could be intruding on a dead man's private thoughts, or he could be honoring his memory. There was no way to tell without asking Gianni himself and, of course, that was impossible. In the end, his curiosity wouldn't allow him to hold the stick in his hand and not discover more about what it contained. So, still buzzing after playing soccer and not wanting to sleep yet, he succumbed to temptation and decided to watch more.

"I had dinner with Anita tonight," said Gianni to the camera.

He was smiling. An expression which didn't involve just his lips but lit up his whole face.

"She's new here and needs to get to know everybody," Gianni continued. "So, we decided to have dinner. I don't know if it was me who suggested it, or her, but we found we had enough credits between us to pay the extra to go to Cameron's Restaurant. I hadn't eaten at Cameron's for a long time and the food's not really any better than the daily rations, but they present it in a way which makes it appear more appetizing and it's nice to be able to sit at a quiet table with just the two of us. I felt… we had a connection."

Gianni paused, like he was thinking back to that moment. "We talked about work at first. Then things naturally moved onto why we had both come to Mars. I started off by repeating all the things I told the recruitment firm about wanting to contribute to the future of humanity on a new world and all that rubbish. But Anita made me feel so at ease that I started to tell her the truth. I told her how it sickens me to see how society resisted adaptation to deal with climate change on Earth, how the news of countries now supposedly under the control of one World Government continue to squabble over depleting resources, how it's impossible to walk down the street without witnessing the result of overpopulation in the poverty of so many people. She listened so intently, I felt that she understood.

"That's when she reminded me of the beauty of Earth." His eyes sparkled at the memory. "The blue of oceans and the soothing swish of waves as they lap a sandy beach. The luscious green of forests, still there despite the global rise in temperatures. Especially after the rain, when the air smells fresh and the birds emerge from their hiding places to sing in the sunshine. Earth is so very different to the relentless dry dust of Mars, she said. It's just a temporary thing, I told her. One day, Mars will be changed so all the natural resources we took for granted on Earth will be able to flourish here, but Anita doesn't buy into all that propaganda. She's a woman with her own mind, a woman who sees things as they really are.

"She looked sad as she reminded me that the Mars terraforming project will take hundreds of years. In our lifetimes we'll see the temperature rise a little, the atmosphere thicken a little, maybe with enough oxygen in it to be more than a trace element. But our generation is only at the beginning. It will be the children of our children, many generations down the line, who will live on a Mars which holds a mirror to the natural beauty of Earth.

"It made me think of the possibility of having children on Mars. For the first time, I was thinking about not just my future on this planet, but a future I could build for a family." He laughed to himself. "I didn't say it, but my mind was racing ahead to the possibility of having a family with Anita. It's stupid, right? After just one meal? But I have a good feeling about us."

Gianni looked like he was about to say something else, then shook his head as if changing his mind. "Time to sleep," he said, and told the window to stop recording.

The diary moved onto the next entry, which seemed to be about some technical issue which Gianni was grappling with at work. Luka turned it off while the man's excitement at his first date hung in the room. He seemed so happy and yet, Luka knew, within six months of making that recording, Gianni would be dead.

CHAPTER ELEVEN

Julie sat back on her sofa in the living room of her apartment, sipping from a glass of water and feeling privileged that, as an executive, she could afford to pay for more than the metered daily allowance. She was using one of her favorite glasses from the pair she kept in the cupboard. It was engraved with a diamond pattern which caught the subdued light from her ceiling and cast tiny rainbows over her hand. In front of her, covering the whole wall, was a window which showed a live feed of the Martian night sky.

When Julie had first arrived on Mars, she had taken one of those nighttime tourist trips where they drive out onto Sinai Planum and invite the wide-eyed newcomers to step out in a rad-suit to view the stars. The tour guide had pointed out Phobos, the closest lumpy rock to be honored with the designation of "moon" , appearing about half as wide as Earth's moon, as it moved across the sky in low orbit. So low, in fact, that it encircled the planet twice a day, orbiting faster than the rotation of Mars itself and appearing to move from west to east. Deimos, both smaller and further away, traveled a slower and more conventional route from east to west. To anyone standing near the equator, it would appear that the two celestial bodies would crash into each other above their heads. Julie remembered the anticipation and excitement as she, and the other newcomers, watched the moons converge on the collision zone. Only for the moons to safely pass each other with more than 17,000 kilometers to spare.

It had been a magical night when she was young and eager. Now even though she was older and more jaded, she still liked to watch the spectacle from time to time, although her days of joining a flock of tourists were over and she preferred to do it from the comfort of her sofa. With so much of her life taken up by meetings and reports, trapped inside some building in Tharsis City, it reminded her of the sense of wonder which drew people to venture into space in the first place. The unique orbits of the two moons was a sight only possible because humanity had the ingenuity to leave the planet where it had evolved and explore the solar system. It didn't matter that Mars' two natural satellites were most likely asteroids captured by the planet's gravity and bore little resemblance to the large globe which was the Earth's moon. It still evoked a lightning strike of excitement to witness the phenomenon.

The small, unassuming, gray lump of Deimos seemed to hang in the sky as it moved almost imperceptibly across the screen on Julie's window. While, from the left, came its faster and larger brother, appearing as if it was ready to knock its sibling out of orbit. But, as Phobos closed in, it merely passed in front of the smaller object, gradually eclipsing it from view before continuing its journey and allowing Deimos to come into view again.

Julie sipped at her water, which always tasted better in her favorite glass, no matter how many times it had been recycled through the city's reclamation system, and resigned herself to the task her WristTab reminded her she had to complete that evening. She told the window to turn off the view of the Martian night sky and activated her standard recording program. Making sure she was nicely framed by the camera, she began to record a message home.

"Hi, Mom, hi, Dad," she said, seeing herself played back in real time on the screen. "Hope you are well. You've probably heard on the news that I've been put in charge of the investigation into the asteroid disaster. It shows I still hold a position of respect around here, I suppose. Although I could do without the extra hassle ..."

Her WristTab bleeped and interrupted her flow. "Who the hell's that?" she said to herself. Realizing she had just screwed up the recording, she told the window to stop.

It was Kareem calling. She diverted the call to her window.

Kareem looked tired. There was a redness surrounding the deep brown of his eyes and stubble was starting to appear on his chin. From the view of empty chairs and desks in the background, it was clear that he was still at work and calling from his screen. He blinked a couple of times as he stared at the screen where Julie's image would be displayed. "What are you doing at home?" he asked.

"It's after office hours," said Julie. "It's traditional for people go home after office hours. You should try it sometime."

He glanced down at his WristTab. "Sorry, I didn't realize it was that late."

"What do you want?"

"Nothing. It can wait until tomorrow."

"You've already disturbed me. You might as well tell me what it is, or I'll be wondering all night what was so interesting to cause you to lose track of time."

"Not over the screen," said Kareem. "Tomorrow is fine. It's not urgent."

"Now I'm really curious," said Julie, a touch alarmed. "Why don't you come over? My place is on the way to yours – if you take the scenic route."

"Only if you promise I can drink water out of one of your posh glasses."

Julie chuckled. "You can sit on my 'posh' sofa, too, if you like."

"Great! I'll see you in a few minutes."

Julie terminated the call. She wasn't in the mood to record a message home anymore and rescheduled it in her diary for another day. She entered her kitchenette, took the second of her favorite glasses from the cupboard and used her account to pay for an extra ration.

Kareem arrived looking, if it was possible, even more disheveled than he had appeared on screen. He sat upright on the sofa, rather than take Julie's relaxed approach of reclining, and drunk down his water in only two mouthfuls.

"Do you want some more?" Julie asked.

"I thought you invited me round to hear what I've found out."

"I was trying to be a good host and pretend that I'm interested in your welfare and not just your brain."

Kareem laughed. She knew he would understand that she was joking, even though she was eager to discover what he had to say.

"Well," said Kareem, scratching the stubble on his chin. "According to my brain – and my research – the piece of metal attached to the asteroid fragment was definitely part of the guidance system. A squashed and severely damaged part of a propulsion engine to be precise."

"Not exactly surprising. It's how CrediCor brings asteroids from the belt."

"It means the piece of asteroid which broke away was close to the vibrations caused by the engine," said Kareem. "Those vibrations could have caused it to fracture and crash on Mars in two different locations: the first well away from a populated area as intended, and the second in Noctis Labyrinthus."

"I thought we agreed the two pieces are probably not from the same rock."

"I sent two samples away for analysis, but I'm not sure anymore. I placed the two rock samples next to each other and they *look* different, but after seeing the engine, I'm inclined to think the simplest explanation is the best. If the asteroid wasn't made of a uniform material and had a hidden flaw, then it could have fractured and two different looking pieces could have come down in different locations."

"Except the CrediCor data doesn't support that. Their scans determined it was a C-type asteroid with no fractures."

"I thought you didn't trust what they sent you."

"I don't, not entirely. But why crash an object into Mars if there was a chance it could splinter on entry? It's not like they're limited for choice in the asteroid belt. How many asteroids are there supposed to be out there?"

"More than million," said Kareem. "Give or take."

"Precisely. So, if this asteroid had been unsuitable, they would simply have chosen another."

"You're saying the scans missed something or CrediCor misunderstood how the asteroid would behave?"

"Maybe." Julie picked up her glass to take a sip of water, forgetting she had already drunk it all. Only a small droplet slid along the inside and touched her lip.

A myriad of thoughts filled her mind as she stood up from the sofa and walked across to the kitchenette for more water. How could CrediCor have miscalculated the asteroid's behavior? They were the experts in all this, after all. It seemed so strange and made her feel unnerved. As she placed the glass under the dispenser, she somehow misjudged the height of the counter, and clonked the glass against the base of the machine. It was knocked from her grasp. She watched helplessly as her beautiful, engraved vessel tumbled to the floor in the relative slow motion of Martian gravity and smashed into pieces.

She stared at the shards around her feet and a sudden, irrational wave of loss came over her. On a planet where resources were tight, personal possessions were few and irreplaceable objects like the glass were inordinately precious.

"Are you okay?" Kareem called from the sofa.

"My glass." Her voice sounded small.

He came over and stopped at the threshold of the kitchenette so as not to step on the shards. "Oh dear," he said in an understated, English way. "Do you want me to clear it up?"

"There's no need." But Julie found she could do nothing but stare at the pieces.

Kareem cleared it up anyway. Stepping carefully into the kitchenette, he picked up the bigger pieces and put them on the side before Julie swept up the rest of the shards and put them in the recycler.

"Are you going to tell me what's up?" said Kareem.

"That was my favorite glass."

"If the glass was the only thing on your mind, I don't think you would have dropped it."

Julie looked at Kareem's concerned face and knew that, as was so often the case, he understood her more than she understood herself. "I don't know... sometimes I feel like it's us two against the world – or Mars – or whatever you want to call it. Even when people offer to help, like with the ThorGate construction crew yesterday, it gets ruined by their Head of Projects."

"You don't know that," said Kareem. "She probably came over to check on what they were doing."

"Didn't you see the men's faces through their helmets when they realized who it was? Anyway, I made sure I was listening to their team comms as we were leaving."

"Isn't that against protocol?"

Julie turned to face him and rested against the back of the sofa. "Are you going to report me?"

"Of course not."

"It's just that you come here and say maybe the simple

explanation is the best, and I'm thinking to myself, maybe you're right. We can put this investigation to bed and concentrate on the thing we came here to do – terraform Mars. I've been so distracted, I don't even know how far behind we are on our greenhouse gas emission targets. Then I consider the evidence and I have all these nagging doubts."

"What doubts?"

"Don't say you don't have them too," said Julie. "For some reason, you ended up staying late at the office working on the asteroid problem. In my experience, when things are simple, people don't do that."

"That's because I found part of the control system for the engine embedded in the rock," Kareem admitted. "They had fused together with the heat of entry. I was trying to get data off the computer chips, but I didn't get very far – they're fairly corrupted."

"But you were intrigued enough to keep trying."

"Well, I…"

She could see it in his eyes. He had as much suspicion as she did, and even if their duty to UNMI was to put the matter to bed efficiently and concentrate on the work they were sent there to do, they had a higher duty to the people on Mars.

"You can't hide it from me, Kareem. There's something about this whole thing which is bothering you, like it's bothering me."

"I enjoy a puzzle, that's all," he confessed. "And a technical challenge."

"Keep trying to solve that puzzle," she said. "Because I'm not ready to let this go yet."

Julie headed back to the sofa and ordered the window to turn on. The confusion she'd felt earlier started to form into an idea.

Kareem followed. "What are you thinking?"

"Course corrections." She pulled up the CrediCor data showing the communications between their control center and the asteroid during landing. The list of times and codes had made her vision blur when she had first stared at them, but now that she knew more, they started to have meaning.

Kareem stared at the screen. "Course corrections?"

"Using gravity alone made sense more than three hundred years ago when people started to talk about smashing asteroids into Mars, but that's because there was no one living here," she said. "It didn't matter too much where they landed, as long as they did it with enough energy to warm the bedrock. It's not the case now. What's more, Bard Hunter's so arrogant he wants to make everyone aware that CrediCor is well and truly in the terraforming Mars race by crashing asteroids where people can see them. You can't be that accurate if you let gravity take over; there are always variables you can't account for. Especially with human activity increasing the volume of gas in the atmosphere."

"So, those are course corrections in the data," said Kareem, stroking his chin again.

Julie stood up and went over to the window. "Right." She pointed to a particular set of instructions that had been sent to the asteroid in flight. "Here, here and here. All minor course corrections causing the engines to fire short bursts during the descent."

"Makes sense. As you say, CrediCor is very specific as to the location of the crashes."

"Except it *doesn't* make sense," said Julie. "Not if a piece of the asteroid broke off – especially if that piece contained one of the engines. Forget about the mass of the asteroid suddenly being smaller – if it suddenly loses one of its engines and has a shifted center of gravity, then those course changes aren't going to *correct* the course, they're going to send it completely *off* course."

"Except the main asteroid landed exactly where it was supposed to," said Kareem.

"The fragment was the only piece which landed where it shouldn't. Does that sound right to you?"

"No. Being bigger, it should be affected less by the engines, but not completely unaffected. But what's the alternative explanation?"

"I don't know yet," said Julie, sensing the lure of the puzzle drawing her in. "But it means, the simplest explanation, no matter how attractive, can't be the real one."

CHAPTER TWELVE

Luka watched more of Gianni's diary. The narration of his relationship with Anita was compelling. Not in a sensual or explicit way, but in a way which pulled Luka into Gianni's life. Almost like he was living it alongside of him. Every day that his diaries told of their love growing deeper, Luka found himself enthralled and rooting for the success of their relationship. The journey of their romance, every moment of every date that Gianni described – from spending time at restaurants and public places, to being with Anita in her apartment, to the blossoming of intimacy between them – was captivating. Even though Luka knew it couldn't last, that Gianni would be dead six months after meeting Anita.

Not all of Gianni's diary was about Anita, however. In fact, a lot of it was about work or commentary about the political situation back on Earth. When he talked about that sort of thing, Luka would keep the entries playing while he did other things around the room. Although he was on his own, listening to Gianni's voice gave him a semblance of company.

That morning, Luka left the bathroom door open while he was getting ready for the day so he could hear Gianni talk about his frustrations with an over-burdened server on the Thor network. He thought he was only half listening until he realized he was holding his toothbrush in his mouth without brushing.

Gianni's entries had segued into talking about Anita.

He dropped the toothbrush, wiped the toothpaste from his mouth and went back to the main room of his apartment.

"Window, rewind playback by one minute."

Gianni's face cut from a worried expression to a thoughtful one. The lights in the recording were down low and Gianni had slung a fleece over his naked chest, as if he was half ready for bed, or had got up in the middle of the night.

"I can't stop thinking about Anita," he said to the camera, not bothering to adjust his disheveled hair where it had fallen partly over his face. "I wish it was in the way I used to think about Anita, but it's not. Something's wrong with her, I know it."

Luka sat on the bed and gave Gianni his full attention.

"We were both tired, I suppose. We didn't talk much, just went to bed. She fell asleep, but my mind was racing, and I lay awake for ages. Eventually, I got up and started looking at things on her window. Not private things, public things like the stats on atmospheric conditions, the latest from ICN, and the news from Earth. I went into the message system, but only to check my own messages. Anita had left herself logged on, so I could see she had a long list of things to deal with. I wasn't going to look at them – I mean, if they're anything like mine, they're mostly work related anyway.

"That was the moment she came out of the bedroom," Gianni continued. "She was furious… crazy, almost. Accused me of all sorts of things like invading her privacy and snooping around in things where I had no right. I tried to tell her, I was distracting myself to calm my head so I could get to sleep, but she didn't even listen let alone believe me.

"I know things have been difficult for her lately. She's been preoccupied and irritable. She's under a lot of pressure with the whole Noctis City project and the migrant workers due to arrive in less than a month, but there was no reason for her behavior. No reason that I could see. I asked her to tell me what was wrong. I said I could help, or if I couldn't help, at least I could be a sympathetic ear. But that seemed to make her angrier.

"It's not like her. I just wish she would tell me what's the matter. I know there are stages in love, and we've got past that early, exciting, passionate stage. I know a relationship has its ups and downs, but I sense this is not about us. She's taking it out on me because I'm the only one there. At least, I hope I haven't done something to upset her. I think she's hiding something from me. I want to help, but if she doesn't tell me what is wrong, how can I?"

Gianni stared into the camera, like there were still thoughts he wanted to articulate. But, after a moment, he shook his head and ended the recording.

The diary moved to the next entry. Luka might have continued sitting there to watch, but his WristTab bleeped.

He put the diary on pause and Gianni's face froze mid-word.

It was a message from Erik to remind him they were due to take a rover out to the Noctis construction site in the next five minutes.

He swore in German. He was late.

Luka stood from the bed, decided his teeth were clean enough, and gathered up his things. As he hurried for the door, he looked back at Gianni's frozen face.

"Window off," said Luka. The rest of the dead man's diary entries would have to wait.

Mist hung in the canyons of Noctis Labyrinthus, creating a mystical landscape of pathways which snaked over the red dust of Mars. The clouds of frozen water shone off-white in the light of the sun which had created them. During the night, the ice droplets had been frost, clinging in a thin layer to the maze of channels running through the Martian crust. As the morning broke, rays of sunshine were enough to warm the frost and turn it into gas which then refroze in the air to become ice fog. Their soft, gray beauty puffed up to just above the top of the ridge in a heavenly maze.

"Wow," breathed Luka, as he gazed out of the rover's windshield. "They said we were building Noctis City where the mist is gray, but I didn't think it would look so magical."

"Yeah," said Erik, who was half staring at the amazing phenomena while also driving the rover. "Quite a contrast to the usual red haze. This view never gets old."

As they closed in on the mist it seemed to dissipate. Partly because they were closer, but also because the activity around the construction site had interfered with the formation of frost and the only ice droplets hanging there had floated in from further up the canyon.

Luka and Erik put on their helmets, checked their rad-suits, and stepped out of the rover to walk the few meters to where the migrants had already started their working day. Central to the activity was one of the robots Luka had programmed. It gathered up a jaw full of magnesium supports and trundled along a pre-determined path to the elevator. Once on the platform, a signal was sent to the central controller, and it descended into the canyon. At the bottom, it used its wide tires and flexible suspension to disembark and negotiate its way to deposit the cargo. Once it had stacked the magnesium poles neatly on top of the pile already there, the robot returned to the elevator to begin the process all over again.

"Looking good," said Erik over Luka's private comms channel.

"That's the easy part," replied Luka. "Building down there in the canyon is going to be more problematic. I don't know how much automation will be possible. It's a difficult site."

"Human operated machines will be needed at the base of the canyon," said Erik.

"That's what I think, but Anita wants to automate as much as possible."

"Ah, Anita." Erik nodded in understanding, which always looked weird on the surface of Mars because his head moved inside his suit while the bulb of his helmet stayed still. "Anita is under a lot of pressure from ThorGate. You have to cut her some slack."

Luka got the feeling Erik was about to say more, but

something distracted him. He turned round and, as Luka did the same, he saw another rover arrive and park next to theirs.

"I didn't realize this was today," said Erik.

"Today?"

"Drilling."

Erik didn't elaborate further. He took himself off Luka's private comms channel and strode over to where Al was talking to some of the other workers. The supervisor waved his arms expressively and it was only when Luka also listened in to the team comms that he caught the tail end of a conversation about stopping the robot and preparing the drilling equipment.

Drilling into the bedrock at the bottom of the canyon was essential to construct the city. The foundations would need to be anchored into the ground, which was what the initial delivery of magnesium was for. Drilling was also necessary to access underground aquifers which would supply the people living there with water. At least for the first few generations until terraforming enabled liquid water to exist on the surface.

The robot arrived back at the pile of building materials, opened its jaw to gather up more and simply stopped.

Erik returned and gestured that they should flick back to the private channel. "Sorry, Luka. No one told me about this."

"No one told you what?"

"The scientists are here to take samples. We can't get access to the base of the canyon until they're done. We'll have to assess robot movements up here as best we can."

"Samples of what?"

"Soil and water. To make sure we're not building over something we shouldn't be. Sort of like an archeological survey."

"On Mars?" said Luka. "What sort of ancient civilization are they expecting to find?"

"Probably nothing, but if there's a colony of little green men under there, there's going to be a lot of red-faced scientists."

Luka had been involved in several projects back home where contractors were required to employ archeologists to assess a site before work could commence. It was a complete pain, and expensive for the contractor – especially if something was found. On one site on the east coast of Spain, archeologists discovered the remains of a Roman villa with a mosaic floor and the whole project was set back by a year. But there was nothing remotely like that on Mars. People had been searching for signs of life since the end of the twentieth century and had not found as much as a single example of alien bacteria.

"I thought the site had already been surveyed," said Luka.

Erik waved his hand dismissively. "It's some concession to the Reds written into the Terraforming Committee mandate, from what I understand. Samples have to be analyzed at the beginning of every construction project."

"Seems a bit like overkill," said Luka. "Wouldn't it be easier for ThorGate to send over a few samples?"

"Easier, but illegal," said Erik. "That's what they used to do until it was discovered some unscrupulous corporations were making sure the samples were clean before they sent them over. Often, they weren't even from the same site. After that, it was made a condition of construction that the scientists personally supervise the taking of samples."

Luka looked across to the elevator platform where some of the workers were loading up drilling equipment while the three scientists watched them. "It won't take long, will it?"

"Hopefully not. I'm going to wait it out in the habitat. Want to come?"

"No, I'll stay a bit longer," said Luka. There was something else he wanted to look at.

"Sure thing!" said Erik, waving as he strode off towards the rover.

Luka glanced further up the canyon to where the asteroid had crashed into the research station and killed Gianni. After spending so much time with the man's diary, he felt drawn to it. To pay his respects if nothing else.

Luka told Al where he was going – as was required by health and safety guidelines – and walked further up the ridge.

The haze of mist which cloaked the asteroid seemed to lift as he got nearer, and the light from the sun climbing higher in the sky revealed a site dusted with red. There was nothing left to show that the research station had ever been there. The debris which had littered the canyon on the day of the crash had all been taken away. Even the blackened exterior of the asteroid itself was now covered in the planet's own particles, as if Mars wanted to hide away evidence of the disaster. Only a few scorch marks remained on the side of the canyon and even they were barely noticeable.

For the first time since he had started to watch his diaries, Luka thought about the way Gianni died. Soon after the asteroid had killed him, the Chair of the Terraforming Committee had stood in front of the canyon and told ICN that there had been no scientists at the research station at the time of the crash, but that didn't explain why Gianni was there. He wasn't supposed to be stationed there; he wasn't even a scientist.

Luka stood for a long time, lost in his thoughts, and looking for answers which he could not see in the haze of Noctis Labyrinthus.

Until he heard his name.

"Luka Schäfer?" It sounded like Anita Andreassen.

He turned back towards the construction site and saw a rad-suited figure approach him. After a few moments, he could see enough of her face to confirm he had correctly recognized her voice.

"Hello, Anita," he said. "Did you need me?"

"I came to discuss construction automation, but Alvar said you had walked off."

"I couldn't do anything useful with the drilling going on. That's not a problem, is it?"

"Only in that we had an appointment. I need you to compile a full report about why human operated machines must be used in the canyon. I know it was in the original budget and it's partly why we brought all the migrants out here, but the ThorGate accountants are nervous after the asteroid disaster. They invested a lot of MegaCredits into that research station and the whole thing got squashed under a rock."

"What were they researching, exactly?" asked Luka.

"Plants," said Anita, simply.

"Plants?"

"Ones which can grow on the surface of Mars, despite the harsh conditions. The canyons of Noctis are considered a prime site because of the moisture in the area. Have you seen the mist?"

"I saw it this morning. It was beautiful."

"It's also the reason the corporations fought for the right to carry out genetic experiments here. Noctis Labyrinthus runs for kilometers, but this is one of the best places, partly because it's next to where the city will be and has access to Valles Marineris. People were furious that ThorGate was given the right to run the research station when people said it should be a corporation with a track record in bioengineering like Ecoline, but ThorGate has more resources and so won the contract. Didn't you see all the arguments on the news?"

"I don't follow politics," confessed Luka.

"I wish I had that luxury."

"But Gianni didn't know anything about plants. He was a computer expert, a programmer, like me. I don't understand what he was doing here when the asteroid hit."

Luka glanced back towards the dust-covered asteroid fragment; a giant tombstone for a man he only knew through his recordings.

"Gianni was stupid," said Anita. "He shouldn't have gone out there alone."

"But I don't understand why he was there at all. No one seems to talk about it."

"They don't talk about it because it reminds them that Mars can be a dangerous place," said Anita. "Everyone knows the risks, but they don't admit it to themselves most of the time because it's easier that way. The ironic thing is, Mars is only dangerous if you forget that the planet was not built for humans. That can lead to carelessness. There have been people who've gone out in their rad-suits without bothering to run through the checks and almost died when their air ran out."

"Was Gianni careless? Even if he had gone out to the research station with someone else, they both would have been killed."

"Gianni…" His name caught in her throat as emotion showed in her voice. "There had been some sort of computer glitch at the research station which affected the environmental controls, so the scientists had to evacuate while it was fixed. Gianni didn't tell me what he was doing. I can only assume he went there to fix it."

"Wasn't the station on the network? Couldn't he fix it remotely?"

"That's the question I've been asking myself since he died. I don't think I'll ever know why."

The hint of tears in her eyes caught the rays of the rising sun. Or it could have been a reflection on her helmet. Either way, Luka's questions had stirred emotions within Anita he had not seen before. It was a glimpse of the other side of the relationship that, up until that point, he had only heard about from Gianni. It seemed that their romantic connection was real, while its memory was fresh and painful.

She switched off her comms, so Luka could no longer intrude on her private moment, turned away from him and headed back to the construction site.

CHAPTER THIRTEEN

Julie had more information to work with thanks to Kareem who – after a little sleep and with a fresh pair of eyes – had managed to pull some scraps of code from the guidance system which had fused itself to the asteroid fragment. Severely corrupted, they were disjointed bits and pieces which meant nothing on their own. The only way to make sense of it was to compare the code she had with the full and uncorrupted version supplied by CrediCor. This was the point where Julie got stuck.

She felt like she was trying to put together a jigsaw puzzle, using a picture on the box which didn't match up to the pieces she had to hand. Even when she thought she had found the part of the code where one of the snippets would fit, there was always something which made her pause. Some small variation which only became apparent when she directly compared the two. The only conclusion she could come to was that the code CrediCor had sent her was not the one used to bring down the asteroid.

Julie contacted the asteroid controller to ask for the correct version. Yet, when it arrived, it was exactly the same one as she had spent the morning looking at. She swore at the computer, as if it were the machine's fault, and kicked the desk.

There was nothing else she could do to extract the correct code from CrediCor, short of a full audit of the offices, and she didn't think Rufus Oladepo would authorize that. Not with the flimsy evidence she had. Assuming, of course, that she was right about the data she was looking at. She couldn't be sure either way.

It was finally time, Julie decided, to seek out her father's coffee. She didn't keep it in the office, but in a secret place at the back of a cupboard in her apartment. If she went to get it, it would force her to take a break and a bit of a walk would probably do her good.

Not as if there was any real "outside" in Tharsis City, only different layers of "inside". So, when she stepped into the street, she was actually moving from the secluded area of the office building into the enclosed environment of the city. The air that she breathed and the temperature she experienced were the same wherever she was. Only her surroundings had changed.

It was the first big city to be built on Mars and consisted of a series of mostly rectangular pressurized buildings linked by walkways. By far the biggest of which was the corporate quarter which housed not only UNMI headquarters, but also most of the other corporate headquarters and the Terraforming Committee offices which lay on either side of its main street. Julie had once described it to her mother as a bit like a shopping center with many separate buildings housed within a main structure. It was a crude analogy which did nothing to reflect the technological achievement of such a construction, but it made her mother happy.

It was not long after the city was built and the first people began living there that the population rebelled to take over the running of the place and created their own cooperative, the Tharsis Republic. UNMI and other organizations, merely rented their space from the Republic and, to a certain extent, had to abide by its rules. This uncomfortable arrangement had led to a lot of the wealthier corporations branching out to build their own cities. Nevertheless, until the Terraforming Committee could agree on the construction of some sort of purpose-built capital to become the administrative hub of the planet, the various organizations had to keep a presence in Tharsis City.

When Julie stepped out of UNMI headquarters, she automatically turned left to head home. But it was only a short walk and the thought of getting straight back to work again – even if it was on her sofa in front of the window – wasn't what she needed. So, she turned back the way she had come and kept walking beyond the corporate quarter towards the Oasis.

The Oasis, a reserve of plant life at the south end of Tharsis City, was more than a park. It was more than a garden. Rather, it was a connection to something primal. Humans had evolved within an all-sustaining ecosystem and, despite their desire to leave their home planet, they couldn't sever the link they had to the natural world. The utilitarian buildings and inorganic materials which surrounded the settlers of Mars fulfilled their basic needs to eat, drink, breathe and stay warm, but their purely utilitarian nature risked dulling the spirit. With only an arid, dusty desert and an unbreathable atmosphere waiting for them on the outside, the builders decided to construct an oasis of plant life on the inside. It was a bit of the natural world they had left behind and a reminder of what Mars might be like when their terraforming plans were brought to fruition – even if they knew they would not survive to see it do so.

Julie could smell the organic aroma as she approached the Oasis. Its sweet oxygen, created by living things, not extracted from oxidized rock, drifted out of the reserve into the last few meters of Main Street. Within the air were other trace gases created by the circle of life. Bacteria in the soil broke down the dead leaves dropped by the plants, while flowers released enticing scents to attract insects to their pollen. There were no insects in the Oasis, of course, as the risk of them flying out into the rest of the city and causing havoc was too great, leaving a human or robot force to do that particular work. But the flowers tried to attract them anyway.

The entrance was a wide, rectangular opening a little taller than head height which was cut into the side of the domed enclosure. Stepping through, Julie transitioned from the solid, radiation-shielded roof of the main city street into a transparent arc of tessellating hexagons which allowed sunlight to filter through. It was one of the first places on Mars where it was possible to look up to the sky without being inside a cumbersome protective suit or stuck inside a rover with only a front windshield. The white disk of the sun, appearing a little more than half the size seen from Earth, shone down through a cloudless pink haze. It was so mesmerizing that Julie almost fell over a small child as he ran out from between two trees towards Main Street. He didn't seem to notice her either, as he had picked up a twig which had fallen from one of the trees and was waving it in front of him like an ancient sword.

As she watched him escape with his contraband – it was strictly forbidden to remove any part of the environment from its designated area – she noticed the barriers at either side of the boundary and the radiation warning lights next to them. The transparent domed roof could only act as a partial radiation filter and couldn't protect people against a major solar flare. They didn't happen very often, but in those circumstances the area had to be sealed off to leave the plants to endure the effects on their own.

She put thoughts of radiation out of her mind as she stepped under a canopy of arching tree branches to move further into the Oasis. Narrow paved strips wended their way through the various areas, from the almost-wild woodland to the right of the entrance, to a meadow-like grassy area where flowers stood tall to reach the sunlight and opened their petals wide in yellow, mauve, and soft pink salutations to the world. Julie stopped beside them and allowed her gaze to sink into their beauty. She forgot all about asteroids, computer code and the investigation. Her breathing became deep and long, her heartbeat slowed and the tension in her shoulders eased a little.

Her WristTab bleeped. "What now?" she said.

She had forgotten to turn off notifications and there were

a couple of messages waiting for her. Her relaxation time, it seemed, was over. She started to look forward to that cup of coffee she had promised herself and turned around to resume the walk back to her apartment.

The smell of coffee filled Julie's apartment with an earthy, bittersweet calm. Above her, the air filters in the ceiling were busy removing its impurities so odorless, clean air could be restored. But, for that precious moment, the aroma was intoxicating.

Julie had never been much of a coffee drinker in her younger days. She would accept a cup if it was offered, and would happily chat over whatever variety was in fashion if she met a friend at a cafe, but she hadn't lived off the stuff like some of the people she worked with at the university back home. Living on Mars meant she couldn't be much of a coffee drinker now that she was older either, even if she wanted to. It wasn't a priority crop for farming, and imports from Earth were both expensive and rare. Which was why her father chose it as a present to send to her and which made each cup she brewed from it all the more special.

She cupped her hands around the hot ceramic mug and took it to her sofa where she rested a moment before switching the window away from the view of Mars to bring up the fragmented code from the asteroid guidance system. It was just as disjointed and incomprehensible magnified on her wall as it had been in her office. Revitalized eyes, it seemed, made very little difference.

Julie sipped at the coffee and savored its strong flavors while the steam settled into tiny droplets of water on her nose. As she waited for the caffeine to hit, she brought up the unfragmented CrediCor version of the code alongside the fragments. Steadily, as she stared, she began to see where the pieces of the recovered code fitted within the original.

The caffeine was starting to weave its magic.

She swigged even more of the coffee and sat forward on her seat to lean closer towards the screen. She realized where she had been going wrong in the office. She had been trying to find an exact match where there wasn't one. What she actually needed to do was find an approximate match and, that way, she could see where the pieces fitted into the original. It was like the jigsaw puzzle had been cut slightly differently each time to form two pictures which were similar, but not the same.

Unravelling what it meant was another problem entirely. The programmers had, helpfully, put in occasional notation in English to describe what each segment of the code did when activated. Mostly, they were words such as "angle" , "thruster" , "altitude" , but sometimes they were more obscure initials. As Julie compared the fragments to the intact original, she began to see notations which weren't in the official CrediCor version. What's more, they appeared to relate to the discrepancies between the two, with each of the five alterations marked up with a single letter: E, R, and D.

Julie sat back and brought her coffee mug to her lips, only to discover she had already drunk it all. She put the cup on the table and took another look at the code on her window.

The initials could mean anything. Engine, Relative, Direction?

Entry, Reverse, Divergence?

It could be Ethel, Roger, and Doris for all she knew!

She rubbed at her forehead as if that would help enliven her brain cells. But the caffeine had weaved all the magic it was capable of. This was a puzzle she didn't have the skills to solve.

Idly, she dragged the fragments over the top of the original code to get a sense of how much of it was missing from the pieces Kareem had pulled from the squashed guidance system. Her gaze was drawn once again to the five initials: E, R, E, D, R. Her mind, designed to seek out patterns in everything it experienced, couldn't help but read the word nestled in the middle of the letters: RED.

"Surely not," she said to herself.

If ever there was an organization opposed to the terraforming of Mars, then it was the Reds. The political party hated the fact that human beings wanted to turn Mars into a second Earth, with green forests and blue oceans because they believed Mars should remain red. The destruction of ThorGate's research station would have thrilled them because what ThorGate's scientists had planned to do was anathema to their ideals. If the asteroid disaster hadn't prevented the scientists from doing their work, they would already be adapting Earth plants to grow within the mists of Noctis Labyrinthus and turning a little bit of the planet from red to green.

The Reds certainly had a motive.

But there were pieces of the puzzle still missing. The first E and the final R in the list of initials could be parts of the word Red, but they could equally spell something else entirely or nothing at all. If someone working for the Reds had marked up the code to remind them where they had made the alterations, they had been sloppy to leave the notations behind – even if they assumed they would never be found. Unless the Reds paid someone within CrediCor to do it and their agent had deliberately left clues out of some sort of divided loyalty. There were many possibilities and spending more hours staring at the code while trying to guess what was in the missing pieces wasn't going to help her get to the truth.

The only thing Julie knew for sure was, once she had seen the word *red*, she couldn't unsee it. And she couldn't ignore it. The code was pointing her to the political party which opposed the terraforming of Mars and she had no choice but to follow. The more she thought about the possibility of the Reds being involved, the more it seemed possible. It seemed very possible indeed.

CHAPTER FOURTEEN

Luka was supposed to be meeting Erik and the others for an early dinner, but instead was sitting on his own in the office they all shared, thinking about Gianni. Ever since his conversation with Anita near the asteroid crash site, he had been trying to make sense of why Gianni would have gone to the research station alone rather than try to fix the computer remotely. He wanted to ask Gianni what on Earth – or, rather, what on Mars – he had been doing. But Gianni was dead. The only ones who had been there and survived were the scientists. It made him want to find out more about them so he could put to them the questions he couldn't ask Gianni.

Publicly available information on the scientists was sparse. There were only five on the initial team sent to begin work at the station, all of whom were specialists in biology and genetics. A statement from ThorGate issued at the time said they would be working on projects including adapting lichen suitable for early terraforming and experiments to harness the resilience of plants brought from the arctic regions of Earth. What happened to them after the asteroid had destroyed the research station was harder to discover and Luka, even though he had new security clearance, felt a stab of guilt as he faked credentials and hacked his way in using a false name to gain access to ThorGate's staff records.

The database showed that three of the scientists had moved back to Tharsis City after the asteroid disaster where they appeared to be still employed by ThorGate although apparently not yet assigned to a new project. Two remained in Thor Town. One lived in an apartment on the opposite side of town to Luka and worked in a department developing future projects for the corporation. The other was Doctor David Kobayashi, who he had seen on ICN looking shell-shocked the day after the crash. What Doctor Kobayashi was subsequently employed to do wasn't listed, which suggested either his work was too secret to be recorded at the level Luka had access to or, which seemed equally plausible, no one had got around to updating the system.

David's personal life, however, was the complete opposite of secret, as he had made it publicly available for anyone who wanted to know. There were swathes of information about his romantic life, which seemed to involve a string of quickly dumped girlfriends, plus some details of his hobbies and interests. He was into martial arts, which had been somewhat of a family tradition after his great grandfather brought his skill from Japan to America and became a superstar within the karate world by winning several high-profile competitions.

Luka would have delved deeper, but the door to the office was flung open and Erik came in with the brazenness of a man unaware that he was disturbing anyone.

Luka jumped in his chair. "Erik, don't you knock?"

"Not usually to enter my own office," he said, heading for his desk which was perilously close to Luka's. Luka surreptitiously entered a few commands into his computer and withdrew from the parts of the ThorGate network where he wasn't strictly supposed to be. He erased the fake credentials, knowing he could never use them again.

Erik grabbed his bag from where he had left it under his chair. "I messaged you to say if you're coming to the dining hall, can you bring my bag. Didn't you get my messages?"

Luka had been too distracted. He hadn't even noticed Erik's bag was there. "Sorry, I was absorbed with work."

"Why don't you leave that now and join us for dinner?"

Luka thought about the information about Doctor David Kobayashi he had just read, but knew he wasn't going to get much more done that evening. He wasn't even sure there was much more he could do from the office, even if he kept rummaging around in the restricted parts of the ThorGate network. "OK," he said, closing down his computer. "Although I'm not sure I'm that hungry yet."

"Blame Pete," said Erik. "He wanted to eat early because of his maternity class."

"Maternity class?"

"Him and his wife are having a baby, didn't you know?"

"I haven't seen much of Pete, we've been working on other projects."

"I suppose you haven't. He must have made the big

announcement before you started with us. She's seven months into the pregnancy, I think."

"Wow," said Luka. "That's a big decision to have children out here."

"Having children is a big decision anywhere," said Erik.

"But growing up in such reduced gravity, they might never be able to go to Earth."

"If you'd been born here, would you seriously want to go to Earth with the way things are back there?"

"I think I'd want the option."

Erik slung his bag over his shoulder and waited while Luka collected his own bag from under his desk.

"You wouldn't have children on Mars, then?" asked Erik. "If you had the opportunity, I mean."

Luka thought about Lena and Oskar. In his mind, they were still six and four, although if they had lived, Lena would be ten and Oskar would be coming up to his eighth birthday. "No, I don't think I would have kids again."

"You have children on Earth, then?"

"Not anymore," said Luka, revealing the plain fact without accessing the emotion attached to it. "They died."

"Oh, mate." Erik's face suddenly crumpled with sympathy. "I'm sorry, I didn't know."

Luka shrugged his concern away. "They were caught up in the Rhine Valley Disaster."

"That awful chemical leak? I can't imagine how terrible it must have been for you."

The pain of the memory came back to him in a rush. Luka had thought he could tell his friend what happened to his family. He thought time and space had put enough distance between him and the horrific event so he was numb to the reality of his grief. But it was suddenly there again, the sense of loss, like a knife through his heart.

"How did you manage to survive?" asked Erik. "I thought the fumes were so bad that virtually no one in the surrounding towns was able to get out."

"I wasn't there when it happened, I was working in another part of the country. I didn't have the chance to save them. Not my children. Not my wife."

A silence fell between them and, in the absence of anything else, the memories returned.

It had been after a successful business meeting where he had secured a major new contract that an ashen-faced woman had taken him aside and suggested he find a quiet place to turn on the news. He remembered the confusion as the screen was filled with images of an unnatural fog hanging over the town of Königswinter. He could still feel the desperation as he tried to call his wife – then her work, the children's school, their friends, their neighbors – and no one answered.

He could still taste the nausea as he watched from the comfort of an office building while firefighters in breathing apparatus staggered out of the toxic haze carrying the limp bodies of people who they lay on the ground where paramedics hopelessly tried to revive them. He was still chilled by the ice that burrowed its way into his heart as he was gripped by helplessness one hundred and fifty kilometers away in Frankfurt.

Someone from the office took him to the airport where he begged, shouted, and cried to be allowed onto a flight back home. There was the feeling of desolation as he sat on a plane shaking and crying while an air steward tried to serve him coffee and a small snack.

He rushed to be with his family, but he was barred from entering what was termed the "disaster zone" and no matter who he approached, who he threatened, or who he attempted to bribe, he couldn't get through the guarded barriers hastily erected by the emergency services. The sleepless, anxious days that followed were lost in a haze of memory, but the calendar told him it was a week before a volunteer led him into a converted community hall to identify his wife and children. They had been laid out respectfully so it disguised the horror of what had happened. But he knew from the testimony of a few survivors that it had been a slow and agonizing death that began with a burning in the throat, then a searing in the lungs until they collapsed and convulsed while gasping their last breaths.

Erik didn't seem to know what to say. There was nothing he could say. Nothing anyone could say.

"Perhaps we should, um… get to the dining hall," said Erik eventually. "The others will be waiting for us."

Luka blinked away the tears from his eyes. "Yeah," he said.

He took the memories of the past which he had inadvertently set free, enclosed them back in the lead-lined box which he kept inside, and did his best to bury them two meters beneath the surface of his consciousness.

"I've actually got something to tell you which I think might cheer you up," said Erik, resuming his breezy, carefree air. Not to undermine what Luka had told him, he was sure, but to relieve the tension.

Luka looked at him warily, trying to get back to the emotional place where he could exchange easy banter with his friend. "Why am I suddenly feeling nervous?"

"It's nothing to feel nervous about. It turns out the coach for the ThorGate football team is a fellow Swede who traveled out to Mars with me. I've sent her a message – I'm sure I can get you a try out."

"Erik…" The thought of socializing with a whole new team of people made him uneasy. "I'm not really interested."

"Nonsense. We can talk about it over dinner – you can start an argument with Pete about whether it's called soccer or football if you like."

"OK," said Luka, managing a smile at Erik's silly joke.

"Good man," said Erik, giving him a friendly slap on the back.

They made their way out of the office, into the street and towards the communal dining hall with Erik chatting about inconsequential things on the way. But even though Luka tried to bury them deep, the painful memories of what had happened to his family continued to burn inside of him. He still carried with him the guilt that he wasn't with his wife and children when they had needed him most. It was a guilt he knew that, no matter what he went on to do with his life, would always be with him.

CHAPTER FIFTEEN

Kirra Morgan, the leader of the Reds political party, was an older woman with a short, bobbed haircut which had turned almost entirely gray. Also gray was the smart suit she wore over a pristine white shirt with a short, upright collar which made her appear more businesslike than many of the business operatives working out of the corporate quarter. The only flash of vivid color about her was a string of red beads which she wore high up on her neck.

She breezed into her own office with the confidence of someone who knows she's important. Julie, who had been sitting waiting for some time, hurriedly broke away from consulting her WristTab and stood to greet her.

"Sorry I wasn't available when you arrived," said Kirra, sounding not sorry in the slightest. "If you had booked an appointment, I would have made an effort to be here."

"I was happy to wait."

"Just as well."

"I don't think we've met," said Julie, offering her hand. "I'm Julie Outerbridge."

Kirra conducted a firm, but perfunctory handshake. "Everyone on Mars knows who you are."

Julie had that horrible feeling again of her fame – or, possibly, notoriety – proceeding her. Kirra, as the Reds leader, was also a public figure, in as much as all the leaders of the political parties on the Terraforming Committee were. Although, out of all of them, the Reds was the party Julie had paid the least attention to. Their whole philosophy sat one hundred eighty degrees from her own and they were never going to win her vote.

"I'm investigating the asteroid disaster at Noctis Labyrinthus," said Julie.

"I also watch the news," said Kirra, with a smile. "But I'm surprised you're here. My assistant said you gave the impression of it being urgent, but I fail to see how the Reds could help your investigation."

Kirra sat down behind her own desk and Julie took it as the cue to also sit.

"It's no secret you opposed the development of research to grow adapted Earth plants in the canyon," Julie started.

"My vote against it in the Committee is a matter of record," said Kirra. "Contaminating the landscape of Mars by trying to turn it into some sort of Little Earth is a violation of the natural order of things."

"Even if it allows the human race to survive?"

"If the human race wanted to survive, it should have made a better job of looking after its home planet rather than going off to ruin another one."

"We're not ruining Mars," Julie insisted. "We're making it habitable. Before the first crewed landing, this planet was barren with nothing but dust, rocks, and mountains. We are giving it a chance to be something greater than that. It may take generations, but one day Mars could be teeming with life and provide an environment for our children's children to live a good life."

"I'm sure that's what your ancestors said when they left Europe to colonize America," said Kirra, " and look at all the terrible things that resulted from that."

Julie grimaced. She was well aware of some of the more abhorrent incidents of human history and didn't need reminding. "I like to think humanity has evolved since then." She calmed herself and resisted the urge to argue further. "But I didn't come here to discuss politics."

"Shame," said Kirra. "I was rather enjoying it."

"I need to ask you about the asteroid crash at Noctis. It must have pleased you to know the research station you voted against was destroyed."

"I wasn't pleased to hear that a man died."

"It suits your agenda, though, doesn't it? One more set back along the road to terraforming."

"Are you accusing the Reds of something, Julie Outerbridge? Because if you are, I would like to know what it is."

"There's evidence to suggest that the disaster wasn't an accident. It's possible that the asteroid fragment was deliberately guided to crash into the canyon and destroy the research station."

By the look on Kirra's face, this piece of information came

as a surprise. "You think, because we opposed the research station in the first place that we would do such a thing? I remind you that we weren't the only people who spoke out against it. None of the other corporations wanted ThorGate to control that site. If you're claiming that the Reds had a motive, then you should also look at Phobolog, Ecoline, Helion, and all the other corporations. You've dealt with these people, you know most of them think the project to terraform Mars is a race, not a collaboration. They would be more than happy to see a rival suffer if it meant they could gain an advantage."

Julie decided to go in hard and hide any doubts she might have from her interrogation subject. "I have evidence, Kirra."

"Against the Reds?" Kirra stared directly at Julie as if evaluating her honesty. "I sincerely doubt it."

Julie linked her WristTab to the window in Kirra's office and both women stood facing it as the fragments of code with their highlighted R, E and D letters were brought up one by one.

"You call that evidence?" said Kirra. Her tone was mocking, but there was a part of her voice which also expressed relief.

"Each of these variations from the official guidance program are marked with a notation which spells the name of your party," said Julie.

"Hardly conclusive."

"It points the finger of blame at you."

"Three initials in a jumble of letters that happen to spell the word Red? Julie, I understood from your reputation that you're an intelligent woman. Are you here to prove that your reputation is undeserved?"

"Don't insult me, Kirra. Answer the question."

"If any member of my party were to do what you suggest, they wouldn't telegraph it like a demonstrator wielding a placard on a protest march."

"So you deny it?"

"Of course I deny it! These letters–" she waved her hand in the direction of the code fragments on the window "– must have been planted by someone who wants to discredit us. Let's face it, with all the corporations and the rest of the political parties against us, the Reds are an easy target. Whoever it was left a little trail of crumbs for you to find, and you dutifully picked them up. You thought you were being clever when you put them together to form a conclusion, but it was a conclusion that someone else led you to."

Julie swallowed the sense that Kirra was continuing to insult her. "But you cannot deny that the Reds had a motive."

Kirra paused and allowed her outrage to soften. "Perhaps I should explain something about the Reds." She stepped away from the window, perched her bottom on the edge of her desk and folded her arms across her chest. "We have no illusions about being on the losing side of the terraforming debate. Corporations are here and they're fighting for a slice of the MegaCredits pie to stake their claim on the new frontier. I cannot put my arguments before the Terraforming Committee and expect the whole project to be put on hold, no matter how right I know I am. I understand that. But we can fight against the most extreme and destructive projects and bring a little sanity to the competitive corporate culture. To do that successfully, we need support. You only need to look at history to know that terrorism and sabotage would merely gain us support from fanatics and lead us to be ostracized from the mainstream. So, even if we were capable of sending an asteroid off course to destroy something we disagreed with, we wouldn't do it. It would be counterproductive."

Kirra's argument was compelling and Julie felt bound to accept it at face value even though it came from the lips of a politician. "You understand that when I saw the word 'Red' in the code, I had to ask you. Regardless of whether it might be – and excuse the pun – a red herring."

Kirra smiled at the half joke. "Indeed."

Julie touched the controls on her WristTab, the fragments of code disappeared from the window and were replaced by the static image of the Reds logo of a red circle, depicting Mars, on a yellow flag. "I shall be in touch if I need anything further."

She walked to the door, fearing her investigation had hit a dead end. Her evidence, as Kirra had astutely pointed out, was hardly conclusive. She wasn't sure what she could pull further from the CrediCor data. Maybe she'd truly hit a dead end.

"Julie, wait a minute."

Julie stopped and turned.

"I don't want us to argue," said Kirra. "I actually have a lot of respect for you. When you ran the terraforming projects here before the Committee was established, you did so with integrity."

"Do you mean that I didn't get very far?"

Kirra laughed. "That's not what I meant, although it's true. Terraforming has forged ahead since the corporations became involved. But that's because they command more resources than a World Government-funded operation ever could. What I meant is, even though our philosophies are different, I respect the way you do business. Much more so than certain other corporation bosses I could mention."

"It's nice of you to say so," said Julie.

"So, you really think the asteroid disaster was deliberate?"

"Almost certainly."

"Let me know if there's anything I can do to help you in the investigation," said Kirra.

"I'm sure there isn't."

"Well, if you change your mind, speak to my assistant and make an appointment. I will endeavor not to keep you waiting next time."

Julie left, disappointed that she had not found the smoking gun in the fragments of code that she thought she had. But also confused as to whether Kirra was someone she liked and respected, or whether she wasn't. The woman had surprised her with her pragmatism, and she would have to give that idea some thought.

Julie sat in her office after hours with the lights down low. It was so quiet, with everyone else finished for the day, that she could hear the faint whir of the air exchangers gently removing the carbon dioxide she breathed out and trace elements like Martian dust, which somehow got inside the building, replacing it with a clean mix of oxygen and nitrogen. Her screen told her there were messages waiting for her, but she didn't open them. They were all to do with day to day UNMI business and she couldn't bring herself to deal with the minutiae of running the organization she was supposed to be running.

Her conversation with Kirra Morgan had been unexpectedly affecting. It was true what she said, that virtually every organization on Mars had a motive for damaging ThorGate's foray into plant experiments. Many people held the view that the corporation, which had grown out of the dying oil industry to pioneer the use of alternative energies, held too much power on Mars. Everyone who lived there relied, to some extent, on technologies developed by ThorGate and their sway over the Terraforming Committee was considerable. She wouldn't be surprised if every one of their rivals had secretly cheered when they heard the asteroid had destroyed one of ThorGate's projects. As for which one of those rivals could be responsible, she would be able to make a case for all of them if she put her mind to it. If only she had some definitive evidence.

Another message pinged into her already cluttered inbox. Her body sagged at the thought of dealing with yet more UNMI minutiae until she saw it was a personal message from Earth from her parents.

Welcoming the distraction, she opened it and the video began to play.

Her father waved at her from the screen and broke into a big smile which revealed his straight, white teeth which he was always very particular about looking after. "Hello, Julie! This is Dad!"

She returned his smile as she remembered the number of

times she had told him he didn't need to introduce himself over the video because she knew what her own father looked like. Although, as she scanned his face, she reflected that he was looking older. He had lost more of his hair, which had been gray for many years, the lines on his face were deeper and his nose had grown bigger.

"Have you started?" came the voice of her mother from off screen. "You're supposed to tell me when you've started."

Julie's mother jostled up close to her husband and gave the camera a smile and a wave. She was also older, of course, but the years since Julie had said goodbye to them on Earth had been kinder to Mom. Her hair had lost all its natural blonde, but its gray strands remained long and thick. There were a few more wrinkles on her face, but she had smoothed them with makeup. Not that she really needed to. Her eyes were bright with life, regardless of the mascara and eyeliner she used to extenuate them.

"Hi Julie, it's Mom!" she said.

Julie's dad nudged his wife in the ribs. "You don't need to tell her that, she can see who you are."

"We heard about you being put in charge of the investigation up there on the news," said Mom. "Very impressive. I've been telling everyone. They said my daughter wasn't featured very much any more after that Terraforming Committee thing, but I tell them, look now! Head of an investigation, no less. That shuts them up, I can tell you."

"What happened with the asteroid?" asked Dad, peering into the camera as if it would help find the answer. "Sounds a horrible business."

"I wish I could tell you, Dad." Julie answered the recording, even though she knew they couldn't hear her.

"You can't ask her that!" said Mom, returning her husband's nudge in the ribs. "I'm sure she can't tell us. It's all top secret up there, you know that!"

Julie found herself smiling again. No matter how many news broadcasts they watched or how much she tried to tell them about what life was like on Mars, they didn't really understand. Their world view was very Earth-centric, if not Baltimore-centric.

"So, I've got something very exciting to tell you," said Mom, her eyes brightening even further. "Rachel came around at the weekend."

Rachel was Julie's younger sister who was doing all the things on Earth that Julie hadn't. She'd married a charming man from Texas called Carl, had a son, Robert, and still taught biology at a college near her home. It all sounded perfect, even though Rachel would complain about her life in the occasional video messages she sent to Mars.

"She brought Robbie all the way from Dallas," said Dad. It was at this point that his small, sunken eyes seemed to take on more life. "He's such a terror, running round everywhere, getting into things. You mother spent the whole week before they got here putting knives and things up on the top shelf. Now every time I go into the kitchen to make lunch, I have to get a ladder out."

"It was so nice to see our little grandson," said Mom. "Rachel also had some news…"

"You can't tell Julie that!" interrupted Dad. "It's Rachel's news to tell."

"I asked her, and she said it would be fine," insisted Mom. "So... one of the reasons she came to visit was to tell us she's pregnant again! Isn't that amazing? We are going to have a second grandchild."

"That's brilliant, Mom," said Julie. She was happy for her sister and her parents, of course she was, but it reminded her of all the possibilities she left behind when she was seduced by the excitement of the terraforming Mars project and boarded a spaceship to make the journey to the red planet.

"We went walking around Druid Hill Park, all five of us," Mom continued. "The weather was beautiful, and we had a nice chat when we weren't running around after Robbie. Where do toddlers get their energy from?"

"You should send Rachel a message when you get the chance," said Dad. "I know you're busy up on Mars, but she'd love to hear from you."

His stream of words seemed to run dry. Mom turned to him. "Have we said everything we were going to say?" she said.

"Um, I think so." He looked down at something outside the frame of the video message. Possibly a list of things he had intended to say. He leaned forward into the camera and put up his hand to shield himself from his wife, like an actor making an aside to the audience during a play. "Don't forget it's your mother's birthday next week."

"I can still hear you, you silly old fool!" said Mom, laughing. "Anyway, give my love to Mars, Julie. Don't work too hard. We're really proud of you. Looking forward to your next message. Bye Julie!"

"Yes, bye," said Dad.

Her parents waved at the camera and put on big cheesy grins for a few more moments until the video cut out and the list of unread messages reappeared.

Julie stared at the screen without focusing, so all her messages blurred into a pattern of unreadable text. She knew her parents were telling the truth when they said they were proud of her, but there was something in the way they spoke about Rachel, Robbie, and her pregnancy that made Julie feel they were happier about that than they could ever be about their other daughter being put in charge of an investigation on Mars. She didn't begrudge them their happiness. It was wonderful to hear that they were enjoying their only grandchild and excited about the arrival of another. It was good news for Rachel too, assuming she was happy about having another baby. But it all seemed to be happening a very long way away in a completely different world to her own.

Which, of course, it was. Even at the planets' closest points, the only family Julie had was fifty-six million kilometers across empty space.

CHAPTER SIXTEEN

Doctor David Kobayashi clenched his right hand into a fist and punched out towards the woman in front of him. She parried so his blow went past her body, reached out to grab his wrist, and simultaneously pushed at his upper arm so he was forced off balance. In terms of a physical match, he should easily overpower her – he was an athletic man in his thirties, while she was slightly younger and more than a foot shorter than him – but using technique rather than strength to defeat an opponent was the whole point of learning karate.

David stepped away from the woman he was demonstrating with, and she let go of him.

"Good," he said, turning to a group of people in various types of exercise wear lined up along the side of the sports hall. "Now, everyone in your pairs."

Luka watched from the safety of the sidelines, where a few rows of seats allowed for a limited number of spectators. He was there ahead of soccer practice with the ThorGate team, as arranged by Erik. Luka had only agreed to it because it allowed him an excuse to get into the sports hall while karate practice was going on. In fact, Erik had tried to get him to attend an earlier session on a different day and Luka had to make up some excuse to ensure he was booked in for the one which followed David's class. It gave him the perfect opportunity to sneak in early to see the scientist and, hopefully, corner him for a private word afterwards.

Nine other adults joined the first woman in the center of the hall. They formed couples, including the woman who paired up with someone more her size and David talked them through the same karate moves in slow motion. Like they were practicing an aggressive form of ballet.

"Now, switch over in your pairs," David called out to his pupils. "If you were the one blocking, you now become the aggressor and vice versa."

As David turned, he caught sight of Luka watching. Rather than ignore him, he stared until Luka felt uncomfortable. Luka returned a friendly smile, but David's expression didn't soften, and he strode towards the spectator seats. Luka looked around to check who else the karate instructor might be looking at, but he was the only person there.

"I'm sorry, but spectators are not allowed," David told him.

"I'm not a spectator," said Luka, suddenly realizing that, by sitting there and watching, that's exactly what he was. "I was hoping to have a word with you."

"If you're interested in joining the class, then I'm afraid there's a waiting list. You're welcome to join that if you want."

"That's not actually why I'm here. Maybe I should

introduce myself." He brushed his palm on the thigh of his sweatpants and offered it to the scientist. "I'm Luka Schäfer. I've taken on the position that used to be held by Gianni Lupo."

David's face paled. "I see."

He let Luka's hand remain suspended in the air until he was forced to withdraw it.

"I want to understand more about what happened," said Luka, and added lamely, "but also about his work, who he was, how we can take precautions to stop an accident happening again."

"I don't know anything. I wasn't there."

"That's actually what I wanted to ask you about. Please, it's important."

"I'll talk to you after the class," said David, begrudgingly.

He returned to the main part of the hall and instructed his pupils to repeat the exercise in real time. Luka continued to watch, feeling like an illicit spectator, as the karate class began to look less like ballet and more like they were practicing for a fight.

After only a few more minutes the class was dismissed, and Luka had to wait for the chatting pupils to disperse before he could come down from the spectator seats. David was sitting off to one side with a large sports bag between his feet and a small towel in his hands.

"I don't know what I can tell you," said David, looking up as Luka approached. "I didn't know Gianni, I never even met him. We had all left before he got to the research station."

"That's what I don't understand," said Luka. "Why weren't the scientists there on the day of the asteroid strike? I'm glad you weren't – obviously – but I thought the research station was supposed to be already up and running."

"There's no mystery. There was a problem with the environmental controls in the building. For two days we all had headaches and were feeling tired all the time. Eventually we realized there was too much carbon dioxide in the air. For some reason, it wasn't being removed efficiently enough and the computer monitoring system wasn't picking up the problem. So we left until it could be fixed."

"Gianni could have accessed it remotely, surely."

"No one could log in remotely, that was the issue," said David. "The computer system was completely cut off from the Thor Network. There was speculation that because we were at the bottom of the canyon the network had difficulty connecting, but radio communications were fine. It didn't make a lot of sense to me, if I'm honest. All we knew was that access to the computer systems was required to understand if the carbon dioxide problem was a mechanical failure – in which case, errors would have been recorded on the computer log – or a problem with the computer system itself. A computer glitch seemed most likely, considering the network problems we were having. One of the people in Thor Town – not Gianni, someone else – tried to talk us through some steps to see if we could fix it but to be honest, we'd been breathing bad air for two days and we just wanted to get out of there."

"Are you sure it wasn't Gianni you spoke to?"

"Definitely. I have Italian heritage on my mother's side. I would have remembered if he had been Italian." David paused. "You know, I owe my life to that computer glitch."

"Gianni owes his death to it," said Luka.

"Yes." The regret expressed in that one word seemed to fill David's body and the toned physique of the karate instructor sagged a little. "I am all too aware of that. My friends tell me I shouldn't feel guilty about it, but I do. I want to ask him why he went out there on his own and why he had to choose that particular day of all days. I want to ask, why did I survive and he didn't? We can't ever know his thoughts on that day, can we? Not now that he's gone."

Luka had no time to process what he had said before the door to the sports hall was flung open and members of the ThorGate soccer team began to file in. In that moment of distraction, David tossed the towel over his shoulder and picked up his bag to leave.

"Hey, Luka!" shouted Erik, the tall Swede clearly visible above the heads of the players. "I didn't know you were here already. The coach is keen to meet you."

As Erik trotted up towards him, Luka saw Doctor David Kobayashi disappear off into the throng of soccer players, swinging his sports bag by the handles as he went.

Luka knew he had asked the last of his questions for that evening.

Luka sat on his bed, still wearing his sweats, after an embarrassing soccer training session. Kicking a ball about in the dining hall and showing off in front of unexpectant diners was easy compared to a serious, structured practice. He hadn't properly dribbled a ball since he was a teenager and quit the FC Cologne youth academy to concentrate on his studies. Trying to do that in Martian gravity that he was still getting used to only resulted in him tripping over his own feet. It was not unusual, the coach told him, for people to fall over the first few times. But it didn't matter what she told him, he was still embarrassed.

He knew his heart wasn't in it. Maybe later, when he had fully settled into life on Mars, he might want to take up some sort of hobby. Possibly soccer, possibly something else. But all he could think of when he was kicking the ball with the people on the ThorGate team – who weren't as bad as Erik made out – was getting back to Gianni's diary. Doctor David Kobayashi had said, "we can't ever know his thoughts on that day," except, maybe Luka could. Gianni had recorded them and left them for him to find.

Luka had been watching all the entries sequentially since he had found Gianni's data stick. But, having spoken to the scientist, he decided to do something he should have done days before – skip to the end to watch his final diary entry.

As the entry began to play, Luka could see how tired Gianni looked. His eyes had sunk back into his sockets and the low light in the room cast ugly shadows underneath them. His beard had grown out into a shaggy mess and his skin seemed to sag around it. It was as if Gianni had aged five years in the six months since the first recording when he had talked excitedly about falling in love with Anita.

"Anita has never been so insistent," he complained to the camera. "She's been treating me like any other indentured ThorGate worker – no, *worse*. It's almost like because we have a relationship – or *had* a relationship, the way I'm feeling at the moment – she doesn't want to show favoritism and thinks she has to work harder to exert her authority.

"She wants me to go out to the biological research station they built at Noctis Labyrinthus and look at their computer system. That's my job, it's not a problem. But the way she talked to me, she made me feel like *un inutile pezzo di spazzatura*. She wants it done today and it has to be me because she doesn't want any of the other idiots on the tech team screwing it up.

"Firstly, those 'idiots' are my friends and I resent the suggestion that it was their incompetence that caused the computer problems on the station. I tried to tell her, the station was connected perfectly well to the network when it was first opened and it's just as frustrating to us that we can't connect remotely as it must be for the scientists.

"Secondly, she has no right to blame the whole thing on the computer system. There's an issue with the environmental controls which isn't being picked up by computer monitoring so, yeah, it could be something to do with the computer system, but maybe it's the environmental control system itself. If that has a fault, then you don't have to be a genius to figure out that it might not be communicating with the research station computer."

Luka paused playback. If Gianni was right, and there was no reason to suspect he wasn't, then Anita had lied to Luka out at the crash site when she had said Gianni didn't tell her what he was doing on the day he died. She had told Luka: she would never know why he went there in person instead of trying to fix the issue remotely. When, in fact, it appeared she knew exactly why he had gone there. Moreover, she had been the one who had sent him.

He resumed playback.

"We argued," said Gianni. "I told her it was all working perfectly when we installed it. I told her that the biggest problem with computer systems is the people operating them. It's not unheard of for a new building to have teething problems when people move into it. People fiddle with things, they knock things. I've even had an instance of someone breaking into a sealed unit and unplugging something they shouldn't. But she didn't listen. I don't think she even cares."

The anger rippling through Gianni's face was picked up by the close framing of the camera as he took a breath and calmed himself. A little. "That's when she ordered me to go to the research station myself, on my own, *today* and sort it.

"So why am I telling you this now, dear diary? Why am I wasting daylight when I could be heading over there right at this minute? Because I have an uneasy feeling. Things have been strained between us recently and we've had a lot of arguments. Anita's under pressure, I get it, we all are. Except, with Anita, it's something more. They say there's this thing called Martian Madness. You know, people are trapped inside the whole time and even if they step outside, they have to be enclosed in a rad-suit. There's no escape. Earth is like a fantasy world we dreamed of and there's no going back to the *gabinetto* of a planet for people who have come to Mars and think they've made a mistake. I'm certainly never going to earn enough to pay off my indenture and buy a ticket to take me back. I remember the reason I left, and I know I made the right decision to come here. But that's not the case for Anita, who talks about missing the rain splashing on the street and walking with the wind in her hair. She's not indentured like me, but the cost of buying out her fifteen year contract is several year's salary and she'll never be able to afford it. The thought of being stuck on Mars for that long is enough to drive a homesick person mad.

"Unless it is me who is the mad one. I'm the one sitting in my room talking to myself, after all."

He chuckled at the irony. But when he looked deep into the camera lens again, there was no smile on his lips. "I'm telling you this because the uneasy feeling won't go away. So, on the off chance I'm not crazy, I'm going to keep this diary safe, *nel caso in cui.*"

Gianni nodded to himself, as if approving the idea. Then he stood up and the recording continued for almost a minute showing him moving around the room and packing a few things into a bag. Then he suddenly turned back towards the camera and glared up close into the lens. The image blurred and then refocused to reveal the tiny red veins in the white of his eyes before he stopped the recording and the window faded to black.

Normally, the diary would move onto the next entry. But not this time. There were no more diary entries. Gianni never returned from the research station to report on what the problem had been. Luka, like Gianni, had to turn off the window without knowing all of the answers.

CHAPTER SEVENTEEN

Julie was about to leave the office at the end of the day when a message came through from Kirra Morgan, the leader of the Reds. She might have dismissed it, if it hadn't been for the title of the message: You Didn't Get This From Me.

There was nothing inside it other than an attachment labelled *Mah Chynna*, the name of the asteroid controller from CrediCor. It appeared to be a list of financial transactions from Chynna's personal account and dated from the months before the asteroid crash. Intrigued, Julie scrolled through the numbers and paused at four large payments into Chynna's account, made once a month from an unnamed account number. It could have an innocent explanation, of course. They could be payments from a relative, the result of a divorce settlement or an inheritance paying out in bits. But the timing of the payments made them look suspicious and the fact that the Reds were the ones who had forwarded the details motivated Julie to look deeper.

If she could trace the account the money came from, she might be able to find out who paid Chynna. Julie looked up the transaction numbers and confirmed the money had come from Earth. However, that hardly narrowed it down because almost everyone on the planet was paid via financial institutions on Earth. After that, it was a dead end. She had hoped they would be linked to an account belonging to a person or a corporation, but she couldn't even work out what bank had been used to process the transactions. She needed Kareem to look at it. He was good at that sort of thing.

Dashing out of her office into the communal space on her floor of UNMI headquarters to find him, she was surprised to see a lot of empty desks and chairs. The usual hubbub of people chatting and working was gone and, without people, it seemed a cold and uninviting place. It was later in the day than she had realized.

One person remained, hunched over a computer screen. It was Alejandro, one of UNMI's more gifted terraforming specialists. He must have heard Julie come out of her office because he looked up from his work and nodded an acknowledgement.

"Alej, is Kareem still here?" she asked.

"No, you just missed him."

"Unlike Kareem to leave on time."

Alej nodded. "Yeah."

She stood in the office for a moment, wondering what to do. She decided to call him. But Kareem didn't answer, so she left a message.

"Alej," she ventured. "I don't suppose you happen to know if Kareem went home, do you?"

It wouldn't the first time she had stopped off at his place after work. Usually to discuss UNMI business, but not always. Sometimes, they sat and chatted for ages. There wasn't a great deal else to do on Mars in the evenings, after all.

"Actually," said Alejandro. "He had a reservation at Chef McCormack."

"Lucky him!" said Julie.

"That's what we all said. He kept going on about it all day, making everyone jealous."

"I bet. Thanks, Alej."

"See you tomorrow," he said.

Julie headed down the stairs, thinking about Chef McCormack. She hadn't been there in a long time. She obviously had enough credits to afford it, but was always looking for that special occasion to justify the expense. Kareem, she knew, was less fussy about that sort of thing. He was very much a "live for the now" person.

McCormack's was only a ten minute walk from UNMI. She could easily make a detour on the way home. Maybe even splash out for a meal. With renewed excitement, she picked up her pace and headed for the restaurant.

She found it was already half full of diners, despite being early evening. The restaurant was a bijou place, designed to be the exact replica of the sort of establishment someone in one of the wealthier cities on Earth might walk into. Chef McCormack prided itself at being exclusive and seating a maximum of twenty people. But that was partly because of the availability of luxury food which it had to fight to secure ahead of an increasing number of other restaurants on Mars.

The smell which greeted her when she stepped inside was incredible. Julie could almost taste the aroma of cooking meat which hung in the air. *Real* meat with a juicy, earthy smell which wakened her stomach and told it to prepare for food. It was a very primitive response and must have been the same for her human ancestors seated around a fire with the prize of the day's hunt roasting in the flames.

All of which contrasted with the design of the restaurant which was the height of sophistication from floor to ceiling. It was dimly lit with yellowish lights to resemble the glow of candles. The walls were decorated with a hand painted floral design which wove itself like a vine around the framed pictures hanging on every surface. They showed an eclectic mix of scenes of Mars, mostly of historic moments like the first human landing, Earth landscapes and the smiling faces of famous people. The floor, although made from the standard compressed brick of Martian soil, had been polished to have a reddish sheen which looked supremely elegant, while also being easy to slip on for someone not wearing the right shoes.

As her eyes became used to the dim light, Julie saw Kareem sitting on his own at the back of the restaurant. Which meant she had no qualms about disturbing him. She passed by the other tables and diners to reach him, with her shoes tip-tapping on the shiny floor as she walked.

Kareem looked up from his glass of water. "Julie!" he said with surprise.

"Alej said you would be here. I hope you don't mind me stopping by. I tried calling you, but you didn't answer."

Slightly concerned, he put down his glass. "Is there a problem?"

"No, no problem. But I was so excited that I couldn't wait until morning to tell you."

"Tell me what?"

Julie sat on the chair opposite Kareem and leant over the table. "I've just been sent the financial records of Mah Chynna, the asteroid controller for CrediCor."

"Who sent them?"

"It doesn't matter who sent them. It's what's in them that matters." Julie pulled up the attachment on her WristTab and sent it over to Kareem. "Look."

Kareem consulted his own WristTab. "What am I looking at?"

"Several large deposits in the months leading up to the asteroid crash."

Kareem sucked in air between his teeth. "That's a lot of money."

"Yeah." Julie watched as Kareem read through the financial report and understood what he was seeing.

"You think someone paid her to crash the asteroid into Noctis Labyrinthus? That's a stretch, don't you think?" Kareem looked up at her.

"Is it? You know the lengths some of the corporations are prepared to go to. We need to do some digging to find out for sure, but that's what it looks like to me."

"So who paid her?" asked Kareem.

The sound of approaching shoes on the shiny restaurant floor made Julie turn. She expected to see one of the staff in restaurant uniform, but it was in fact a woman in a flattering blue dress which plunged low at the neck and pulled in tight at her slim waist. She had sleek, black hair which hung down to her shoulders and deep brown eyes with pupils which had grown large in the dim light.

"Julie, this is Areesha," said Kareem, lowering his WristTab and looking up at the woman. "Areesha, this is Julie, my boss."

"Oh." Suddenly embarrassed, Julie got up from where she was sitting. "I'm sorry, I didn't realize you were expecting company."

Areesha, who had seemed somewhat put out by finding someone else sitting in what was evidently supposed to be her seat, changed her expression to a respectful smile. "Pleased to meet you," she said.

"Likewise." Julie shot a reprimanding look across to Kareem. "You should have told me you were expecting company."

"You didn't exactly give me the chance," he said.

"Sorry. I was too excited. I didn't think."

"Excited about what?" said Areesha.

"Work," said Kareem.

Areesha seemed intrigued. "Something exciting's going on at UNMI?"

"Not really." Kareem glanced across to Julie. "Areesha is employed by Inventrix. We promised we wouldn't talk to each other about work."

"Glad to hear it." Julie took a respectful step away from the couple as Areesha sat down in the seat she had just vacated. "I should probably go and let you have your meal in peace."

"We can talk about that thing in the office in the morning," said Kareem, tapping at his WristTab.

"Yes, see you in the morning. Nice to meet you, Areesha." Feeling herself go red, Julie turned to make her escape and came face to face with a member of staff who had come up behind her in soft-soled, near-silent shoes. She muttered an apology, sidestepped him, and rushed out into the street.

She felt a complete idiot. She hadn't stopped to consider that Kareem had a life outside of UNMI and he might have had a reason not to answer when she called. Not everyone was like her, devoting most of her waking hours to her job.

Sometimes she wished she could be a bit more like other people.

CHAPTER EIGHTEEN

Julie felt exalted and free running on the top of Olympus Mons, the greatest volcano on Mars and the tallest mountain on any planet in the solar system. She was inside the caldera complex, a series of circular and semi-circular depressions eighty kilometers across, created when the volcano stopped erupting and the ground partially sank into the spent magma chamber beneath. Ahead of her, the edge of the crater ascended into a three kilometer cliff to meet the orange haze of the atmosphere that barely disguised the blackness of space at the high altitude. Unencumbered by a protective suit and wearing only training sweats, Julie skipped across the channels created by ancient lava flows, as she breathed in oxygen-rich air and willed her legs to keep running.

It was all an illusion, of course. A projection of what it would look like to be on Olympus Mons, as captured by a video imaging team a decade ago. With every thump of her foot on the treadmill, she understood she was still in Tharsis

City. In reality, no one could run on Mars without a rad-suit, let alone on the top of Olympus Mons.

The illusion was suddenly broken as Kareem stepped onto Olympus Mons right in front of her.

"What the–?" She pulled up short, even though she was running on the spot and in no danger of colliding with him.

The emergency stop of the treadmill cut in and almost threw her forward before she grabbed hold of the safety handles and steadied herself.

"Julie, what are you doing here?" said Kareem. He stood on the floor of the gym booth, about ten centimeters below where the projection judged the volcanic plateau to be, so his feet appeared to be stuck inside the rocky surface.

"Kareem, what are *you* doing here?" She panted out the words as her lungs continued to demand more oxygen.

"You haven't seen the news?"

"No, I've been running." She started to feel nauseous after stopping so suddenly and set the treadmill on a slow walk to recover.

"You *have* to see the news. Why do you never watch the news? I can't always be making sure you're up to date with current events." He glanced round at the projection behind him. "Can you turn this thing onto ICN?"

The gym pod was capable of displaying almost any backdrop the user desired. Julie turned on the ICN channel and Kareem became surrounded by the live feed from the Interplanetary Cinematics studio where the regular newscaster was interviewing a shell-shocked looking scientist. Julie knew him from the days when UNMI received regular updates from the Advisory Board for

Martian Science. He was a no-nonsense Russian with a sense of the didactic who, under interrogation from the calm but probing journalist, looked almost green.

Along the bottom of the video feed, partly written across Kareem's legs, was a headline banner: *LIFE ON MARS.*

"Life on Mars?" questioned Julie.

Kareem nodded with wide-eyed excitement. "Yeah. They've finally found it: the greatest discovery in history."

CHAPTER NINETEEN

Julie returned to the UNMI offices, still wearing her sweats which were slightly damp from her run. She should have felt dirty and clammy, but all those feelings were eclipsed by a range of emotions about the discovery of life on Mars all fighting for supremacy inside of her. Kareem's excitement was contagious, but she also sympathized with the shell-shocked Russian scientist who had been dragged into the ICN studio.

"It's impossible," said Julie, feeling the ache in her legs as she climbed the stairs of UNMI headquarters.

"Right," said Kareem, following her.

"We've been searching for life on this planet for three hundred years and found nothing: zero, zilch, zip, nada."

"I know!"

Julie reached the second floor and opened the door that led both to her office and the communal office of UNMI's terraforming experts. The excited rumble of many voices filled the space. Almost no one was sitting down at their desks. They were mostly standing, talking to others in groups and huddled around several screens where ICN was playing. Only a few sat in quiet contemplation at their own desks, staring at the news feed with its unrelenting headline writ large along the bottom: *LIFE ON MARS.*

Julie passed by them all. No one seemed to notice her. Or if they did, they ignored her. The head of UNMI arriving in sweaty exercise gear barely registered on the day's news radar.

Inside the privacy of her own office, Julie turned the window onto ICN and watched the same feed that all the UNMI workers were watching outside. The same feed that everyone on Mars was probably watching, if not everyone in the solar system. A clip from the interview with the green-pallored Russian scientist replayed in front of her.

"I can confirm that a routine sample of water taken from beneath the construction site for Noctis City contained microbes which we believe are native to Mars. So, as you say, it appears that we have found the much-anticipated proof that life developed on Mars independently to that of Earth, and still continues to exist in microbial form on the planet, at least in this particular aquifer. But, I have to stress that these are preliminary results. It is unfortunate that they were leaked to the media before we were able conduct further studies."

"You're not suggesting that this historic news should have been kept from the public?" said the ICN journalist.

"Not at all," replied the Russian. "Not at all. But we would have liked to have gathered more information. At the moment, we have one isolated test result. We need to return to the site to take additional samples and further testing needs to be conducted. Early analysis suggests DNA distinct from any microbes found on Earth, so we don't think it can be contamination from any people or equipment we brought with us. But, as I say, these are early test results. We need to find out more. Until then, I'm afraid that I'm not going to be able to answer many of the questions that I'm sure you want to ask me."

Julie flopped herself down in one of the armchairs. "Window, mute," she said, and the sound from the ICN feed abruptly stopped.

Kareem sat down in the armchair beside her. "What do we do now?" he asked.

Julie raised her hands in a helpless gesture. "I don't think we can get anything done today. Everyone's going to be talking about life on Mars."

"I meant, what are all of us going to do now? We came here thinking Mars is a dead world. Now that there could be native life here, that makes us invaders."

She gave him a hard stare. "You've been listening to too much Reds propaganda."

"I listen to all the arguments so I can come to an informed view," said Kareem.

"We do what we always do: we continue to colonize the planet and we continue to terraform it until there are oceans and forests and humanity can survive on the surface without rad-suits. It doesn't change the situation on Earth, it doesn't mean that humans don't need a new home, it doesn't mean that we can't take advantage of the resources here. The Martian microbes don't need to build farms and cities and mining communities. We do."

"You sound very certain."

"We talked about it a lot here at UNMI before the formation of the Terraforming Committee. Just in case this sort of thing happened."

"Even so, I feel different about what we're doing here after that." He nodded across to where ICN was still playing with images of an empty Noctis City construction site where all work had ceased.

"It's understandable. But we can't all get on a spaceship and go back to Earth tomorrow. The reasons why we left still exist: there's not the room for us, nor the resources for us to eat and live. Humans are on Mars to stay and we have to make the most of it. Regardless of what microbes might lay beneath our feet."

"I suppose all these arguments will be trotted out endlessly on ICN all day," said Kareem.

"All week, I imagine."

"I don't know if I can just sit about watching it, but I don't know if I can get on with anything else – do you know what I mean?"

Julie nodded. She knew exactly what he meant. "I wanted to set up another meeting with Mah Chynna about her financial records, but that's not going to happen today."

"Everyone's too distracted."

"We'll have to wait a few days. This news has shocked everyone."

"Indeed."

Julie shifted uncomfortably on her chair. When she got

up that morning, she had planned to come into the office and have a quiet word with Kareem. The auspicious news had derailed her plans somewhat, but as the conversation ran dry, her embarrassment at her actions at the restaurant came back to her.

"Kareem," she said. "I wanted to apologize for intruding last night. I wasn't thinking."

"It doesn't matter."

"It does. I was so caught up with what I saw in those financial records, that I didn't think about it being your private time."

"It's fine. Areesha was actually quite excited to meet you."

"Excited?"

"You forget, for people who were back on Earth when UNMI started terraforming Mars, you were somewhat of a celebrity."

"I really wasn't." She felt herself blush. "So… Areesha… is she the reason you shaved off your beard?"

Kareem self-consciously rubbed his bare chin. "No," he said, defensively. "I fancied a change, that's all."

"Well, it looks good on you. Areesha's very lucky."

A hesitant knock caused Julie to look up. The office door opened slowly and Alejandro tentatively entered. "Sorry to disturb you," he said. "ICN are outside asking for a comment about life on Mars. What shall I tell them?"

Julie sank further into her chair and groaned. She had hoped her days of giving statements to the media were behind her following the formation of the Terraforming Committee, but apparently not. "Tell them to go sit out on Syria Planum without a rad-suit!" she snapped.

Alejandro's eyes widened in shock. "OK," he said, and hurriedly backed out of her office, closing the door behind him.

"No, don't actually tell them that!" she called out after him.

Kareem laughed.

Julie pulled herself from her seat and rushed to the door. By the time she opened it, Alejandro was almost at the stairs. "Alejandro! Tell them I'll be down in a minute. Got that?"

"Got it."

He disappeared down the stairs. The few people who had stopped watching ICN to look at her, went back to staring at the news feed.

Julie returned to her office and stood before Kareem while she smoothed down her sweat top and brushed back her hair with her fingers. "How do I look?"

"Like you've just come out of the gym."

"Good," she said. "I'll use that as an excuse not to say anything profound."

She turned and walked out of her office, composing a bland statement in her head as she went, in the hope of disguising her true feelings on the matter.

CHAPTER TWENTY

Rovers raced towards the Noctis construction site, one leading with two flanking on either side, sending up clouds of Martian dust behind them. All the rovers on Mars looked the same, but there was something about the way they traveled in formation that felt ominous, like an army advancing on their position.

The news they were bringing traveled ahead of them. *Life on Mars!* was the chatter over the comms.

What?

They've found life on Mars!

What are you talking about?

Martian microbes. In the aquifer.

Here? Not here! Are you sure?

More voices crowded onto the team comms channel until it was just noise buzzing in Luka's helmet.

Luka secured the prongs of the forklift-type loading machine he had been working on and turned to see the

other migrants had also abandoned their work and were
standing to watch the approaching rovers.

They pulled up near to where Luka had parked his own
rover and a rad-suited figure stepped out of the lead vehicle.
Through the bubble of his helmet, Luka could see the man's
serious green eyes. He held up his hand with the palm facing
forwards, like a police officer halting traffic, and waited for
the comms chatter to subside into an expectant silence.

"My name is John Wilson." His strong, confident voice
boomed out of the speaker in Luka's helmet. "I have an
important announcement. You may have already heard the
news that a significant scientific discovery has been made
in this part of Noctis Labyrinthus. It is so significant that
we cannot allow any more work to be carried out on this
development. I have, therefore, been authorized to close
down this construction site by order of the Terraforming
Committee."

What?

No!

You can't do that!

Others came out of the lead vehicle. Then more suited
figures emerged from the two flanking rovers until there
were twelve people standing before the construction
workers. The show of strength was not lost on Luka, nor
on the workers around him whose voices over the comms
became increasingly confused, worried and angry.

"I understand…" John's commanding tone somehow
projected itself over the noise and urged the workers to
listen. "I understand this is all very sudden, but the terms
of corporate engagement on Mars are clear: this important

scientific discovery must be protected. Construction at Noctis Labyrinthus must cease until such time that the Terraforming Committee decrees that work can recommence."

A rad-suited figure weaved their way through the standing crowd of workers and walked directly up to confront John Wilson. Luka could tell by the way he walked, and by the way the others stepped aside to let him through, that it was Al Vertanen. Luka couldn't see his face because it was hidden by his helmet, but he imagined Al's moustache was bristling with rage.

"This is unacceptable!" came Al's voice over the comms.

"I understand you're upset," replied John, in a conciliatory tone.

"Upset? Upset doesn't cover it! Do you see all these people here?" Al held out his hand to indicate the onlooking workers. "All these people were brought from Earth to construct this city. You can't just throw them out of work!"

The idea, which must have occurred to at least some of them, came as a shock to others. Concerned murmurs whispered in Luka's helmet.

"You tell him, Al!" shouted one brave, or perhaps scared, worker.

"No one's being put out of work," John insisted. He turned to the crowd. "I'm sorry that this announcement has come as a surprise to you – as it has to all of us – and I understand that you might be worried, but there really is nothing to be done. I suggest you leave quickly and quietly so the scientists can do their work."

"What if we don't?" said Al.

If John had sensed the threat in Al's voice then it made no dent in his resolve. Indeed, he seemed to stand taller and more defiant in front of ThorGate's workforce supervisor. "We could remain here and face each other for the next few hours while we wait for our air to run out and the power in our suits to fail, but what would that achieve?"

John's question remained unanswered as the people in front of him undoubtedly considered the consequences of a standoff. In Luka's peripheral vision, he could see the sharp metal prongs of the loading machine primed and ready to be brought into action. They could do a lot of damage to a person if used as a weapon. Behind him, there was other powerful and robust machinery for drilling, digging, and carrying which, in the hands of an angry workforce, would be an effective substitute for tanks and guns. And, if the thought had occurred to Luka, it had probably occurred to some of the others around him.

Al took a conciliatory step back and pointed an accusing finger at John. "I shall be taking this up with your superiors."

"Please do," said John. If he was trying to hide the sound of relief in his voice, then he had failed. "I only have the authority to carry out the closure order, I don't have the authority to change it."

Al turned to the workers. "Everyone! I want you to go back to the habitat." He gestured with his arms to wave them away from the canyon.

"Al, come on!" shouted someone who Luka couldn't see. "You can't be serious."

"Deadly serious. Leave whatever you were working on and get back in the bus. All of you. *Now!*"

Reluctantly, but inevitably, people began to move away from the canyon. Luka stopped to make sure the loading machine was secure and joined the melee. Although, in his case, he walked back to his rover rather than the construction bus.

Life on Mars, he thought to himself as he walked. *Here, under my feet.*

He touched the control on the outside of his rover and, as the hatchway opened, he looked out across Sinai Planum. The dust kicked up by the fleet of vehicles had settled back onto the carpet of red dirt which stretched out to the horizon. It seemed such an immense, desolate place that it was hard to imagine what the planet might have looked like in its ancient past when it was a warmer world with a thicker atmosphere and where liquid water could exist on the surface. Many had speculated that, back then, conditions had been ripe for the spark of life to be ignited.

But Mars was too small to hold onto its heat and was never able to maintain an environment to allow life to evolve and flourish like it had on Earth. The molten core of Mars cooled and hardened, its magnetic field faded and the blanket of air which once surrounded the globe was slowly eroded by radiation and the solar wind. Conditions on Mars became so harsh that any life which might have existed almost certainly died out. For three centuries, scientists hoped that some primitive microbes might have clung on beneath the surface where, despite the darkness, there might have been enough moisture and warmth for them to survive. But the scientists had found nothing. Not even the fossilized remains of a single celled organism. The only conclusion they could come to was that Mars had never given birth to life of its own. It was, and always had been, a dead world.

To discover that those assumptions were wrong was extraordinary. It was revolutionary. It was also unsettling. As Luka journeyed back to Thor Town, allowing the navigation systems on the rover do most of the driving, he wondered what it all meant for the future. Not only for the future of the migrants who had spent half a year traveling to Mars to work on a project which had been suddenly and unceremoniously closed down, but also for the rest of humanity living and working on the red planet.

CHAPTER TWENTY-ONE

The whole of ThorGate's operations on Mars were in turmoil after the shutdown of the Noctis site. The corporation still had a lot of projects running, but the atmosphere in Thor Town was tense. Luka tried to distance himself from the fear, speculation and anxiety and spent much of his evenings going through Gianni's diary. He repeatedly watched the videos to understand how he had become the frightened and suspicious man who Luka had seen in his last diary entry.

Watching him talk about Anita across the six months of their relationship was like watching a movie in which the slow decline of a man is compressed into a few hours. At the beginning, the love he had for her was real and deep and the joy of the early entries seemed to spill out of the window. What started as a crush and a tentative first date became more intimate and intense. Then, as time moved on, Gianni got more and more frustrated. He kept talking about something bothering her, about Anita refusing to talk to him about it and how it was souring their relationship.

There was one entry which seemed to be key. It was from a week before Gianni died and was recorded late at night. As Luka watched it again, he not only listened to the words, he paid attention to Gianni's body language. He came across as nervous and distracted, speaking to the camera in an urgent whisper, often averting his eyes from its probing lens, as he recounted the events of that evening and tried to make sense of them.

"I was looking for Anita," he said. "I wasn't stalking her or spying on her. I actually wanted to spend the evening with her. I'd just received a small bottle of *Barbera del Monferraato Superiore* which my parents had sent in the recent shipment from Earth – I can't imagine how much it cost them – and I could think of no one that I would rather share it with than Anita.

"I wanted to surprise her," Gianni continued. "But she wasn't at her apartment. I went to her office, but it was all locked up. That's when I realized she hadn't picked up my messages. I called her again, but there was no response and her WristTab was out of range. That meant she wasn't in Thor Town and that's when I got worried. If she hadn't been so secretive over these past few weeks, I might have assumed she had business at Tharsis City and forgot to tell me. So, I checked the computer systems."

Gianni shot a guilty look at the camera. "I suppose you could call it an abuse of power, but I'm in charge of the systems, so I can cover my tracks. Which is more than

Anita had done. Records showed the last known location of her WristTab in Thor Town was at the rover depot. She had taken out a rover and, according to the time noted on the log, it was already getting dark out on the surface when she did so. No one takes a rover out at night unless it's an emergency. Satellite navigation works just the same and the rover's headlights are enough to illuminate the ground ahead to avoid any big rocks, but visibility is still reduced. Not to mention the cold. She knows that temperatures can drop to minus seventy out there and keeping the inside of the rover warm takes a lot of power. So, I went down to check it out. Like I said, I was worried.

"I found one maintenance guy who confirmed that a rover was missing. He pulled up more detail on the log and found Anita's authorization code, but it wasn't linked to a planned route. Safety protocols insist people log a route when taking out a rover – for heaven's sake, she shouldn't have been able to take it out at night at all! But she'd got round the rules somehow. I suppose, the Head of Martian Projects can do what the hell she likes.

"I tried calling her on the radio, but there was no response. The maintenance guy was nervous about being blamed and asked if we should alert someone and send out a search party, or commandeer the satellite network to trace her. But I knew she had deliberately left Thor Town under the cover of darkness and not told anyone where she was going, so I said it wasn't anything to be concerned about. That it wasn't his fault. She had the authority, although I'm not sure that's the truth. He didn't believe me – he must have seen I was worried – but he didn't question it when

I said I would wait until she came back. He said he had responsibilities at home he couldn't ignore, and that no one would be in until morning. I didn't mind if he left me alone at the end of his shift.

"I sat there for…" Gianni paused as he thought back. "It must have been a couple of hours before the airlock warning alarm sounded and the automatic systems sealed off the bay to allow Anita's rover to return. When it repressurized, I went back inside and watched as the hatchway opened and waited for Anita to appear. She looked shocked to see me, but it wasn't her expression that made me realize she had been doing something secret out on the surface. It was her clothes. They were covered in red, rusty Mars dust. The stuff gets everywhere when you step out onto the planet. You try to be careful when you take off your rad-suit, but it still seems to find its way into your hair, on your skin and all over everything you're wearing. The more contact you've had with the dust, the more it seems to want to go home with you. A lot of it had attached itself to Anita tonight.

"She was furious and accused me of stalking her and spying on her. I tried to tell her I'd been worried, but that only made her swear at me. When she ran out of rude words in English, she swore at me in Norwegian. That's when I caught a glimpse of the equipment she had with her inside the rover. I only saw it briefly before she climbed out and closed the hatch, but it was definitely some sort of drilling and lighting equipment – the sort you might need if you were working outside in the dark. She tried to explain away the dust, the equipment, and the fact that it was the middle of the night by claiming the rover got stuck in a pothole and she had to manually dig herself out of it. But I didn't believe her. And, by the look on her face, she knew I could see through her lies."

Gianni looked directly into the camera, so Luka felt he was looking across the passage of time. "So, what do I do now? Tell someone? Who do I tell? She's my boss! And tell them what? That she's been behaving suspiciously? They'd say I'm reading something into nothing. They'd say I was upset with her because our relationship isn't what it was. They might even be right – about that last bit, at least.

"I don't know. Maybe I'll just open that bottle of *Barbera del Monferraato Superiore* on my own and get drunk and forget about tonight. Maybe, in the morning, I will have the courage to say I don't want to see her anymore."

Gianni seemed to hold onto that last thought, as if it was the first time it had occurred to him.

Luka paused the image so he could study Gianni's face closer. He looked so sad. Like a man who had realized a great love affair was over. Even so, subsequent diary entries revealed that he never had the courage to break up with Anita. Perhaps, deep down, he didn't want to. Perhaps, deep down, he still loved her.

But one thing was certain: in the message that Gianni had recorded a week before he died, he didn't appear paranoid. He was angry, hurt and frustrated, but apparently completely sane. Which meant that Anita really had been up to something secret that night in the rover. Something that, when Gianni found out about it, caused her to be furious with him. So furious that after Gianni had spoken about it in his diary, he made sure to hide away those recordings for someone else to find, *nel caso in cui.*

Which Luka had translated from the Italian and discovered meant "just in case."

CHAPTER TWENTY-TWO

Julie looked up from her computer screen as Kareem walked into her office. He was carrying a full-sized Tab, which was the shape of an old-fashioned book, with the back resting on his forearm and the bottom sitting on the line of his waist. Like he had been in the middle of doing something else when he wandered through her door.

"You wanted to see me?" he said.

"I did?" Julie tried to think back over everything that was going on in her life. "Oh yes, I did! Shut the door and sit down, could you?"

"Sounds serious." He did as he was asked and placed his Tab on the desk between them.

Julie closed down what she was looking at on her screen and gave him her full attention. "I want you to look at our greenhouse gas emissions."

"I look at them every day," said Kareem.

"I mean, for the Terraforming Committee. The annual

funding review is coming up and I've been so caught up with this asteroid thing that I haven't been able to give it my proper attention."

"I'm sure you don't need to worry."

"But I do worry. I need to report on our progress so far and draft proposals for how we plan to continue. I know that UNMI is supposed to have privileged status when it comes to giving out the Universal Tax MegaCredits, but they're not going to give it to us if we hand in our homework late. On the other hand, if I stop work on the asteroid thing to concentrate on the review, it will annoy Rufus and we won't get approval for what we need to do."

"I'll work on it," said Kareem. "Not everything has to weigh on your shoulders, Julie."

"Thanks, Kareem. That would be a real help."

Her WristTab bleeped a reminder at her. "I have to go," she said, getting up from her chair. "CrediCor have finally agreed I can formally interview their asteroid controller. Not as if I imagine she'll confess to taking a bribe. I don't suppose you had a chance to trace back those large payments into her account?"

"As much as I could. I've been meaning to write it up and send it over," said Kareem.

"And?"

"The short version is, I got about as far as you did – I traced the money back to Earth, but the actual account number is a dead end. It doesn't exist and appears never to have existed. I imagine someone used specialist software to disguise where it really came from."

"Whoever made those payments seems to have known

what they were doing," said Julie. "Sounds like a sophisticated operation."

"Not necessarily. That software is freely available on the black market – for the right price."

"Yet another example of human skullduggery making its way to Mars," Julie reflected, heading for the door. "Hopefully, I can get some more information out of Mah Chynna."

Kareem followed her. "There's something else you'll probably want to know before you go."

Julie looked at her WristTab and knew she had little time to dawdle. "Can you tell me the short version?"

"I finally had back the analysis from the two asteroid samples."

"And?"

"They are almost certainly from different pieces of space rock."

"So there *were* two asteroids?"

"Looks like it. I'll send you over the data." Kareem touched the controls on his WristTab.

Julie ignored the bleep of an incoming message. She didn't need to read past the headline to know what it meant. "That suggests that all the scans and everything CrediCor provided were correct, but they were for the main asteroid. It crashed exactly when and where it was supposed to without fracturing."

Kareem nodded. "It was quite large, so it could easily have masked a second, smaller asteroid being brought down on the same trajectory. Until, at some point during the descent, it received instructions to change course and crash into

Noctis Labyrinthus – right on top of the ThorGate research station."

"Which means the research station was deliberately destroyed."

"But, to everyone watching, it would seem like a tragic accident. Like the asteroid splintered in the atmosphere and a rogue fragment veered off the flight path."

"Mah Chynna must have been the one who sent the course corrections."

"The question is," said Kareem, "who paid her to do it?"

Julie turned to open the door. "That," she said. "Is what I'm hoping to find out."

Julie sat across the desk from Mah Chynna in the same boss's office she had taken them to when they first met.

The woman she remembered as bright, talkative and – on the whole – cooperative, sat with her head bowed. She stared into her lap where she clasped her hands together so tightly that the knuckles of her interlocked fingers were white. Her long, black hair had been pulled back into a ponytail to reveal the almost-hollow cheeks of her gaunt face. If Julie hadn't known better, she would have thought she was a completely different person.

Sitting next to Chynna was an overweight man with a receding hairline. He stared at Julie with self-important authority and introduced himself as a CrediCor appointed lawyer subcontracted from the Teractor corporation. He was there to ensure protocol was followed and to represent the interests of both CrediCor and Mah Chynna. Behind both of them, the office window was not showing a live view of

Mars out towards Olympus Mons, as it had on her first visit, but an animated form of the CrediCor logo which continued to play on a loop. The purple background fluttered like a flag in the breeze while a white graphic similar to the symbol for gold darted in from the bottom left like a flying asteroid as a MegaCredits emblem faded up in the middle.

If the intention was to make Julie feel intimidated, then it didn't work. The lawyer's very presence meant the corporation was scared of what she was going to say. Which only meant Julie held the balance of power in the room, not anyone employed by CrediCor.

"I hope you don't mind if I record these proceedings," said Julie, reaching for the controls on her WristTab.

"And I hope you don't mind if I do the same," said the lawyer, whose name was Peterson. He had also given his first name, but Julie had instantly forgotten it.

A few strands of her hair came loose from Chynna's ponytail and hung down by her cheek. She tucked them back behind her ear, but they weren't quite long enough to stay put and fell forward again.

"I hope you don't mind me using your window to display some crucial documents which are relevant to your client?" said Julie. She phrased it as a question, but gave the lawyer no opportunity to respond before she connected her WristTab and caused the CrediCor logo to vanish. It was replaced with a series of documents which implied Chynna's guilt.

The lawyer turned to look at Chynna's financial history, the course corrections recovered from the guidance system at the crash site, and Kareem's data showing the two asteroids which came down that day were not from the same rock.

The lawyer scoffed. "I don't know what that's supposed to be prove!"

Julie looked across the desk at Chynna who didn't so much as lift her gaze from her lap. "This points to you as the one who deliberately sent the asteroid on a collision course with the ThorGate research station."

"I've advised my client she does not have to say anything to you," said Peterson.

Julie ignored him. "If you have anything to say to defend yourself, Chynna, now would be the time."

Chynna tugged at the loose strand of her hair and forced it back behind her ear again. It rebelled and returned to hang at her cheek.

"If you tell me the truth," said Julie, "I might be able to help you. But if you stay silent, the evidence will have to speak for itself."

When Chynna finally looked up, there were tears in her eyes. "No one was supposed to die!" she whispered.

"You're talking about Gianni Lupo?"

The color drained from the lawyer's face. "I think my client has said quite enough!"

"I think your client can speak for herself." Julie glared at him. "Chynna?"

"I took the money, it's true," she said, through her tears. "But it wasn't all for me! I had to pay someone out on the belt to find the second asteroid and attach the guidance system. They made sure it would come down on the same trajectory so everyone thought it was the same asteroid.

Then, once it entered the atmosphere, I fed through the course corrections so it would divert into the canyon and destroy the ThorGate research station. But the man wasn't supposed to be there!"

Her confession trailed out into sobs. Like everything she had been bottling up for weeks was spilling out of her. Much to the annoyance of the lawyer hired to keep her quiet.

"Who paid you, Chynna?" Julie pressed.

"There wasn't supposed to be an investigation," she said through continued sobs. "Not a proper one. I mean, we haven't even got a real police force on Mars."

Chynna didn't have a hanky, so she lifted her arm and wiped her nose on her sleeve.

"Chynna, who paid you?" Julie repeated.

"I don't know," she sniffed.

"You don't know? Or you won't say?"

"I swear, I don't know. I tried to find out when they stopped returning my messages, but it was a fake name hiding behind a fake corporation. Then they closed the account and my messages bounced."

"Could it have been the Reds? Another corporation?"

"I don't know," Chynna sobbed. "I don't know, I don't know, I don't know!"

The door to the office was thrown open from outside. All three of them jumped in their seats as the handle slammed hard against the wall.

Standing in the doorway, filling it with his tall, wide presence was Bard Hunter. The multibillionaire founder and CEO of CrediCor was unmistakable in his trademark white cap which, as always, covered his bald head.

"You!" he pointed at Chynna. "You've just been fired."

Bard pointed at the lawyer. "You! You're paid by CrediCor to keep everything confidential, am I right?"

"Well…" The lawyer blinked several times as if his brain was working overtime to catch up. "There's a standard confidentiality clause…"

"Good. I expect you to honor it. If anything that was said in this room gets back to Teractor, I will have you struck off. Are we clear?"

The man nodded his head profusely. "Absolutely."

Bard smiled as he turned to Julie and his whole demeanor switched from officiousness to reverence. "And you must be Julie Outerbridge, the head of the United Nations Mars Initiative." He stepped forward and clasped one of her hands between his two large palms like a precious object. "My name is Bard Hunter."

"Yes," said Julie, too stunned to snatch her hand back. "I know who you are. I've seen you on the news."

CHAPTER TWENTY-THREE

Bard dismissed Chynna and the lawyer, but insisted Julie stay. She watched him with a wary eye, expecting him to make demands for her to back off on her investigation. But Bard, it seemed, was a more subtle operator than that. He invited Julie to sit on one of the more comfortable armchairs in the room, while he walked up to the window where the evidence against Chynna was still displayed.

"I was horrified – *horrified* – when I heard what happened with the asteroid," he said.

"As were we all," said Julie, injecting a warning tone into her voice. "So I hope you're not here to get in the way of my investigation."

"Get in the way?" he exclaimed, as if the very idea was blasphemy. "Precisely the opposite. As soon as I heard you were in the CrediCor offices, I came to find you to assure you that I will do everything in my power to discover what went wrong and what caused this horrific disaster. I am completely appalled at the possibility that one of my own employees allowed themselves to be bribed by a nefarious outside organization, and I am determined to discover who that was."

"I'm pleased to hear it." Julie couldn't work out if he was being truthful or was putting on an earnest display for her benefit. Either way, she wasn't going to be taken in by his infamous cunning.

"In fact," said Bard, "I was hoping you could tell me who bribed my employee."

"That's something I'm working on," said Julie. "It could have been anyone with a motive for damaging ThorGate's operations on Mars."

Bard took off his distinctive white cap, scratched his bald head and replaced it again. "That's every other corporation on the planet, not to mention half of the political parties."

"Including CrediCor itself."

Bard's face furrowed in anger as he tapped at Chynna's financial records with his index finger. "CrediCor had nothing to do with this."

"Chynna was your employee," said Julie. "And she confessed she had people out in the asteroid belt helping her. All of which are also your employees."

Bard came back over and sat down in the armchair opposite. "I want to explain something to you, Julie Outerbridge. I like terraforming, especially when it involves hurling asteroids at Mars. I have a hunch it's going to pay off and not only warm the planet, but put CrediCor in a position to be a major player. I wouldn't jeopardize that for some vendetta against one of ThorGate's little projects, even if I believed the contract should have gone to another corporation."

"Then I welcome your help in unearthing who paid Mah Chynna and who else at CrediCor might have played a part."

"I sincerely doubt anyone else at CrediCor played a significant role. It stands to reason that this was a rogue element within the corporation which I – as much as you – want to ensure is stamped out. I am only embarrassed to say that I was completely unaware of it until now."

"Are you sure you were unaware?"

"I hope you're not accusing me."

"I'm not accusing anyone – yet," said Julie, pointedly reserving the right to do so in the future. "Just asking the question."

He leant back in his chair in an attempt, Julie felt, to appear undisturbed by her veiled suggestion. "I'm only frustrated I couldn't be here to personally take charge of the situation much earlier," he said.

"I would have liked to have spoken to you, but I was told you were unavailable on a yoga retreat on Earth."

"Ah." Bard grinned. "That was a little ruse to explain my absence during the journey here. I didn't want anyone questioning where I was and discovering I was locked in a spaceship halfway to Mars."

"Would it have made any difference?" asked Julie.

"Of course!" Bard stood up and paced up and down the small room like he had energy he needed to release. "My arrival was to have been a great surprise and I was to step onto Mars in a blaze of publicity. I was to use it to announce my new, grand scheme which I will personally supervise.

But then this whole 'life on Mars' thing happened and completely stole my thunder."

Only a man with an ego the size of Bard's would consider the greatest discovery in history to be a personal slight to his ambitions. "How unfortunate."

"Exactly!" said Bard, completely missing her sarcasm. "Instead of dominating ICN and being the talk of the planet, as I'd planned, the announcement of my arrival was going to be a footnote on the news. I didn't come all this way to be a footnote, so I slipped in quietly – in as much as it's possible to slip in quietly when landing a spaceship. I've been busy over these last couple of days turning this little 'life on Mars' setback into an opportunity. I think you'll agree that what I've managed to achieve is an exciting, unprecedented deal."

He looked at Julie with expectation. She resisted the implication that she should ask what it was and calmly returned his gaze. Although, she had to admit, she was curious.

Bard smiled while he stood and waited. Julie got the feeling that he would stand there all day if he had to, just to make sure he got the reaction he wanted. In the end, she decided it would be childish to try to stare him out and capitulated to ask the inevitable. "What unprecedented deal?"

"I can't tell you that!" Bard declared, walking up and down the room one more time. "No, Julie Outerbridge, to tell you that here and now would spoil my grand announcement."

Julie stood up to go. There clearly wasn't room enough for both her and the CrediCor CEO's ego in the same room. "Then I should be getting on with my investigation."

"No, wait!" said Bard, as she headed for the door. He rushed over to intercept her. "Can you drive a rover?"

Julie stopped as her path to leave was blocked by the large man who waited expectantly for her answer. "I've been on Mars half my life, of course I can drive a rover."

"Excellent! Then you can drive me out to where they dug up those Martian microbes. I want to see where it all happened."

Julie looked at him, suspiciously. "Don't you have staff who can drive you?"

"Yes, but where's the fun in that?"

"Anyway, you can't go there, the site is out of bounds."

"Don't worry about that. I know they will let me in. I have a grand announcement to make which, I believe, will benefit the whole of Mars. If you drive me out there, you can come and watch."

Julie leant back against the parked rover near to the closed Noctis City construction site. She had stopped alongside other parked vehicles which, she presumed, belonged to the investigating science team and the ICN crew who she could see on the ridge less than one hundred meters away. In the middle of all of them was Bard. He was striding around the site, introducing himself to everyone across the general comms channel like a member of some old Earth royal family. Their reaction ranged from awestruck to bewildered, but within minutes everyone was aware that the infamous, maverick CEO of CrediCor had arrived. Not least the news crew, who followed him around like he was the Pied Piper of Hamelin.

Once Bard had secured the attention of everyone on the ridge, he found a place to stand where the sun lit him from the side and he had the expanse of Noctis Labyrinthus behind him. Just like Rufus Oladepo not long before him, he knew how to use the majestic Martian landscape to great effect.

"I am so privileged to be standing here at this momentous place and at this momentous occasion," he said over the comms, opening his arms wide as if to embrace the whole labyrinth of canyons behind him. "I was traveling through space when I heard the news about the discovery of Martian life and, like many of you, I could barely contain my excitement.

"But it comes after a great tragedy which, as the founder of CrediCor, I feel responsible for." His voice struck a sorrowful, even melodramatic tone. "The asteroid disaster happened on my watch and, although I was unable to do anything about it from my spaceship, I still feel responsible."

Julie rolled her eyes. He was laying it on a bit thick. On the one hand taking responsibility, but on the other distancing himself from the whole thing.

"My reasons for coming to Mars, in the light of these two events, now seem trivial. It is why I have been working hard to move Mars into a new era of discovery and innovation. Since my arrival, mere days ago, I have been talking to some of the representatives of the corporations based here on this planet and I am pleased to announce that CrediCor is ready to embark on a unique collaboration with Ecoline. Ecoline's expertise in biology is unsurpassed, while CrediCor has the financial resources to fund an exciting new project.

We will do this, not as a business opportunity or a money-making scheme, but as a philanthropic gesture to all the people who live on Mars now and who will live on Mars in the future.

"The discovery of native life is of profound significance to humanity, but it is clear that we cannot leave Mars to the Martians. We are already here, and we are here to stay. So we must live in harmony with Martian life. This collaboration with Ecoline will be at the forefront of establishing how we do that. At the same time, we will rebuild the science research station which was so tragically destroyed by the asteroid. Except, this research station will be on a grander and more ambitious scale. I will personally oversee this new endeavor to genetically engineer Earth plants to grow in the harsh conditions of Mars as we continue to pursue our dream of terraforming the planet."

Movement among the crowd of spectators suggested several of them had broken into applause which was strangely silent in the thin atmosphere of Mars, where sound barely carried and where they were all cocooned in their rad-suits.

"What about Noctis City?" shouted one of the crowd, presumably a member of ICN.

"It is such a shame," said Bard. "ThorGate's plans were so ambitious, but it is difficult to see how it can be built on this historic site. I wouldn't want to pre-judge the science or the decision of the Committee, of course, but the study of these amazing Martian microbes should be the priority. It is my belief that CrediCor and Ecoline's new research center will be at the heart of that, right here where the discovery was made. We can learn how these microscopic organisms were able to survive and thrive on this planet and use that knowledge to help humans do the same."

The next question was about Bard's yoga retreat cover story and Julie mentally tuned out the answer. She was thinking about CrediCor's collaboration with Ecoline. Bard may have been a maverick egotist with a flair for the flamboyant, but his plan was clever.

People had criticized ThorGate for having too much power and securing Universal Tax funding for the best planetary projects, but they couldn't criticize the collaboration of two supposedly competing corporations at no cost to the taxpayer. Especially when one of them was Ecoline, a relatively small organization. Their development of fast-growing lichen, suitable for early terraforming, made them a competitive player on the Martian stage, even though they lacked the resources and business acumen to exploit it. That could all change with CrediCor at their side.

As everyone else continued to watch Bard, Julie turned away and saw that a rover was approaching, sending a cloud of dust up behind it as it sped across Sinai Planum. Traveling at an inadvisable pace, it bounced over the uneven ground and skidded to a halt a meter before hitting the parked rovers. Its wheels scattered a rain of grit and dirt over the vehicles and over Julie. Slightly affronted, she brushed herself free of the debris.

After a few moments, the hatch opened and a rad-suited figure stepped out. None of the people watching Bard saw her arrive, but they couldn't miss the angry voice of the woman in the suit as she shouted over the comms and strode towards them.

"What the hell is going on?" Her angry tone gave her away as Anita Andreassen. "This is ThorGate's site!"

Bard's impromptu press conference was abruptly halted as everyone turned to watch Anita. When she reached the crowd, she stopped and put her hands defiantly on her hips. "You can't do this!" she yelled.

Julie wished she could see Bard's face. He must have been annoyed that someone was usurping his big moment. However, all she could do was listen to his indignant response. "I'm sorry, who are you?"

"I'm ThorGate's representative on this planet and you are trespassing."

"I don't think so," said Bard. "This site is under the jurisdiction of the Terraforming Committee."

"The Committee which says *they* have a right to be here." Anita indicated all the others standing around her. "*You* do not."

"I'm sorry, let me introduce myself." He stepped into the crowd and they parted to let him through like he was some kind of messiah. He reached out both his gloved hands to Anita to greet her in the same way he had greeted Julie back in the CrediCor office. "My name is Bard Hunter."

Anita pulled back from him and Bard was forced to drop his arms back down by his sides. "I know who you are," she said. "How dare you conspire with Ecoline to take away a project that belongs to ThorGate!"

Bard remained calm, despite her angry words. "Why don't we take this conversation onto a private channel?"

"So no one else can hear about your despicable behavior?"

"So we can discuss things in a sensible way."

There was some more discussion before they agreed to switch to a private channel. The crowd began to drift away and left Bard and Anita to their discussion. Which, judging by their gestures, was more like an argument.

Someone said over the general comms that the wind had started to pick up the dust and it looked like a storm was on its way. The news crew headed back to their rover and the science team began to pack up their equipment. Julie looked out across Sinai Planum and saw a haze that wasn't there before. The day also seemed to have become darker, even though the sun was approaching its highest point in the sky.

She walked over to where Bard and Anita were still talking and flicked onto their private channel. She heard the tail end of Bard saying something about offering ThorGate an exclusive deal for power generation technology before she interrupted.

"Sorry to disturb you, but it looks like a dust storm is brewing. We should go."

Bard turned towards her and, for the first time since he had breezed into the office back at CrediCor headquarters, she saw a ruthlessness in his eyes. "In a minute."

"We've got a long journey back."

"I said I'll be there in a minute!" Bard snapped.

"I'll wait for you in the rover," said Julie. "Don't make me leave without you."

She switched away from the private channel before Bard could say anything else and walked back the way she had come, wiping off a film of dust which had settled on her helmet. She wished she hadn't allowed him to talk her into coming out to witness his announcement firsthand when she could have easily watched it later on ICN. But it had been little more than a year since control of Mars had been taken away from her and part of her still wanted to be at the center of things. It seemed she was about to pay for her curiosity. The storm was drawing closer while she waited for Bard and threatened to make their journey back more difficult than it might otherwise have been.

Light levels around her diminished further, like night was coming in early, and eddies of dirt swirled around her legs. She opened the hatch to let herself into the rover and kept it open for Bard to join her, while the wind blew in a sprinkling of dust and she lay in a course to Tharsis City.

By the time Bard had finished his negotiations, she could no longer see the canyons of Noctis Labyrinthus through the windshield. The storm was raging and she was preparing to drive right into it.

CHAPTER TWENTY-FOUR

A red mist descended. For an Earth-dweller, that expression meant an anger so intense that it was as if they could see the blood in front of their face. For someone living on Mars, it meant the very dirt that made up the surface of the planet was coming to batter them. Mars didn't have an atmosphere thick enough to create gale force winds like the ones which could knock someone off their feet on Earth, but it had enough strength to lift the dust into the air. Dust which was so dry and so small, having been ground down by millennia of storms, that it was easy to play with and throw at the humans. As if the planet itself was attacking the invaders from another world.

Driving through a dust storm was unpleasant, but it wasn't dangerous. Satellite navigation would guide the rover along the well-worn Martian tracks and Julie only had to pay attention to make sure they didn't encounter any unforeseen hazards.

Although, she would have preferred it if Bard had finished

his negotiation when she had asked him to, not wait until the storm was at its height.

"I hope that conversation was worth it," Julie said to Bard, who was sitting next to her in the passenger seat.

"Oh yes," he said, and fell silent.

"Is that all you're going to say?"

"Put it this way, both Anita and I got something we wanted."

Bard peered through the windshield at the haze of dust reducing the visibility in front of them. The rover's headlights were on, but all they did was shine light off the particles of dirt in the air which was reflected back at them. Like driving through mist on Earth.

"Can't we sit here and wait for this to be over?" asked Bard.

"We don't know how long the storm's going to last. There's always a chance it could last longer than the air and power that we have in the rover."

"But you're safe to drive in this?"

"This isn't my first dust storm," said Julie. Although, she had to admit to herself, she had never been out in one that bad. In the past, she had always done the sensible thing and driven back to the city at the first sign of the winds picking up.

She maneuvered the rover away from the canyons and onto the track which led to Tharsis City. She had hoped to be able to speed up a little once they were on their way, but the visibility was too poor and progress was slow. Bard eventually got bored of looking out at nothing and climbed into the back of the rover. After a while of listening to the sounds of him rummaging around, Julie glanced back to see what he was up to. Bard had one arm in and one arm out of his rad-suit. "What are you doing?"

"Getting out of this blasted suit," he said, trying to extricate his second arm.

"You need to keep that on in the rover."

"What on Earth for? The stupid thing is uncomfortable."

"You're not on–"

The rover jolted.

The front left side sprung up in the air like leaping off a ramp and came back down so hard that Julie was catapulted across the controls. Bard fell forward and banged his head against the back of the passenger seat.

The rover came to a complete halt and tipped over sideways by about twenty degrees so the whole cabin was at an angle. Julie pulled herself upright and turned off the drive motor.

"What was that?" said Bard.

"I don't know," said Julie, trying to sound calm. "I think we hit something."

She put the vehicle into reverse and tentatively applied power to the motor. The machinery whirred and sent vibrations through her driver's seat, but the rover didn't move one centimeter. She changed to forward gear and tried again. Still nothing. Increasing the power did nothing either and the motor merely growled angrily as it propelled them nowhere.

"Weren't you looking where you were going?" said Bard.

"Of course I was!"

Apart from that brief moment she had turned to look at

Bard. She cursed herself for allowing him to distract her. "This is why you're supposed to keep your suit on for the whole journey – in case we need to get out of the rover in a hurry, or something happens and the hull is punctured."

Bard frowned. "We're getting out?"

Julie got up out of the driver's seat and leaned over to one side as she walked on the sloping floor to get into the main part of the cabin where she had left her helmet. It had rolled off the bench and was upside down in a pile of dust at the hatchway. "I need to see what the problem is. I'm going to have to depressurize the cabin before I open the hatch. So, if you want to breathe, I suggest you put your suit back on and secure your helmet."

She helped Bard complete his suiting up, they secured their helmets, carried out disembarkation checks, waited for the rover to suck the air from the cabin back into its reserves and then opened the hatchway.

Julie stepped out into the storm of whipped up tiny particles which were so small they hissed rather than clattered against her helmet. The wind was blowing from the side strong enough for her to feel it, but not so much to knock her sideways. She walked around to the front of the rover where the headlights shone out into the dust. She had to shield her eyes from the glare as she looked back towards it, but it was obvious the rover was impaled on something. The front left side was suspended in the air, with the wheel dangling helplessly over the ground.

She crouched down to look underneath and, as her eyes adjusted to the relative dark, she saw the underside of the rover was resting on top of a rock. She stared at it for many moments and the horrible feeling in her stomach got worse as she realized they were well and truly stuck. She would have to go back into the rover and call for help, but no one would want to come out in the storm.

"That doesn't look good," came Bard's voice over the comms.

Julie turned around and saw that Bard had followed her outside. "No."

He crouched down beside her to see for himself. "How did you manage to hit a rock?"

"The road should have been clear," she said. "We must have gone off track somehow. These tracks are only the width of a rover, so it's not impossible if the satellite navigation was out by a meter or two. Either that or some idiot dumped debris in the wrong place – I wouldn't put it past some of the corporation worker teams out here."

Bard walked over to the corner of the rover and grasped its underside with both hands.

"What are you doing?" asked Julie.

"I think I might be able to lift it off. Everything on Mars weighs not much more than a third of what it would weigh on Earth, right?"

"That still doesn't give you powers to lift it up like some kind of superhero."

Bard bent his knees to get his weight under it and tried to lift. Julie could tell he was tensing his muscles, even through the bulk of his rad-suit, but the rover didn't budge in the slightest. "Damn!" he said, as he let go. "My strength must have really atrophied on the journey out here."

"Rovers are heavy. There's the battery, the drive motor,

not to mention the thick hull, and all the environmental controls inside one of these things."

"Are you saying that to make me feel better?" said Bard.

"No, just helping you come to the inevitable conclusion that we'll have to call for help and wait it out."

"I'm not ready to give up yet." He turned and walked back towards the open hatch. "There might be something in the rover we could use."

"I doubt it," Julie called after him, even though raising her voice wasn't necessary over the comms.

"It won't take a minute to look." He stepped inside.

"Turn off the headlights while you're in there, let's not run down the battery any more than we need to. And bring a flashlight."

Julie took another look at the rugged boulder on which the rover was resting. It appeared to be firmly embedded in the ground. Not only was the swirling dust gathering at its base, the weight of the rover itself almost certainly acted like a hammer and jammed it hard into the dirt.

It suddenly darkened all around her. Bard must have turned off the headlights. She stood back up straight and, as her eyes got used to the available daylight in the haze of the dusty atmosphere, she saw Bard approaching from out of the rover with the beam from a flashlight dancing about the ground in front of his feet. Under his arm was a pole about a meter and a half long, like the ones used to mark out land for surveying or development. Except, without the usual flag on top.

"I found this," he said, stabbing the ground with the pointed end.

"A marker pole," said Julie, wondering what he expected to do with it.

"If we can get some leverage, we might be able to lift the rover off the rock."

She looked at the thin pole and then looked at the large vehicle. She didn't hold out much hope, but figured it couldn't do any harm. "Worth a try, I suppose."

He went back to the corner of the vehicle, got down on his hands and knees, and shone the flashlight onto the rock. "Hold this for me, would you?"

Julie came up behind him and took the flashlight as he handed it back to her. She focused it on the rock as Bard maneuvered the pole so the center rested on one of the jagged bits at the top of the rock. Holding onto the other end, he flexed it up and down so it pivoted on the boulder. Julie could see that if he pushed down on the end of the lever sticking out from under the rover, then the other end would connect to the underside and lift it up. In theory.

Bard stood up straight again and grabbed hold of the other end of the pole. "Here we go," he said, and pushed down.

But he pushed too hard and fast. The other end of the pole hit the underside of the rover so quickly that it bounced off its pivot point on the rock.

For the first time, she got the sense that his plan might have real merit and they could soon be on their way. "Nearly," she said.

He tried again. This time, he took it slow. The far end of the pole connected with the rover, and he kept gently pushing as the sound of his heavy breathing was picked up by the comms.

The rover lifted free of the rock by only a couple of millimeters, but it was enough for both of its front wheels to hover in the air.

"That's it!" said Julie.

But Bard couldn't hold it any longer and, with a grunt, let go of the pole and the rover landed back in its impaled position. Anticipation turned to frustration as they were clearly back where they started.

He leant forward and rested his hands on his knees while he got his breath back. "I can lift it, but I can't move it sideways. It needs to be shifted clear of the rock."

"If you could lift it, maybe I could push it far enough so it's free of the boulder," she suggested.

Through the bubble of his helmet, Julie could see Bard smile at the idea. "That could work," he said.

With the dust still swirling around them, Bard replaced the pole on the rock so the other end was touching the center of the underside of the rover. Julie walked round to the front left side near to where the wheel was dangling.

"Ready?" said Bard.

Julie wiped some of the dust off the bubble of her helmet and put her hands on the corner of the rover. It was difficult to grasp through the fabric of her gloves, but if she braced her palms against the flat metal sides and curled her fingers under the rim, she could get a firm enough hold.

"Ready," she acknowledged.

"On three," he said. "One, two, three!"

Bard grunted as he pushed down on the pole. The force vibrated through Julie's gloves and the rover lifted a hairsbreadth above the rock. She pushed to move the vehicle sideways, but it was stubborn. With the front elevated, most of the weight had shifted to the back wheels, forcing them further into the dirt and resisting her efforts to move it. She dug her boots into the ground, leaned all her weight against the side and, at last, the rover begrudgingly began to turn. It was hard work because the more she pushed, the more the angle caused the underside to scrape on the top point of the rock. It was so frustrating – if it was just a little higher, she felt sure she could push the rover clear of the obstacle.

"Can you lift it up any more?" called Julie over the comms.

"I think so."

Bard forced all his bodyweight down onto the pole with a grunt of effort so sudden and violent that the corner of the rover was ripped from Julie's hands. It tipped up and lurched forward, heading straight for him. He jumped out of the way as the front end struck the ground where – moments before – he had been standing.

But it didn't stop. The momentum kept the rover tumbling and Bard turned to run as the crashing machine flipped over and plummeted towards him. He had taken only two steps before the bumper struck the back of his knees, throwing him forward, and he went sprawling to the ground. The roof of the rover crashed down on Bard's legs, and he screamed as the force of the impact rippled through the ground.

"Bard!" Julie cried.

"My legs! My legs!" he shouted in desperation and panic.

Julie stared at the horrific reality of what had just happened. Bard lay face down in the Martian dirt, the top half of his body sticking out from the rover and his bottom half trapped underneath.

She ran to him and crouched down where the bubble of his helmet was pressed into the ground. Through the side, she could see him grimacing in pain as the color drained away from his face.

"No, no!" he cried out, He wriggled the upper half of his body as he tried to scramble free, but he could only scratch at the dirt beneath his fingers. "I'm stuck!"

"Don't do anything hasty," Julie tried to calm him. "We need to assess the situation first."

"I can't stay here!" Bard put his hands in the dirt on either side of his chest and tried to push himself away. His torso lifted from the waist, but his legs didn't move. They were completely trapped under the rover. With an exasperated gasp, he stopped pushing and collapsed back down.

"Breathe deep," Julie told him. "Save your strength and let me take a look."

With dust swirling around her, she craned her head to look under the upturned machine where Bard's legs were pinned to the ground. In the reduced light of the storm and the shadow of the rover, the only thing she could see clearly was the beam from the flashlight radiating from beneath the vehicle's roof. It shone out in the direction of Bard's left boot and highlighted its grotesquely twisted angle with the toe pointing up and his leg turned unnaturally sideways.

"Can you move your legs at all?" she asked.

Bard let out a painful gasp as he tried. His right leg shifted a little bit, but his left leg stayed where it was. The pain was clearly too much, and he stopped trying.

She looked away from his contorted limb and tried to hide the concern from her face. "I think your right leg is fine."

"But the left one? What about the left one?"

"It's going to be fine," said Julie, using a tone which she hoped was soothing. "Have you got any warnings coming through on your rad-suit?"

"Warnings? What warnings?"

"If the integrity of your suit has been breached, there will be an audible warning in your helmet. They should have told you about that in your training. I can't hear anything over the comms."

"No," said Bard, breathing quick and heavy. "No warning."

"That's good," said Julie. "That means your suit's not been ruptured."

"Good? You've got to get me out of this! Find the pole. Can you find the pole?"

Julie knew she wasn't strong enough to lift the rover off him, even if she retrieved the pole, but she owed it to him to try.

She paced around the upturned rover and soon found the pole, which had been partially covered by accumulated dust and was half sticking out from underneath. She grabbed hold of the pointed end and pulled, but it was well and truly stuck and didn't move even a little bit. It also looked like it had been bent where the rover had landed on top of it and, even if she could get it out, it would be completely useless.

Julie stepped back and glanced across at the open hatch. The entrance was upside down, but it would be easy enough to climb in. "I'm going to call for help," she said. "I won't be minute."

"Don't get in the rover!" said Bard in panic. "You'll put more weight on my leg."

"I'll be quick. We need help." Julie glanced back at his prone, stricken body for a moment, then put her hands on the edge of the upside-down hatch and hauled herself inside. As she put out the distress call, she worried that rescue would not come quick enough, despite the eagerness due to loyalty or expecting a reward. There was no telling how bad Bard's injuries were. He could be bleeding internally for all she knew, and without medical attention his crushed leg could be killing him from the inside. All she could do was express the urgency of the situation over the radio and hope that whoever heard it was willing to battle through the storm to save them.

CHAPTER TWENTY-FIVE

Julie jumped out of the upside-down hatchway and fell forward as her feet hit the surface of Mars. Her gloved hands struck the dirt in front of her and she pushed herself back up to standing. Particles hissed against the outside of her helmet as the winds continued to hurl dust through the air.

She approached the front of the rover and, through the hazy atmosphere, saw Bard where she had left him – lying face down and pinned to the planet. The man who had appeared so big and impressive when he had arrived in dramatic fashion at the CrediCor office, looked suddenly small and helpless with half his body hidden under the white, upturned mass of the stricken rover.

She sat down next to him. "I've called for help."

"I don't know how much longer I can stand this pain." Bard's voice was shaky. Julie feared he was going into shock.

"They'll be here soon."

"How long?"

"Soon."

There was nothing more she could say. "Soon" was pure speculation. She had put out the distress call but didn't want to leave Bard alone long enough to discover who, if anyone, was going to answer it.

In the few minutes that she had been gone, more dust had accumulated against the side of Bard's body so he was half buried in a sand dune. She brushed as much of it away as she could and tried to think of something she could say to keep him talking and distracted.

"Why don't you tell me about your grand announcement?" she said.

"Because I'm concentrating on breathing," said Bard, his voice straining through the pain he must be in.

"Talking is better," said Julie. "It'll take your mind off the pain. Tell me about your grand announcement."

"I told you already. You were there."

"Not that one. The one you said brought you all the way out to Mars in the first place. You told me you had planned to announce it in a blaze of publicity before the whole 'life on Mars' thing got in your way."

Bard turned his head sideways so he was no longer facing the dirt. He grimaced at the discomfort, but it must have allowed him to see Julie out of the edge of his helmet. "I can't tell the head of a rival corporation my future plans."

"Credit me with some integrity," said Julie. "I'll sign a confidentiality agreement when we get back if that will make you feel better. Or talk to me about something else. But keep talking. It will help me as much as you."

"OK, I'll tell you," he said, then paused. Perhaps for dramatic effect, or perhaps because he was really reticent about revealing his plans to the head of UNMI. "I want to bring Deimos down."

"You mean crash it? Like one of your asteroids?"

"Why not? We don't use that moon anyway."

Through the side of his helmet, despite his anguish, she could see the glee on his face at the outlandish idea. "You can't bring down one of Mars' moons!"

"If I can bring an asteroid all the way from the asteroid belt and crash it onto the surface of Mars, then I can bring down a little rock from orbit."

"But people go out at night to look at Phobos and Deimos. They're almost part of the planet."

"You're thinking like an Earth woman, Julie Outerbridge. Those two small, jagged rocks are nothing like Earth's moon. They don't have a strong gravitational pull on Mars like the Moon does on Earth. They don't affect its rotation, they don't affect the tides – I know there are no tides yet on Mars, but there will be one day when we have oceans. Deimos is a useless rock that I can make use of. And not just to create a breathtaking spectacle when it smashes into Mars and becomes part of the terraforming effort. I can use it as black polar dust. It's so dark, I can grind it up and sprinkle it on the poles so it absorbs sunlight and melts the water and carbon dioxide locked up in the ice."

"That's a huge project," said Julie. "You'll probably have to repeat it every year when the carbon dioxide refreezes over the top."

"But think how amazing it will be to watch the whole of the white polar regions turn to black."

Julie was familiar with the idea as one of many which had been put forward over the years, but she had never before considered how dramatic it would be. "You think the Terraforming Committee will let you go through with it?"

"I know they will."

Julie could almost hear the smug smile in his voice, even though his breathing was becoming more labored and he was struggling to keep the conversation going.

"Why come all the way out to Mars for that? Surely, your team is perfectly capable of doing it without you."

"Because I'm spending a lot of money on this planet, and I wanted to see some of the things I'm paying for. The older I get, the harder it is to journey into space. When Deimos comes crashing down, it will be the most amazing spectacle. I want to be here to see it."

Something made Bard want to move his body – perhaps a sudden stab of pain he was trying to hide – and his torso wriggled in the dust. But he quickly went still again as he let out an agonized groan. "If I survive that long," he said.

"Of course you'll survive," she said, trying to convince herself as much as him. "The rescuers are on their way."

"I can't feel my leg." His voice was a whisper, as if he could hardly bear to admit it to himself. "How long will they be?"

Julie was getting worried. She looked at the storm and thought she could see less dust blowing around them and more light reaching the ground. But that could have been wishful thinking. Either way, Mars was not yet finished punishing them with its weather and anyone hearing their distress call, if they were willing to come out in such conditions, would be taking it slow.

"Soon," she said, praying that what she told him was true. "They'll be here soon."

A warning bleeped in Julie's helmet and the voice of its control system spoke to her. "Low oxygen warning."

"Please no," she whispered.

"What?" said Bard.

"My oxygen levels are getting low."

"That means my oxygen must be getting low too. I have to get out of here." Bard clawed at the dirt in a pointless attempt to push himself free of the rover. But all his frantic movement did was to shuffle himself further down into the dirt.

"Stay still," Julie urged. "The calmer you are, the less oxygen you will use up."

"I'm gonna die out here on the surface of Mars!"

"You're not going to die. There's enough oxygen for us in the rover. If I transfer most of my remaining oxygen to your reserves, I can go back inside and breathe whatever's left in the cabin. I can also monitor the radio more easily."

Bard reached out suddenly and grabbed Julie's gloved hand. "Don't leave me."

"It's OK. Rescue is on the way."

"Please."

He gripped even tighter.

"Just for a minute then." Julie tried to draw her hand away, but Bard wouldn't let go.

"Do you know the other reason why I came to Mars?"

He sounded desperate, like he was reaching for a way to persuade her to stay.

She remembered her own words to him and the need to keep him talking "No," she said. "Tell me."

"I know that CrediCor can't go on forever crashing asteroids," Bard admitted. "I hear that the people who live here already complain every time a rock strikes the surface of the planet. That stupid incident with the crash at Noctis Labyrinthus is only going to make it worse for us. I had to come here to make sure there was a future for CrediCor on the new frontier. We need to diversify. We need to be part of all the technologies going on Mars. The genetically engineered plants, farming, creating oceans, creating forests – everything involved in terraforming this small, red planet. That's really why I had to make the deal with Ecoline. Do you understand?"

Julie nodded. "Yes, I understand."

"Even if I never get to see it, at least I will have started the process rolling. Even that ThorGate woman won't stand in my way now. Or, rather, in CrediCor's way."

"Stop talking like you're going to die."

"But it's bad, right? I know it's bad. Even if I survive, even if they get me out, I'm afraid I'm going to lose my leg." Bard sniffed inside his helmet and Julie had the feeling he was on the verge of breaking down.

The warning bleeped in Julie's helmet again. "Low oxygen warning."

"Let me get back to the rover," she said. "I can fill up my oxygen reserves from in there, come back out and attach a line to fill up your tanks. You'll be fine, it won't take long."

Bard took a deep breath. "OK. But you will be quick?"
"I promise."

Julie put her free hand on top of where Bard's fingers were clasped around hers and gently pulled her hand free. She stood up into the storm and turned to face the prevailing wind as it threw dust against her. She had only taken a single step towards the open hatch when she thought she saw something through the haze ahead of her. She stopped and stared at what she realized were the two headlights of an approaching rover.

A voice broke over the comms. "Hello! Are you the people who said they needed some assistance?"

"Yes!" Julie lifted her arms and waved at the two shining eyes of her rescuers. "Bard! It's another rover! They've made it!"

"Hey, we're over here!" yelled Bard. "Over here! Over here!"

She trembled with excitement and relief as the rover stopped less than two meters away. Her legs went weak and she had put out her hand on the base of the hull to steady herself.

After a few moments, the rescue rover's hatchway opened and three suited figures stepped out into the swirling dust.

"You've got yourself in a right old pickle there," said the first of the suited figures, whose voice revealed him to be an Australian man.

"Thanks for coming out in the storm," said Julie.

"No worries," he said with a jovial air. "We were only at the Noctis City construction site and, seeing as we're not allowed to do any constructing at the moment, we figured we might as well help."

"I'm really grateful, but it's my–" Julie couldn't think of how to describe Bard, "–my traveling companion who needs help."

She led them to the front of the rover where Bard was trapped.

"Don't worry, mate," said the Australian. "We'll get you out from under there in a jiffy."

CHAPTER TWENTY-SIX

An anger that Luka had thought he had hidden away inside began to wake. Like boiling water in his stomach, it bubbled and scalded him as he watched the ICN report.

Bard Hunter was on Mars.

Bard Hunter was delivering a self-satisfied speech about his plans for Noctis Labyrinthus. Bard Hunter's brazen attempt to snatch ThorGate's grand plans out from under their noses was despicable enough, but it was nothing compared to the crimes against humanity he had committed on Earth. All in the name of corporate greed.

Luka would have turned off the window to hide the man's evil face from his eyes, but he was standing in the communal space of the construction habitat watching the news with about twenty other migrant workers and Erik, who stood next to him. Before the storm hit, the two of them had been at one of ThorGate's more distant solar arrays to implement Luka's new program for the dust cleaning robots. When it was clear the storm was going to be bad, they decided it wasn't worth trying to make the long drive back to Thor Town and stopped off at the much nearer construction habitat to wait for the winds to die down.

It was a much more tense atmosphere inside than Luka had remembered. The migrants had had nothing to do since the discovery of life on Mars and their frustration was so palpable that it filled the air and vibrated through the walls. For them to sit there and listen to Bard gush about plans for the Noctis site – plans which didn't involve them – added insult to injury.

"He can't do that! The Terraforming Committee won't let him do it," said one of them.

"I think he's already done it," said another.

"It's fine for rich tyrants like him. They don't care about the ordinary people on the ground."

Luka knew all the voices who spoke, all their names and all their personalities. But they all blurred into one as he stared at Bard's smug face on the ICN footage. Even with his helmet on, the man still wore the famous white cap that he used to cover up his bald head. Luka would like to take that white cap and shove it down his throat until he choked. Then he would hold it there and watch him suffer as he struggled to breathe. Like Luka's wife and two children had struggled to breathe when the chemical leaked from the factory and poisoned the air in the town where they lived.

"Are you all right?" asked Erik. He peered his head round to look Luka in the eye. "You've gone a funny color."

"Bard Hunter," said Luka, with distain.

"Apparently so," said Erik.

"I didn't know he was on Mars."

"No one did. It was supposed to be a surprise, apparently."

"Yeah," said Luka. "A big, fat surprise. I thought if I came to Mars, then at least my feet wouldn't be sharing the same planet with that man. But it seems there's no escape."

"What's your problem with Bard Hunter?"

Luka let out an ironic chuckle. How soon people forgot the horrors of the past. "The Rhine Valley Disaster," he said simply.

By Erik's shocked expression, Luka could see he remembered their conversation about his deceased family. "But that wasn't CrediCor," said Erik. "That was... some other corporation. I can't even remember who it was now."

"But who financed the corporation who ran the chemical factory in the valley?" said Luka. "CrediCor. Who called in their loan so the factory was forced to make cut backs? CrediCor. Who ignored the warnings that lack of finances would put safety at risk? CrediCor. Bard Hunter has blood on his hands, and now he's brought his immoral practices to Mars."

Erik was halfway through bumbling a sympathetic sentence when Morten came rushing in from the corridor. "The rescue team is back from helping that stranded rover," he declared to the room. "You'll never guess who was out there – Julie Outerbridge and Bard Hunter!"

The ears of the workforce pricked up at the names of the two corporation leaders, while Luka acted on instinct. He rushed out of the communal area to the entrance to the airlock where those arriving had to disembark. Before he saw anyone, he heard the cries of a man screaming, "My leg! My leg!"

From around the corner came Julie Outerbridge. Looking world-weary and still in a dusty rad-suit with her helmet off, she leant on another woman as she was led down the corridor. Following were two other members of the rescue team carrying a stretcher between them. Lying on it, with his face contorted in pain, was Bard Hunter.

"Is he going to die?" asked Luka.

But no one answered. A medic from the habitat came up behind him and pushed Luka out of the way as he rushed up to the stretcher and leaned over to speak to Bard. "Don't worry, sir," he said. "We'll get some good pain relief into you and take a look at that leg."

The medic waved on the stretcher bearers and they turned off the corridor into one of the rooms that sometimes doubled as a medical bay. Luka continued to stare at Bard as he was carried past him, and felt the scalding heat of his anger burn a little more brightly.

Erik joined some of the other migrants in a board game being played on a screen set into a table in the communal area, but Luka declined the opportunity to join them. He was not in the mood for games. He plugged a headset into his WristTab and listened to music as he tried to push away the emotions that he had traveled across space to escape. As he sat there, Julie Outerbridge was brought in by one of the medics who placed a cup of something beside her before saying a few words which Luka couldn't hear and then leaving her to sit on her own.

He thought back to the first time he and Julie had met, albeit briefly, at the site of the crashed asteroid. It allowed his thoughts to drift away from Bard Hunter and the crimes he had committed on Earth, to the subject that had obsessed him since he had arrived on Mars: Gianni.

This was his chance to talk to the woman who was investigating the crash that killed him. If he didn't take up that chance, he might never have another. So, even though she appeared to be having some private time, he decided to approach. If she declined to talk to him, then he would respect her wishes.

She was staring down into the cup of tea the medic had given her and shaking a little. As he approached the table, he saw her face was ashen. Although she appeared physically uninjured, it was obvious that whatever had happened to her out in the dust storm had been traumatic.

"Excuse me," he said, tentatively.

She looked up from her tea, a blank expression in her eyes. "Yes?"

"I don't know if you remember me. I'm Luka Schäfer, we met when you needed help to get a sample of the asteroid at the crash site at Noctis Labyrinthus."

"Oh yes," she said. Her words suggested she remembered who he was, but her expression remained blank.

"If you don't mind, I would like to ask you about the investigation," ventured Luka. "Of course, if you prefer to be left alone…"

"You can sit, it's all right. The company would be nice."

Luka pulled a spare chair up to the table. But she didn't look at him. She just kept staring into the liquid in her cup.

"Are you sure you're OK? I mean, do you want me to get you something?"

"I have something." She picked up the mug and sipped. Her face wrinkled at the taste. "It's so sweet."

"I can get you another one that isn't sweet if you like."

"No, I need the sugar." She sipped it again, grimaced again and replaced the mug on the table. "So, what is it you wanted to ask me?"

"Have you found out how the asteroid disaster happened?"

"I have found a few things," said Julie. "But I can't really talk about it until my report is complete."

"It's just that I'm the one who has taken over from Gianni Lupo here at ThorGate. I'm doing his job, I'm living in the same room he used to live in, and I feel like the two of us have some kind of connection. I just want to know a bit more about how he died."

"The investigation is ongoing and it would be wrong of me to speculate. But, as I understand it, there's no question that he was killed in the asteroid crash."

"I'm sure that's where he died, but I have a feeling it wasn't a coincidence that Gianni was the only person in the research station when the asteroid struck."

For the first time in their conversation, there seemed to be something going on behind Julie's eyes. "What sort of feeling?"

"I found some diary entries which Gianni left behind. I think he was scared for his life."

"Interesting," said Julie. But that was all she said.

"What I don't understand is, what made him so scared? No one could have known that the asteroid was going to break up in the atmosphere and, if they did, they couldn't have possibly known where it was going to land. I've been thinking it over a lot, and it doesn't make sense to me."

"Unless they did know," said Julie.

A chill passed through Luka as she presented a devastating possibility he hadn't even thought of. "Unless they did know what?"

Julie stared out into space. Almost like she was talking to herself rather than Luka. "I haven't looked into why Gianni was there. Perhaps I should have done. I'm sorry about that."

"But you've looked into the accident. I mean, it *was* an accident?"

"All I can say is, for an asteroid to split in two and for only one part to go off course is highly unlikely."

"Are you saying you think someone brought it down on the research station deliberately?"

"I'm not saying anything."

"They got the scientists out but allowed Gianni to go there?"

"My information is he wasn't supposed to be there."

"Do you think…" The idea was just forming in Luka's own mind. "Do you think he was sent there on purpose?"

Luka watched for some sort of recognition on Julie's face. To get a sense if this was one of the things she couldn't talk about until her report was complete. But her face remained impassive. "That would be a lot of effort to go to, to murder someone," was all she said.

Luka was going to ask her more questions, but the medic returned. Julie stood as he approached the table and Luka's chance to find out more slipped away.

"Is Bard OK?" asked Julie

"He's stabilized," said the medic.

"You were able to save his leg?"

"That's for the specialists back at Tharsis City," he said. "But the blood supply is getting all the way down to his toes, so I'm hopeful."

Julie went up to the man and shook his hand enthusiastically. "Thank you. Thank you so much."

"The dust storm is receding now," he said. "You should be able to head back without a problem. I'll get one of my medics to make the journey with you to be on the safe side."

Julie walked out with the medic, without acknowledging that Luka was even there.

She forgot her sweet tea too, which sat half drunk on the table in front of him. He picked it up and took a sip. It was lukewarm and incredibly sweet. As he swallowed and waited for the sugar high to kick in, he thought about what she had said. If someone in Julie Outerbridge's position could believe the asteroid might have been deliberately targeted, then Gianni's suspicions were not a product of Martian Madness.

Yet, he had no proof of what had happened, only suspicions. He wasn't even sure he believed it himself. As Julie had said, dropping an asteroid from space was a lot of effort to go to to murder someone.

CHAPTER TWENTY-SEVEN

Luka told the others he couldn't join them for dinner because he had to stay late in the office to get some work done. It wasn't true. The minute Erik, Pete, Myra, Inger, and Roman were gone, he breathed deep and allowed himself to relax. Relax in a nervous, fearing he might be caught, kind of way.

He had been waiting all day for this moment and, now that it was here, he wondered if he was doing the right thing. Spurred on by his conversation with Julie, he needed to find the proof to back up his suspicions or confirm his doubts about what happened to Gianni one way or the other. That meant looking closer into the woman at the heart of Gianni's diary entries: Anita.

He had considered confronting her directly, but he doubted she would reveal anything to him voluntarily. After all, she had completely blown up at Gianni on the couple of occasions he had questioned her. Luka needed more evidence first and that meant breaking into Anita's personal files. Not a difficult thing. As a member of the tech team, he had access to the ThorGate network. He only needed to bypass any extra security she might have set up and make sure that his delving around didn't leave any traces which could lead back to him. None of this was difficult, but it was probably illegal and almost certainly immoral.

Luka's finger hovered over the control for his screen. He contemplated turning it off and forgetting about the whole thing. It wasn't too late to chase after the others and spend an hour or so joining in with their frivolous chatter over dinner. But, after that, he would still have to go home and, in the quiet solitude of his room – the room that Gianni used to live in and where he had recorded his diary entries – the questions would come back into Luka's mind. Questions that he would never have the answers to unless he took a risk.

With his rumbling stomach complaining it was dinner time, Luka connected to the back end of the ThorGate network and went into the message server. He found Anita's messages easily enough without having to jump through any security hoops, but the result was disappointing. They only went back a couple of weeks, and they were all boring and work-related. There was a long list of correspondence with Rufus Oladepo, the chair of the Terraforming Committee, about the continued shutdown of the Noctis City construction site, and some more recent ones about the CrediCor/Ecoline proposals for Noctis Labyrinthus. Others were suggestions around how to occupy the migrant construction crew with work on other ThorGate property and there were some very officious notices from corporate headquarters on Earth about a budget overspend.

Luka placed his elbows on the desk, interlocked his fingers, and rested his chin on the bridge of his hands. He sat like that for several minutes, looking at the messages he had uncovered, before he admitted to himself that he was at a complete dead end. Nothing he had found would have caused Anita to be furious at Gianni. None of her messages appeared personal, they weren't even that confidential from a business point of view. There had to have been something else on her window in her apartment that had caused Anita to react as she did.

He didn't think he would be able to gain access to her personal window through the ThorGate network and, indeed, he couldn't. He could see where it was connected, but he couldn't get past the security protocols to probe any further. The system was designed to keep out the most sophisticated hackers from other corporations, so Luka knew he had no chance of breaking through. The only way to see what secrets she might have stored locally was to sit in front of her window and look. Just like Gianni had done on that night that Anita had become angry and accused him of invading her privacy and snooping around in things where he had no right.

Luka waited in the street, pretending to be interested in a small flower which was growing in a one meter square of grass set into the paving between two rows of accommodation blocks. He kept his head down and his back towards the apartment building where, according to ThorGate records,

Anita lived. Ahead of him, if he angled himself properly, he could see the reflection of the main access door in the glass of a window – a traditional window which allowed someone on the inside to view the outside – and waited for her to come out.

At last there was movement in the reflection in the glass and Luka watched as a small woman emerged from the building and began to walk up the street. He couldn't see her face, but her body shape and hurried, confident stride, told him it was Anita. Luka tuned his hearing into the sound of her shoes on the paving and watched them coordinate with her steps. When the angle of the glass was no longer able to show her reflection, he kept listening until the sound became so distant that it merged into the hubbub of Thor Town.

With Anita safely out of the way, he took a slow and casual stroll towards the door, running through in his mind the various scenarios for persuading someone inside to buzz him in. But he didn't need to. Another woman came out as he approached and held the door open without him needing to ask. He was a ThorGate employee after all. He had the right to be here. They exchanged a smile and he ventured inside. Luka stopped and listened to the door click shut behind him.

He noticed the security camera at the base of the stairwell out of the corner of his eye and hoped the temporary malfunction he had arranged was still working as he climbed up to the second floor. Entering the corridor, he looked right and then left as if crossing a busy road back home in Germany, then padded past the first two doors to the apartment where Anita lived.

Lifting his WristTab, he ran a program to access the Thor Town system and override the security settings on Anita's door. Most security personnel were few, due to the absence of a police force but also the need for human efforts to go elsewhere. Building security was mostly regulated by the machines, with a security detail addressing various problems in Thor Town as required. As he waited and stared at the small, red light of the lock mechanism, he felt the moisture from his nervous sweat soak into his shirt. It was a long thirty seconds but, just as Luka feared it wasn't working, the door sounded a series of electronic bleeps, the red light turned to green and it clicked open.

Luka placed his index finger on the panel of the door and pushed it slowly out of his way. Stepping inside, he listened for sounds of movement, but all he heard was the faint tweeting of birdsong and what sounded like the whisper of a wind blowing through trees. He closed the door behind him and, hearing the click of the lock shut again, a little bit of the tension fell away. He was certain he was in there alone.

Anita's lounge was large, luxurious, and dominated by a large window along one wall. It stretched almost as wide as the wall itself and was about a third as deep. Most people kept their windows turned off when they were not there – it was a Terraforming Committee directive to stop unnecessary use of power – but Anita had left it on to show a live view of snow-capped mountains towering over a lush, green forest. It was clearly the source of the sounds of nature which played out of speakers hidden in the ceiling. It was a beautiful memory of Earth, even if it was an idyllic one that few people who lived there would ever have the chance to experience.

Facing the window was a small table with a dirty cup, plate, and cutlery gathered up in one corner. In front of it was a sprawling two-seater sofa big enough to fit four people sitting side-by-side. At the back of the apartment was a kitchenette area – a rarity on a planet where limited food resources meant everyone was required to eat mass catering most of the time – and two internal doors which almost certainly led to a bathroom and a bedroom.

But Luka was not there to be jealous about how the privileged lived. He was there to snoop into Anita's personal and private files. She would be gone for hours at the office, but with a bit of luck he would be in and out in ten minutes.

He sat on the same sofa that Gianni had sat on that night when he couldn't sleep and turned off the view of Earth. When he did so, just like Gianni, he found that Anita had left herself logged on. "Good," Luka said to himself.

He easily accessed her messages and saw the same ones from the last two weeks that he had been able to access from his office screen. As he scrolled down, he felt an enormous sense of validation as he went past the last few weeks and saw older messages. Hundreds of them. She obviously stored all her files locally and kept very little on the network.

A few of the messages had intriguing titles which promised to reveal more, but turned out to be just as boring as those with mundane titles. Some were audio files. He played a couple of the ones which looked interesting.

"Hi Anita, it's Jakob," said one. "I really need a decision

on what to do about the migrant habitat for the Noctis City site. If you could get back to me, that would be great."

"Don't you ever answer your WristTab?" said an irritated male voice in another. "This whole new solar farm order's doing my head in. Can you at least acknowledge my meeting request? This is Alan, by the way, in case you didn't realize."

He frowned. It could take hours to listen to them all.

As Luka continued to scroll through, he expected to see messages from Gianni. The two of them had been lovers, after all. But there were none. That's when he took a closer look at the dates and realized there were six months of messages missing. Everything from around the time that Gianni's diary entries had started to the day before his death had been deleted.

Luka had friends back in Germany who, after a particularly bitter relationship breakup, had tried to distance themselves from the painful experience by getting rid of everything that reminded them of the other person. One had even used liquid fuel to set light to a stash of mementos and, in his enthusiasm, accidentally set fire to an outbuilding and had to call out the fire service. Deleting a whole six months of messages, including everything to do with work and some that might have been important, sounded like the actions of a woman who wanted to wipe every trace of memory of a man who had hurt her. But, even in Gianni's diary entries when he talked about the arguments they had, Luka hadn't got the impression that they had split up acrimoniously. He didn't even think they had split up at all. Anita had certainly exhibited grief when Gianni was killed. It didn't make sense for her to destroy everything in that way.

Unless the reason she had deleted the messages was the same reason that Luka was looking for them: they contained evidence that she didn't want anyone else to find. If he was right, that was what Gianni had inadvertently stumbled upon during the night he couldn't sleep, and it was why Anita had been so furious. Luka sat back on Anita's sofa and looked at the list of messages he had risked so much to see. All they revealed was an absence of evidence. An absence of evidence was no evidence at all.

But just because Anita had deleted the data from her home system, it didn't mean it was gone for good. Some years ago, when he had worked for the Climate Corporation on Earth on a project to rejuvenate the Black Forest, he was called in by an executive who was tearing her hair out because she'd accidentally deleted details of a contract negotiation which had gone awry. Her system told her that everything had gone and was irretrievable, but in fact the data still existed in areas which had not yet been overwritten. That might also be the case for Anita's missing messages. There were ways, of course, of ensuring deleted files were genuinely deleted, but he was willing to bet that Anita – like most people – either didn't know about them or had failed to implement them.

Luka came out of the user interface and delved deep into the background systems which controlled Anita's computerized window. There, he found junk data that wasn't indexed or obviously linked to anything else. Luka's brain, trained to look for meaning and pattern, picked out the occasional word nestled within the mass of symbols and letters, such as *ThorGate* or *Gianni*, but jumbled and out of context they didn't mean very much.

He did find one intact audio message, however, from Gianni that was dated the day he died.

He played it and listened to Gianni's familiar, but frustrated voice. "Anita, I know you're angry at me, for whatever reason, but you can't ignore my calls when we still need to work together. I need more information about what's wrong with the computer system at the research station before I go over and take a look at it. Will you *please* call me back."

Interesting. Confirmation that he had contacted her about the reasons for going to the research station on the day he died, when Anita had claimed she didn't know why he was there.

He ran a recovery program and tapped an impatient thumb on the sofa cushion beside him as the computer systems tried to form something meaningful out of the apparently meaningless.

Titles of deleted messages began to appear. Some of them were gobbledygook, having been corrupted while lost in the back end of the window's operating system, but most appeared intact.

As he watched, one name came up repeatedly: Sara Hansen. Luka didn't remember seeing that name in any of Anita's other messages. The titles were uninteresting at first glance – Mars Temp Stats, Power Output Variance, Postpone Lunch Meeting – so he opened one at random.

It consisted of one short sentence: *The power plant must be empty of all power on the date,* it said. *Failure to achieve this objective will nullify the agreement.*

Luka stared at it for a moment. It seemed, on the face of it, fairly innocuous. He opened another message. This one was corrupted in a few places, but was still readable: *I've arranged for some samples to be deli$&red to your office. If you could let me know the color you x%^ld prefer.*

Individually, the messages were ordinary and made some kind of sense, but, together, there was something strange about them. The first one, about a power plant was logical because ThorGate was the leading provider of electricity on Mars. Whereas the second one about color samples seemed to be about interior design. Putting aside the fact that the opportunity to choose the color of anything on Mars was usually limited to the one color that was provided, for the same person to be messaging about both was very odd.

Luka didn't remember hearing of Sara Hansen before and accessed the Mars global system to look her up. But there was no record of a Sara Hansen working on Mars in the current list of personnel or in the archive. Luka went back to check if he had mis-read the messages and perhaps they had come from Earth instead, but the address confirmed they were sent locally. Following the address back to its origin revealed that it had come from a server belonging to Ecoline.

Sara's messages, he felt, had to be the key. There was no record of anything from her before or after the six months of deleted messages, and the ones he was able to recover were all written in the same, strange format. They were always short, of no more than a few sentences and completely without any pleasantries. No "hi Anita" or "thanks for your last message" or "looking forward to hearing from you." Highly unusual, especially for two people who seemed to have communicated a lot. The more he read, the more he believed that the messages – on completely different topics – were written in a thinly veiled code.

There were two in particular which Luka stared at for a long time. The first had to refer to the area where the Martian microbes were found:

I agree that the aquifer below the cons%20&xxtion site is the best target area. Drilling must be deep enough for protection against radiation and extreme temperatures.

The second alluded to some form of payment:

The offer will be substantial enough to buy out your contract. Returning to Ea&*h or staying on Mars isn't something that concerns us.

Their meaning, it seemed to him, was clear.

Luka glanced at his WristTab and realized he had been in Anita's apartment for two hours. So much for his plan to be in and out in ten minutes.

He was going to have to transfer all the data he had and decide what to do with it later. He initiated the process, but it had barely started before he heard a series of bleeps coming from the door. He shuddered as he realized someone was accessing the electronic lock. Quickly, using his WristTab to control the window rather than voice commands, he covered up what he was doing by switching the display back to the snow-capped mountain overlooking the forest.

The sound of birdsong and wind rustling through the trees returned to the speakers. Luka stood, trying to calm his thumping heart, as he looked around for somewhere to hide. But it was too late, the lock clicked, the door swung open, and Anita stepped in through the doorway.

She stopped mid-stride when she saw him. "Luka Schäfer? What the hell are you doing in my apartment?"

Luka forced an innocent smile to his lips. "I've fixed your window for you. There was a problem connecting to the network, but it should be fine now."

Anita glowered at him. "I didn't report a problem."

"Oh, didn't you?" Luka's mind was racing almost as fast as his heart as he tried to think of a reasonable excuse for breaking and entering. "Well, someone reported it. But, as I say, it's fixed now."

He stepped forward to leave, but Anita backed up and pushed the door shut behind her. She lifted her WristTab to her mouth. "Security, this is Anita Andreassen. There's an intruder in my apartment. I need assistance immediately." She lowered her WristTab and regarded Luka with suspicion. "You have five minutes to tell me why you're really here, or I'll have you detained and questioned."

CHAPTER TWENTY-EIGHT

Luka looked at Anita as she stood defiantly between him and the only way out of her apartment. She was smaller than he was, he could probably push her out of the way and get to the door before she could recover enough to stop him. But where would he go? She controlled Thor Town and, in a city of around five hundred people, it would be difficult to hide for very long.

Perhaps it didn't matter. When he had considered confronting Anita before, he had nothing but speculation and suspicion to hold over her. Over the past couple of hours, that had changed.

"Gianni suspected you were engaged in something that you weren't telling him," said Luka. "Now I think I know what it is."

"Gianni?" Anita looked genuinely surprised. "Gianni's dead."

"Did you kill him?"

"Kill him? What craziness has got into you, Luka? I *loved*

him. When I hired you to take Gianni's place, I thought you had a sensible head on your shoulders. Now I see that my grief clouded my judgement."

"I think it was the fact that you hated living on Mars that clouded your judgement." Luka glanced across at the window with its idyllic view of a lush green forest, the pristine white of a snow-capped mountain and the gentle blue of an Earth sky. "You surround yourself with images of the planet you came from. Gianni said that you talked about it with nostalgia and told him how much you missed the rain."

She placed her hands defiantly on her hips. "You couldn't possibly have spoken to Gianni. He died the day you arrived."

"But he left behind his video diaries."

Anita's composure wavered for just a moment before she restored her steely expression. It must have meant she was anxious about what information Gianni might have left behind, even though she denied it. "We made no secret of our relationship. Whatever he might have said about our private conversations, it's nothing I'm ashamed of."

"He said that you're homesick, Anita, and you're stuck here on a long term contract you can't afford to pay off for many years. I think, when you realized how long it would be before you could return home, you became desperate enough to do anything."

"You're talking nonsense."

"Am I?" Luka turned off the image of Earth on the window and revealed the two messages he had recovered from Anita's personal files. "I think the meaning is clear: *The offer will be substantial enough to buy out your contract. Returning to Earth or staying on Mars isn't something that concerns us."*

She shrugged it off. "I had a job offer, so what? There's a limited number of people on Mars and corporations find it cheaper and quicker to poach someone from a rival than to bring an employee with the required skills all the way out here. I was tempted, I admit it, but negotiations came to nothing."

"That might be believable if you hadn't been so angry when you found Gianni sitting here looking at these messages."

"You're making this up," she retorted. "I don't believe Gianni left behind any video diaries. If there were any, they would have been found when his room was cleared out. I know that none were because – as the one person on this planet who was close to him – that task was left to me."

"Perhaps that's why he hid his diaries where you wouldn't find them."

"You're talking out of your ass, Luka. He loved me. He wouldn't hide anything from me."

"But you hid things from him, didn't you? I think that's why you were so furious when he accessed your messages. Because I don't think this message is about a job offer. I think it was an offer of a bribe. One that you tried to hide. But what you didn't realize is that sometimes deleted messages can be recovered."

She shook her head. "I didn't take up the job offer so I didn't need the message anymore. I don't know what you're accusing me of – good housekeeping?"

"This wasn't the only message you received from Sara

Hansen. You attempted to get rid of them by deleting everything you received in that six-month period. Sara Hansen didn't send a single message before or after that time. Sounds like you did your housekeeping in a bit of hurry."

Anita looked away from him in disgust and spoke into her WristTab. "Security, how long until you reach my apartment?"

"Uh..." came the reply. "We're coming as fast as we can. Should be there in three minutes. Are you OK?"

Anita responded with a superior grin. "I can hold my own for three minutes."

So, Luka thought, could he. In fact, three minutes was all he needed.

"What about the time Gianni caught you coming back in a rover in the middle of the night?" said Luka, getting increasingly high on his discovery and the guilt he could see stirring within her. "If it was an innocent trip, why were you so furious with him? If you had nothing to hide, why did you sneak out under the cover of darkness?"

"Oh that! I got stuck in a pothole and had to dig myself out. It was dark by the time I got back. I hope you're not reading anything into that."

"Gianni didn't believe that explanation on the night and I don't believe it either. He saw you had drilling and lighting equipment with you in the rover and wondered what you were doing. Unfortunately, he never got to live to hear about the Martian microbes discovered under where ThorGate was supposed to build Noctis City."

"What are you suggesting?"

Luka knew she was seriously worried. Buoyed up by the knowledge his suspicions were being confirmed, he looked across to the window where the other incriminating message was still displayed. "I think that's what this message refers to: *I agree that the aquifer below the construction site is the best target area. Drilling must be deep enough for protection against radiation and extreme temperatures.* Does this refer to what you were doing on the night Gianni caught you? Were you out at night planting microbes in the aquifer? Microbes which people would later believe were Martian life?"

"You're as crazy as Gianni was. Crazier! I knew men were more susceptible to Martian Madness than women – and you two are the proof."

"The proof," said Luka, "is in the messages you tried to delete. They only appear innocent if you don't know what you're looking for. Like the one about delivering samples to your office. I don't think it's talking about fashion or furniture samples. I think it means microbe samples. I've traced the messages back and the woman who is supposed to have sent them doesn't exist, but the digital signature of where they came from was still embedded in the code. They came from Ecoline: the corporation that thought it should have the contract to conduct plant experiments in the canyon where the ThorGate research station was destroyed. The same corporation set to benefit from the deal with CrediCor to restart plant research in the exact same place. Probably the only corporation on Mars with the skill to genetically engineer Earth microbes to make people think they came from Mars. Am I right, Anita?"

She nonchalantly waved away his suggestions, but the anxiety on her face told a different story. He was right and she was scared.

The door opened and Anita spun round as two security officials in ThorGate uniforms ran in. The men were unarmed, but large and muscular enough to easily overwhelm him.

Anita staggered backwards towards the kitchenette, pointing an accusing finger at Luka. "He's the intruder! The burglar! The trespasser!"

Luka glanced at the men approaching her, then turned to Anita. Without concern for himself, he continued his tirade against her. "What happened when you realized Gianni would know what you had done when they found the microbes?" he cried. "Is that when you decided he had to die?"

One of the men took Luka firmly by the elbow. "Come on, sir."

Luka shook his arm free. Still determined to confront Anita, he wasn't ready to leave yet. "Is that when you conspired to make sure he was in the research station when the asteroid crashed?"

Two pairs of hands grasped his upper arms. Luka wriggled to shake them free again, but this time the men had him tight. He wondered how many times they'd actually had to restrain someone and figured it wasn't much. "Because you knew it was going to happen, didn't you?" he shouted at Anita. "You had to conspire to make sure the scientists were evacuated from the research station before the crash – that's what the message from Ecoline meant: *the power plant must be empty of all power on the date.*"

The men tugged at Luka's arms, but he resisted and used all his strength to stay in front of Anita.

"You were part of a conspiracy to make sure ThorGate's project was destroyed, but none of the people working on it were killed."

"I want him locked up!" Anita screamed at the men, her face red with fury. "Take him away and put him in the securest room you can find!"

"They were paying you to tie up loose ends at ThorGate, weren't they? Is that what Gianni was? Another loose end?"

The men dragged Luka away, his feet flailing uselessly against the floor. He struggled in their grip, but they were more than twice as strong as him and he couldn't stop himself from being pulled closer to the door.

"You arranged for him to go to the research station on the day of the disaster," Luka yelled as his presence in the room was pulled away. "You knew the asteroid was going to destroy it and you knew Gianni would be killed. Because you couldn't risk him realizing you had planted the microbes at the Noctis City site and telling everyone that you had been paid to do it by Ecoline."

Luka saw the horror of discovery written across Anita's face for a brief moment before the men tugged at his arms one final time and yanked him from her apartment.

CHAPTER TWENTY-NINE

Rufus Oladepo looked across his desk at Julie, then returned his gaze to her asteroid crash report on his screen.

"You really think the crash at Noctis Labyrinthus was deliberate?" he said.

"The CrediCor asteroid controller admitted as much," said Julie.

"But we don't know who paid her."

"No," Julie admitted. "I haven't been able to trace the payment."

"You also think the scientists were evacuated from the research station on purpose?"

"The chances of it being a coincidence are too great."

"But you don't think this controller woman was involved in that?"

"I don't see how. She said no one was supposed to be there. I got the impression she agreed to orchestrate the crash because she was told no one would die."

"But someone did die," said Rufus. He peered at the screen to read the name. "This Giovanni person."

"That's a bit of an anomaly. He was one of the tech crew based at Thor Town."

Rufus leant back in his chair and clasped his hands behind his head so his elbows spread out wide to emphasize his already dominating presence. "It seems to me, Julie, you haven't got very much."

She leaned forward across the desk as if she hadn't heard him correctly. "I have financial records which prove Mah Chynna took a bribe and I have her confession. I have analysis of the two asteroid fragments which ninety-nine percent prove they were never part of the same rock. I have a mangled piece of guidance equipment which caused the crash in the canyon, and I have the extracted data which differs from the official version logged by CrediCor."

"Yes, but does anyone care?"

Julie's mouth opened to argue, but for once in her life she was lost for words. "Of... Of course they care," she managed, eventually. "A ThorGate project was effectively bombed from space using a terraforming project as cover. How can you not care?"

"But look at all the positive things that have come out of it," said Rufus. "CrediCor and Ecoline are teaming up to build a bigger and better center for conducting plant experiments. One, I might add, that isn't costing the Terraforming Committee one single MegaCredit. We have all the excitement surrounding the discovery of life on Mars. I know it might mean sacrificing the Noctis City project, but think of the scientific significance locked up in those native microbes. The asteroid crash is yesterday's news."

"But you will publish my report?" said Julie.

"Naturally."

"I want to hold a press conference to announce my findings and make sure all corporations, the World Government and every news outlet receives a copy."

"No," said Rufus, sitting upright in his chair again. He reached over to his screen and closed down the page which showed Julie's conclusions.

"I beg your pardon?" Again, she could barely believe what she was hearing.

"It will be published in the Terraforming Committee archives."

"Where no one will see it?"

"They will when the archives become public. Which is, I think, in twenty years. I believe that's the timescale we agreed on."

"Rufus, you can't seriously be suggesting we sweep this matter under the carpet. You hired me to do this job. You chose me to find out what was really happening."

"I know, but Julie, you can't seriously be suggesting we drag CrediCor's reputation through the mud when they're investing so much in the planet's future."

Julie's eyes narrowed as she regarded Rufus with renewed suspicion. "Has Bard been speaking to you?"

"I've had words with him, naturally."

"How much did he offer to pay you?"

His face reddened in anger. "How dare you imply that I would accept a bribe. That may have been how you ran things back in your day, Julie Outerbridge, but I can't be bought. Even by someone as rich as Bard Hunter. I merely assured him that his new project – which, may I remind you, is of considerable benefit to the people of Mars – will not be hampered by some unnecessary witch hunt."

"Unbelievable!" Julie stood up so fast, her chair was knocked over backwards. It clattered to the floor where she left it. "You're going to turn a blind eye to corruption? I thought better of you, Rufus Oladepo."

She turned, unable to live with the disgust she felt by looking at him any longer, and headed for the door.

"Julie," Rufus called after her. "Don't think you can leak this information privately. Remember, the Terraforming Committee has its review coming up soon and UNMI will have to apply for universal tax funding to keep its projects running. My members will not look favorably upon an organization whose leader goes behind their backs."

His threat stabbed her in the stomach. Julie felt sick, betrayed and outmaneuvered. She didn't give him the satisfaction of turning back so he could see the hurt on her face. She threw open the door and allowed it to slam against the wall as she stormed out and headed for the street.

Julie sat in her office and stared at the live view of Mars on her window. It was that very stark beauty of the planet and its virgin potential which had inspired her to move her whole life to that rusty, red, rocky dust ball all those years ago. But her optimism and excitement had been undermined by some of the people who had followed her out there. People who had poisoned the Earth with their self-important ambition and disregard for others and were now spreading that same poison across Mars.

The anger still raged inside of her, even though it had been hours since she had been face to face with that self-centered, conniving...

She sighed and told herself not to waste any more energy on that weasel of a politician. She had devoted the last few weeks to discovering what really happened in the asteroid disaster and Rufus had thrown it all back in her face. He didn't care about the truth, all he cared about was his image. He had stood beside the smashed remains of the ThorGate research station and announced that there would be an investigation because it played well in front of the cameras, not because he wanted the truth. Once he learnt that Julie's report made for uncomfortable reading, he conspired to bury it. What mattered, it seemed, was progress in the terraforming project. How humanity made that progress was immaterial.

That was not what Julie had signed up for or what she wanted to be associated with.

Her WristTab bleeped that she had an incoming message. She glanced down to dismiss it, but saw it was a video message from her parents.

"Window," she said. "Play latest video message from Mom and Dad."

The view of Mars disappeared and was replaced by the image of her mother. She looked older than she had done in her last message. She wasn't wearing makeup and her face was so pale, it was almost gray. The light in her eyes had dulled until they were almost glassy. Mom attempted to smile at the camera, but the movement of her lips didn't engage the other muscles of her face and only made her look sorrowful instead of happy.

"Hello, Julie, it's Mom."

"Hi, Mom," said Julie, even though the recording of her mother couldn't hear her.

"I've… got some bad news. I don't know if you're sitting down, but… you should sit down."

Mom's eyes glanced away and she took a breath. Julie stopped breathing as the coldness of dread spread through her body.

"Dad died last night. A heart attack, we think. He was rushed to the hospital, but there was nothing they could do. He was already gone." Mom's voice was croaky, like someone who had cried herself hoarse. But there was no longer any sign of tears. She appeared numb, washed out and in shock. "It was sudden, which is a blessing. We think it happened in his sleep, so he died peacefully. That's all any of us can ask for, isn't it?

"But I don't want you sitting up there on Mars worrying about me. Rachel's traveling here and all the neighbors have been wonderful. I've got the funeral to sort out, so that's going to keep me busy. I know you're doing important work in space and Dad wouldn't want it any other way. I'm going to go now, I'm tired. But I'll keep you informed. Just keep yourself safe up there."

Mom tried another smile and reached over to end the recording.

"Window, freeze image," Julie ordered.

The window obeyed and a still picture of her mother remained on the screen. Julie stood up and walked over to it. Close up, she could see the individual pinpricks of light which made up Mom's face. She had wanted to be closer to her, but instead it only emphasized that the video was an artificial reconstruction of the person she loved. Nevertheless, Julie reached out to touch Mom's cheek and, as her palm connected with the membrane of the window, she imagined the soft, warm touch of her mother's skin.

Imagination was all she had. She wasn't there when Dad died and, unlike her sister who was only a plane ride away, she couldn't be there to comfort Mom. Even if she walked out of her office at that moment, even if there was a ship scheduled to leave the planet imminently, even if it had space to take her, it would be many months before she would arrive back on Earth. Long after the funeral and long after Mom had struggled through the early stages of grief.

Because Julie had chosen to come to Mars. Because she thought she was participating in a noble cause. Because she thought she could help build a new future for humanity. But all she had really done was turn her back on her family to be part of a world where corruption was king and nobility was for fools.

Julie rested her head on the back of her hand as it touched the screen and felt the weight of the day press upon her with a gravitational force as strong as Jupiter. She had once thought that human ingenuity was so strong that, eventually, it would bring rain to Mars. But, in 2316, the only water that fell on the planet was her own tears.

CHAPTER THIRTY

There were no prison cells on Mars. The people who had built the first few cities must have believed that crime was something that they could leave behind on Earth. But Anita's demand that Luka be locked up meant he had to be put somewhere and so the two security officials put him in a disused accommodation block in Thor Town. It had a bed, a toilet, and a sink – and nothing else. No other furniture, no access to the computer network, no window. The security officials had even remembered to take away his WristTab.

Luka sat on the bed and considered his predicament. He was a criminal, it was true. He had broken into Anita's home and violated the privacy of her messages, but he had done so in search of the truth. Strictly, he had broken the law, but morally his conscience was clear. Where that left him, however, was so deep in trouble that he had no idea how he could possibly climb out.

His thoughts were interrupted by the bleeping of a security code being entered into the door lock. There was a click, the door released and opened to reveal a security official. Not one of the ones who had dragged him from Anita's apartment, but just as large and intimidating. "You have a visitor," said the man.

He stepped aside to reveal Erik Bergman standing in the doorway.

"Erik!" said Luka, standing up to greet him.

"Sit down!" barked the security official.

Luka jolted at the sound and sat back down on the bed obediently.

The security official remained standing by the door with his hands clasped in front of him, on guard, while Erik gave Luka a kindly smile. It was the sort of saccharine, sympathetic smile someone might give to an injured child. "Are you all right?" he said.

"Yeah," said Luka. *Apart from being totally screwed.* "I guess so."

"What were you thinking?"

"Anita knew the asteroid crash was going to happen. She made sure Gianni would be at the research station when it was destroyed."

"Whoa!" exclaimed Erik, waving his hands as if to bat Luka's words away. "I don't want to hear it. I've got enough craziness in my life without listening to any more."

"Craziness? It's true, I have proof…"

"Oh, mate. I'm sorry to see you like this. I get it with Gianni, he was Italian, hot-bloodied and driven crazy by love. But you… German, dependable, experienced… I never expected you to be affected."

"You think I am mad?"

"Martian Madness isn't something to be ashamed of. No one knew what would happen to the human spirit when we left home to live on another planet. It's understandable."

"I'm not crazy! Erik, you have to believe me."

Luka got up to approach his friend, but the security official barked his order again. "Sit down!"

This time, he didn't obey. Instead, he glared at the man and dared him to do something about it.

"You better do as he says, mate," said Erik.

"Why?" Luka remained standing. The security official took a threatening step forward. "What more can he do to me?"

"I think it's better that you don't find out."

Luka glared defiantly at the official, then saw Erik's concerned face and, reluctantly, sat.

The official stepped away but continued to watch intently.

"What happens now?" said Luka.

"That's not up to me," said Erik.

"You must have some idea."

"There's some talk of getting a doctor to evaluate you. After that… I don't know."

"You have to get me out of here."

"No can do."

"If not for me, then for the good of the corporation. Anita took money to betray ThorGate. She planted the Martian microbes!"

"She what?" The surprise on Erik's face morphed into an amused smile. "You think Anita created life on Mars? Now I know you're crazy."

"Erik, I'm not, I swear. I have evidence to prove it, I just need to get out of here and get it to someone."

"My advice, Luka, is to stay here and face the consequences. Tell them you had a mad moment, take the therapy and the medication or whatever they offer you and find a way to get your life back on track. Because there's nowhere else for you to go. Outside of this room, you'll still be in Thor Town and Anita *owns* Thor Town. Even if you manage to take out a rover and escape, there's a limited number of other places and I doubt any one of them will want to take in someone with your reputation."

"Erik…"

"Not that you could do that anyway. We're being hit by a solar flare so the planet's in lockdown."

"You have to help me."

But his pleas went unheard. "I'll have a word with Anita," said Erik. "It's the best that I can do. In the meantime, you should think carefully about cooperating with whatever they want you to do and forget all this conspiracy business. For your own sake."

Erik gave Luka another kindly, sympathetic smile before he turned away from him and exited the room, what Luka was starting to consider his cell. The security official, keeping his eyes on Luka the entire time, backed away and closed the door so Luka was once again alone.

Luka shuddered as the electronic bleep sounded and the lock secured the door shut with a hollow click which echoed around the tiny room. He felt abandoned. He had one true friend on the whole of Mars and even he was more loyal to his treacherous boss than he was to him. How foolish he had been! He had had a plan for getting himself into trouble, but no plan to get out of it.

He leaned back against the cold, hard wall behind him and closed his eyes against the four walls and the locked door which contained him. In the privacy of his mind, he tried to think of a plan which would get him out of his predicament, but Erik's words kept coming back to him: "take the therapy and the medication or whatever they offer you… because outside of this room, you'll still be in Thor Town and Anita *owns* Thor Town". There seemed to be little choice. If he clung onto what he knew to be true, then he would never be free to tell anyone. Either way, there would be no justice.

The sound of the door opening again caused Luka to open his eyes and pull his head away from the wall. It was the security official again, this time entering with a tray of food.

"Your friend said you should eat this," said the official, placing the tray on the end of the bed. It contained a mug of water and a bowl of some sort of brown stew with a spoon resting alongside.

"Erik?" said Luka.

"He wanted me to give you a message that even if you're not hungry, you should try to keep your strength up and at least have some of the stew. He seems like a good friend. You should listen."

"Stew!" Luka spat out the word like a piece of moldy bread. "I'm stuck in here and he expects me to eat?"

The official shrugged. "We haven't really detained someone before. Honestly, I don't care what you do. I was told to bring this to you. You should be grateful."

Luka stared at the unappetizing offering as the official withdrew and locked him in again. It felt he was being offered a last meal. But at least it was a distraction from thinking about the hopelessness of his situation. He pulled the tray forward and took a mouthful of water from the mug. It was lukewarm and tasteless, but it moistened his dry mouth. He sniffed at the stew. It didn't smell of much, probably because it had gone cold and a skin had congealed across the surface. Picking up the spoon, he teased at the liquid at edge of the bowl and lifted out enough to taste. It was tepid and slightly salty with a background hint of a meaty flavor. It might have actually tasted nice if it had still been hot. Maybe if he gave it a stir, it wouldn't look so unappetizing.

The spoon clonked against something at the bottom of the bowl. He hesitated, wondering if there had been some catering mishap and something unsavory lay underneath the thick, brown gloop.

Carefully, he stirred again. His spoon hit the object a second time. He scooped it up and brought it to the surface.

Sitting on his spoon, with drips of brown sludge falling back into the bowl beneath, was a WristTab.

Luka picked it off the spoon and held it up to examine it closer. He dropped the spoon back into the bowl and pushed the tray away. It was definitely a WristTab. He wiped it on the bedsheets to get rid of as much of the residual stew as he could, pressed the button to turn it on and waited.

WristTabs were supposed to be tough, able to stand up to everyday knocks, and resistant to water, but he had never heard of any experiments to test how one would survive being immersed in a bowl of tepid, fake-meat stew.

The power came on and a wave of elation ran through Luka's body.

"Thank you, Erik!"

The WristTab was new and completely blank of any personalization. But it had two messages. One was a booking for a rover at the Thor Town depot and the other was entitled "door code." Curious, he opened it and the WristTab began transmitting. Hoping against hope, he approached the door. Electronic bleeps sounded from outside. Followed by a click and the door was released from its frame.

Gingerly, he pulled open the door and peered outside. The security officials had gone, once more trusting security to the machines. Either he didn't feel the need to guard a locked door or Erik had used some rouse to lure him elsewhere. Either way, the corridor was empty, and he was free.

CHAPTER THIRTY-ONE

Luka walked through Thor Town's main street with his heart thumping loudly and adrenaline buzzing through his body as he resisted the urge to run. He needed to get to the rover depot as fast as possible, but he needed to do so without attracting attention. If he had been on Earth, he could have gone the back way and hidden in the shadows, but in the small, enclosed development on Mars, there was only the front way through the main street. He kept his head down, trying to look like he wasn't keeping his head down, and walked as quickly as he could towards the rover depot, hoping he didn't look like someone who had escaped from custody.

He had used the rover depot many times since taking on Gianni's old job at Thor Town. It was the only one serving the whole complex and lay at the farthest end of the street where its modest entrance was marked by a simple sign above a normal door.

As Luka approached, he saw there was a second sign

dangling from a piece of wire looped over the door handle. Laminated and printed in bright red lettering underneath a ThorGate logo, it read: *Rover Access Temporarily Suspended Due to Solar Flare Activity*. Underneath, someone had stuck a handwritten note which said: *no, we don't know when it's going to end, so there's no point asking*.

Erik had mentioned something about a solar flare, but Luka had forgotten about it in his eagerness to escape. He paused. Coming to Mars had already exposed him to more radiation than would have been the case if he had stayed on Earth and minimizing unnecessary exposure had been drilled into him and the other migrants during their journey. But he knew he really didn't have a choice: a little bit of radiation exposure was preferable to being recaptured.

He tried the door and found it to be open.

Inside was a small area, like a waiting room, with a couple of visitor chairs and an admin desk where Luka would usually discuss his rover booking with a member of staff. But, with rover access suspended, no one was there. Luka's heart calmed: with a bit of luck, he would be able to take out the rover without having to explain himself.

Beside the desk, an airlock door led to the hangar where all the vehicles were kept and serviced until they were dispatched. Above it, a green light indicated the hangar was fully pressurized. Luka placed his hand on the control and, with relief that access hadn't been restricted, listened to it respond by firing off a loud but brief warning buzzer. The locks uncoupled and the airlock door moved backwards and sideways on automated arms to allow Luka to step through.

On the other side of the airlock door was a large room full of parked rovers, half of them dusty and the other half clean and pristine white. There were, he counted, ten of them, all parked nose to tail in formation. He hurried down the first row, reading the serial numbers off the sides and looking for the one that matched the booking details on his contraband WristTab. But none of them did.

He tried the hatch of the rover at the end in any case but it was locked and the control panel only responded with a stubborn red light when he tried to access it.

He went around the front of the rover to check the next row and almost ran into a woman coming round the other way. He yelped as his adrenaline surged.

The woman, wearing a set of dusty, denim-blue overalls, merely looked up from the full-sized Tab resting on her arm and regarded him with curiosity. She was young, not even twenty, tall and slim bordering on the underweight, with long dark hair which she had pulled back into a ponytail. "What are you doing here?"

Luka put his hand to his chest as if to slow his heart, pretending that she had merely surprised him, not scared the life out of him. "I didn't think anyone was about."

"I heard you come in, but I thought it was someone from maintenance. You know all rovers are off limits until the solar flare's over?"

"Yes, but I've got a booking." Luka lifted up his WristTab to show her.

"I don't care if you've got a signed letter from the Queen of Sheba, we're in lockdown."

"But it's an emergency."

"Is your grandmother dying in the hospital at Tharsis City?"

Luka took a moment to process the bizarre question. "No."

"Then it's not an emergency." She turned and walked off between the two rows of rovers, heading towards the reception area.

He rushed after her. "Can you please just look at the booking?"

The dispatcher halted, did an abrupt turn, and frowned. "Name?"

"I'm not sure."

"You're not sure about your own name?"

"A friend booked it. He might have used his name, my name, the company name…" Possibly a false name.

Luka showed her the booking on the WristTab. She peered at it and consulted her own Tab.

As he waited, anxiously, with the sound of his own blood pumping in his ears, he evaluated the slender woman in front of him. If it came to it, he could almost certainly overpower her. He could probably knock her unconscious and carry her out of the hangar before he vented the air if he had to. He prayed it wouldn't come to that.

She raised her eyebrows at the Tab's screen. "It seems you're right, you do have a booking. Erik Bergman, is that right?"

"That's my friend." He was surprised that Erik was brazen enough to use his own name.

"And, um… you're right, it has emergency status which clears you to leave during the solar flare." She lowered the

Tab and looked directly at him. There was genuine concern on her face. "Are you sure you want to go out there?"

She nodded towards the large airlock doors which ran floor to ceiling and were the barrier between the rovers and the planet outside.

Luka looked at them too, the warnings from his training still nagging at the back of his mind. "I'll be wearing a rad-suit, it'll give me some protection, won't it?"

"Rad-suits only protect against normal background radiation."

"But the rover itself has some shielding?"

"Nowhere near as much as you get in a city."

"If you combine the protection in the rover and suit…"

"You're still looking at a dose larger than recommended," she said. "Especially on top of what you're exposed to every day living here."

Luka felt the anxiety twist in his stomach. He didn't have time for a discussion. He had to leave before anyone realized he was gone. "It doesn't matter, I need to go. Are you going to check out the rover or am I going to have to take this to a higher authority?"

She paused, thinking. He closed his fingers into a fist and tensed his muscles in preparation.

"Your booking gives you authorization," she said. "I can't stop you."

Luka released his fist and allowed his body to relax a little.

"But, if I were you, I would have a serious think about who you consider to be a friend."

The dispatcher went back the way she had come, towards the front of the row of vehicles and pointed to the rover at the head of the second row. "This is the one he booked out for you. According to this–" she checked her Tab "–it's all set to go."

Luka placed his hand on the control and the hatch opened.

"I presume you know that satellite navigation is unreliable during a solar event?"

"Obviously," said Luka. Although, in truth, he hadn't even considered it. "I'll follow the tracks in the dirt."

"Just don't get lost. They can be obscured by dust blowing over them sometimes."

"I won't. Thanks."

Luka stepped inside.

"Can I ask," said the dispatcher, as he turned around to close it. "What's the big emergency?"

"It's about getting justice," said Luka.

She didn't look impressed. "Well, good luck with that. I'll go open the airlock."

Luka watched her walk back down the row of vehicles and closed the airtight hatchway behind him. At the sound of sealing himself inside, he relaxed a little more. In only a few more minutes, he would be out of Thor Town and heading for Tharsis City. He needed to explain what he had discovered to the one person who would understand: Julie Outerbridge.

CHAPTER THIRTY-TWO

The computer sounded an alarm the moment the rover left the depot: "Radiation warning: levels of radiation are above recommended limits. Please return to a city or a shielded habitat immediately."

Its inappropriately cheerful female voice tugged at Luka's instincts to obey, but he kept going, holding onto his need for freedom and his desire to secure justice for Gianni.

Nudging the rover further away from Thor Town, he brought up the navigation system in the hope he could get enough signal to steer him in the right direction. But the dispatcher in the rover depot had been right: the satellite system was completely unresponsive. The interference from the solar flare meant that Luka couldn't even get a fix on where the rover was, let alone where it was supposed to be going. But, by using the landmark of Thor Town behind him, eliminating the path he knew would take him to Noctis Labyrinthus and examining the crisscrossing dirt tracks on the ground, he was able to calculate the route he needed to take to reach Tharsis City.

After twenty minutes, the familiar landmarks he knew from his occasional trips out in a rover were gone and he was staring out at a seemingly endless plain of Martian dessert. He kept staring at the horizon, hoping for the structure of Tharsis City to appear in the distance, but it was still just the red of the land meeting the pink of the sky.

"Radiation warning," chimed the irritatingly cheerful computer again. "Levels of radiation are above recommended limits. Please return to a city or a shielded habitat immediately."

He didn't need to be reminded of the danger. He tried to turn it off, but it was part of the rover's safety systems and couldn't be deactivated without delving into the code and carrying out some intricate reprogramming. So, he was forced to listen to the computer's pointless periodic warnings. They were his only companions on the journey because the radiation had also knocked out radio communications.

Staring at the dirt was hypnotic and driving the rover became subconscious as his thoughts turned to what Anita had done. There was a lot to explain to Julie Outerbridge and he wanted to make sure he had it all straight. He was so preoccupied with it all that he didn't see the tracks in the landscape become fainter and fainter as he drove until they became lost in the dust, like a mirage that evaporates in the desert.

A bump of a small rock under one of the rover's wheels snapped back his attention and he watched for several, horrible moments as he realized he was traveling blind. He pulled the rover into full stop and checked the cameras to get a three hundred sixty degree view. The only tracks he could see in the dirt were his own. If he had been following the right path, then his wheels would have driven over and obscured any tracks which were there before. So there was no point backing up to check he was on the right path. There was simply no telling where he might have gone astray.

He breathed deeply and tried to think through things logically. Even though he hadn't been able to rely on satellite navigation, he had been going in more or less a straight line since he left Thor Town with the small, white disc of the sun well past its midday peak on his left. He had followed a clearly marked trail from the beginning and, even if he had diverged from it, he couldn't have gone too far without realizing. The chances were he was still going the right way because, as the woman in the depot had pointed out, dry dust blew around the Martian landscape every day and it was normal for it to settle and disguise even large objects left on the surface.

He restarted the rover. He had to trust himself. Keep going straight, try harder to concentrate and maybe he could pick up the trail again. If not, he had the resources of the rover to keep him safe until the solar flare had passed and he was able to call over the radio for help. Even if the radiation was "above recommended levels," he would probably survive, even if it meant trading off some of his future health.

A shadow up ahead caused him to stare harder out of the windshield. It could be cast by a rock or be a dip in the land, but as he closed in he was relieved to see it was a track left by another rover. His closed his eyes and said a silent thank you before reopening them again and making sure he was traveling on the same trajectory.

"Power warning," chimed the rover's computer. "At current usage, power will fail in ten minutes. Please recharge or reduce power consumption."

"What?!" Luka checked the dashboard and brought up the resources data screen. The power indicator was in the red. He didn't understand it. The rover should have had enough power to take him to Tharsis City on one charge. It should even be able to take him back again if he needed it to.

Keeping one eye on the tracks ahead of him, Luka checked to see what was draining the power, but it was only operating the life support systems and the motor. Nothing out of the ordinary. Then he checked the power history and discovered it hadn't been put on charge after returning to the depot from its previous trip. He was running on residuals and they were running out.

While looking through the data screens, Luka had also come across the data relating to the rover's oxygen supply. That, too, hadn't been replenished.

"Oxygen warning," said the inappropriately cheerful voice. "At current usage, optimum oxygen levels are expected to be maintained for approximately fifteen minutes. Please return to a city for resupply."

Luka felt himself shaking, and not from the vibrations of the rover as it trundled along in the middle of nowhere. Optimum levels were twenty-one percent. In theory, humans could survive on only fourteen percent, as had been proved by mountain communities who had lived at high altitude on Earth for generations. It was the reason the goal for terraforming Mars was to reach fourteen percent oxygen, but Luka wasn't acclimatized to those conditions, and he would start to feel it as oxygen levels fell.

With trepidation, he checked the supply in his rad-suit, the only one he had found in the rover. Its power and air supply were sitting just above the warning zone. It, too, hadn't been replenished after it had last been used.

"Erik," said Luka to himself.

He remembered the words of the woman who had checked out the vehicle: "have a serious think about who you consider to be a friend."

The rover had had enough resources to take him out onto the desolate surface of Mars and strand him there. During a solar flare when interference meant he couldn't use the radio to call for help.

Luka pushed fear aside to focus all his attention on getting out of the mess he found himself in. His first option was to shut down everything that was using power apart from essential life support systems. That would prolong the amount of time he had in the rover's cabin until the heating failed or the oxygen ran out and he was forced to use the reserves in the suit. It could double his available time, but if radio communications weren't back before the supplies in the suit ran out, he would be dead. Even without factoring in how long it might take for a rescue team to reach him.

Sitting there waiting to die had little appeal.

His second option was to keep going and hope he could get close enough to Tharsis City – assuming that's where the tracks were leading him – to somehow summon help. If he couldn't, using up resources quicker would mean he would die sooner.

Either way, he was dead.

He would rather die fighting than wait for death to take him.

He kept following the tracks in the dust.

At last, he saw a red shape begin to emerge on the horizon. At that distance, it could have been a mountain or an abandoned habitat, but as he got closer, the recognizable geometric angles of Tharsis City caught the light of the fading sun and warmed Luka with the hope that he could make it.

A minute later, the rover ground to a halt. All power was gone. Apart from the tiniest emergency amount for opening the hatch and running the useless communications system.

Luka hung his head. He knew that the moment had been coming, but he had prayed that the rover's data systems were being overcautious, and he could squeeze more out of the battery than they claimed. Instead, they had been horrifyingly accurate.

He put on his helmet and listened for the seals to click into place. His rad-suit began to draw on its limited resources to provide him with heat and air.

With the last of the electricity left in the rover's dying battery, Luka pulled all the air out of the cabin and connected a line from his suit to siphon the last of its oxygen supply. It bolstered the suit's reserves a little, although not as much as he had hoped. Then he opened the hatch and prepared to leave.

His final action inside the rover was to initiate a distress message, explaining that he had left on foot for the long walk to Tharsis City. If the radiation from the solar flare subsided enough for radio communications to be possible, and if the power lasted that long, then perhaps someone would hear it and come find him.

Luka felt the Martian dirt crunch under his boot as he stepped out onto the surface. With another step, he left the safety of the rover and felt a shiver of doubt as he wondered if he was doing the right thing. When he had been in the confines of the cabin, he was in control of his small domain. Whereas, on the dusty plain with the vastness of the untamed Martian surface stretching out in every direction, he felt small and vulnerable. But the vehicle which had brought him that far was dead while he was still alive and so he pulled renewed determination from within himself, patted the side of the rover like a good, but spent horse and begun the next phase of his journey.

Ahead, catching the afternoon sun and casting angular shadows across the dust, the city seemed further away than it had done in the rover. Luka feared he would be lucky to make it in the fifteen minutes the rad-suit said it could sustain him. He considered reducing the amount of oxygen available in his air supply, but his muscles would need it for the walk and he couldn't risk it. Getting lost and disoriented or falling unconscious because of a lack of oxygen would be fatal.

He needed to go as far as he could on the resources he had and hope that, unlike the programmers of the rover, the people who had programmed the rad-suit's monitors had calibrated them to err on the side of caution.

Luka jogged with long, energy-conserving strides, keeping his eyes on Tharsis City and ignoring the data about the power and air left in his suit. With each breath he heard within the bounds of his helmet, he was conscious of turning precious molecules of oxygen into useless molecules of carbon dioxide. The suit's systems estimated that the amount of power he had available to stop him freezing to death would outlast his air supply and he diverted a small part of the battery's energy to running the suit's comms to send out a distress signal. It couldn't broadcast very far, not like a rover, and it was unlikely anyone inside a city would be monitoring channels usually used for suit-to-suit communication, but even if there was a small chance someone might respond, he had to take it.

Normally, when listening out for a reply, the comms filtered out most of the static so voices sounded as clear as possible, but Luka wanted to hear anything that might be a human being trying to communicate with him. So he turned the setting off. White noise hissed from his helmet's speaker and accompanied him on every trudge across the dusty ground.

Luka knew each stride took him closer to Tharsis City, but each time he looked it, it seemed just as far away. His mind drifted to his childhood and a school trip to Heringsdorf when a friend had suggested spending the afternoon at the famous seaside pier and, rather than pay for a bus, they had decided to walk. The magnificent structure jutting out into the sea looked so close that they thought they would be there in half an hour. But, after half an hour, it looked just as far away as when they had started. Rather than admitting they were wrong and finding a bus stop, they kept going because they convinced themselves it couldn't be that much further. By the time they got there, it was the end of the afternoon and they were so exhausted that all they did was buy a drink to quench their sizeable thirst and pool the rest of their money to get a taxi back to the hotel.

It was like that walking to Tharsis City. Luka knew he was getting closer, but the building continued to look far away. The only change in the city appeared to be in the size of its shadow, which grew longer as the sun lowered in the Martian sky.

With each step and each breath, Luka's mind closed down to any other reality. His life consisted only of the walk, and the need to reach safety. There could be nothing else. His survival depended on it.

The rad-suit warned him of depleting oxygen and he realized he didn't have long. He reached for the controls with a shaking hand to do the thing he had ruled out when setting off: reduce the mix of oxygen in the air. He was not a young man, but he wasn't old either, and if his lungs needed to work harder to get him to his destination, then they would have to do that. The sound of his breath reverberated louder in his helmet and, mixed with the white noise of the comms, he imagined it was the sea at Heringsdorf crashing onto the sand and leaving a line of white foam on the beach as it pulled away back into the ocean.

Luka sweated like his body was gripped by a fever. The rad-suit should have removed excess moisture from the air so the sweat evaporated away, but he was working so hard that the systems were struggling to cope. Luka himself was struggling to cope. He looked again at the angled structure built of Martian brick on the horizon and realized he could see individual features on the outside. Evidence – finally – that he was getting closer. There was a large recess in the front which looked like it was the entrance to a rover depot. To the side of it, glinting in the sun, was the transparent dome of the famous garden which visitors to the city always talked about. From what he heard, the people that lived there called it the Oasis in the Martian desert.

His pace quickened with excitement as he convinced himself he would be able to reach it. He knew he could do it. Just a little bit further.

But the rad-suit protested. He had maybe five minutes to breathe what oxygen was left in its tanks, after that the levels would be too low to sustain him. Luka overrode the safety warning and turned the mix of oxygen down even lower. If the terraforming experts believed humans could survive on Mars with only fourteen percent oxygen in the air, then it was his duty to prove them right.

An excruciating headache squeezed his brain while nausea churned his stomach and his lungs strained to find sustaining oxygen. Gasping, with pain searing through his chest, he stumbled and fell. Fearing his body was failing him, he put his hands out to break his fall and ended up on all fours. He stopped for a moment, breathing deep while his heart thumped hard and fast to transport oxygen depleted blood to his muscles. He knew he must go on, but his body begged him to stop. To rest, to get back his strength. He wanted to obey it, for just a moment and he closed his eyes.

"Luka?" a woman's voice spoke out of the static on his radio.

"Yes!" He forced his eyes open and struggled to focus as he gasped a reply. "Hello? Can you hear me? Are the comms working?"

"Everything is working," she said. "Everything is going to be fine."

She was speaking in German. A language he had barely heard since he left Earth.

"Are you coming to rescue me?" he replied in his native language.

"No, I cannot rescue you," she said. "You must rescue yourself, my precious Luka."

His wife used to call him that. She used to say it ironically, often when she was cajoling him into doing something he didn't want to do. The voice had the same soft tones as his wife, but he knew it couldn't really be her. "Sabine?"

"Yes, Luka."

"I don't understand."

"Don't talk. You don't need to understand. You need only to keep walking."

With effort, he lifted his eyes and saw, standing on the red dust of Mars ahead of him, the figure of his wife beckoning him forward. "Sabine!"

He staggered to his feet, stumbled again and just about stopped himself from falling a second time as he stared at the impossible. She was as he remembered, dressed in her favorite T-shirt she liked to wear on weekends, with her long, brown hair loose to beneath her shoulders and gently blowing in the Martian wind. She wasn't wearing a rad-suit.

That made a sort of sense, Luka thought. Ghosts have no need of radiation protection, heat, or air.

"Walk towards me." She beckoned him again.

Luka's eyes filled with tears as his heart beat even faster and his lungs pumped as hard as they could to propel him forward one step at a time. He reached out a hand to touch her, but she moved backwards. Always a little out of reach, continuing to urge him on.

"That's it, my precious Luka," she whispered. "Keep going."

The sound of children's laughter carried on the wind towards him. He turned his head and saw, playing in the dirt, a little girl and a little boy.

"Lena?" he gasped. "Oskar?"

Lena, wearing the blue and white summer dress that Sabine had bought her for her sixth birthday, ran around Oskar, giggling as she tickled him with the petals of a sunflower she had picked from the neighbor's garden. Oskar clutched the scruffy brown teddy he had had since birth, as he batted away the flower and chased after her.

The joy of seeing them lifted the pain away from his aching body and his mind flooded with euphoria. "It's Daddy!" he tried to call out, but his rasping breath could barely manage a whisper.

"Don't waste air talking," said Sabine. "Go be with them. That's right. Walk. Find the energy within yourself."

The euphoria carried him, and Luka willed his body to move. He staggered, gasping and fighting through the pain, to be with his children once again.

To his dismay, they turned and ran from him, heading for

the transparent dome that people said contained an oasis of Earth. The thought of losing them again was unbearable and he tried to follow, but his oxygen-deprived body couldn't keep up with their young legs. Their ethereal bodies ran straight through the barrier of the dome and disappeared within.

Luka tried to call their names, but he hadn't the breath. He stumbled to reach the unseen door that they had passed through and his gloved hands banged against the material of the dome. His eyes struggling to focus, he looked for his children, but all he saw was a forest of trees. Like they had run inside to play and got lost within the branches.

The pain of losing them a second time tore through him, deeper and more tortuous than the screaming of his lungs and the pressure on his brain as his body failed him. He opened his mouth to cry out, but there was nothing left in his lungs to make a sound.

He was dizzy. So very dizzy. His legs no longer had the energy to hold him upright. His body rested on the outside of the dome and he closed his eyes. Gravity pulled him to the ground and a lack of oxygen pushed him into unconsciousness.

CHAPTER THIRTY-THREE

Julie walked into the medical bay where Luka was sitting up in bed. He had a drip plugged into his arm and a nasal tube supplying extra oxygen to his nostrils. He was gaunt and pale with beady eyes which seemed to have sunk into their sockets. His hair was greasy and swept back, while a dark stubble had grown on his chin. Her mother might have described him as "like death warmed up" which, indeed, was what he was.

Luka managed a smile as Julie approached. "You got my message, then," he said. His voice was croaky from the trauma he had put his lungs through.

"I did," she said.

"I wasn't sure that you would see me."

"Oh, I had to see the crazy man who walked to Tharsis City in a rad-suit during a major solar flare."

"Crazy, am I?" said Luka.

She felt embarrassed at possibly offending him. "That's not what I meant."

"Did they tell you I hallucinated my dead wife and children out there?"

Julie nodded. The doctor treating Luka had told her to go easy on him. Mentally, as well as physically, he was still fragile. "It was understandable."

"I knew, deep down, it wasn't real. But if it hadn't been for them, I don't think I would have made it."

"You nearly didn't," said Julie. "You were unconscious when they found you. They had to connect an oxygen line to your suit and give you CPR out on the planet's surface."

"How did they find me? I asked the doctors, but they said they don't know."

"You collapsed in full view of one of the outside cameras. Several people had their windows tuned to a live view of the Martian landscape from that side of the city. You were lucky they saw you and reported it. There was no one in the Oasis to see you banging against the transparent dome – it gets sealed off during a major solar event."

"It must have given people a shock to have their pleasant window view interrupted by a desperate man." He laughed at the thought. Then broke into a fit of coughing.

Julie reached over to a jug of water by his bed and filled the mug sitting next to it. She offered it to him as the coughing subsided and he took several small sips between wheezy breaths.

"Thank you," he croaked. "One good thing about being in hospital – you get extra water rations."

Julie smiled. At least he had maintained a sense of humor. "So, how are you? That cough doesn't sound good."

"There's some damage from the hypoxia which I'm

probably going to have to live with. But, I'm going to live, which is bonus. They don't think there's any brain damage, but they want to run some more tests. Obviously, I got an inadvisable dose of radiation, so I still feel sick all the time and the long term consequences of that are... best not dwelled upon."

"Are they giving you the gene repair therapy?"

"I can't afford that! I'm indentured labor, I have no money. Even if I was still in ThorGate's good books, they don't expend special treatment to their migrant workforce."

"Maybe I can do something," said Julie. "UNMI has resources the other corporations don't have."

"That would be amazing, but it's not why I asked to see you."

"I know that, but we can enroll you in a research program or something. I'm sure I can find some scientists determined to test how their therapy works on someone who went out for a walk during a major solar event."

"Thank you."

"So, why did you ask to see me? I'm assuming it has something to do with the reason the woman who runs ThorGate is demanding to have you extradited back to Thor Town."

"Anita Andreassen wants me extradited? Can she do that?"

"I can oppose it, but ultimately it's the Tharsis Republic's decision. This is their city."

"I can't go back there, said Luka. "Not while she's in charge."

"What did she do to you?"

"It doesn't matter what she did to me. It's what she did to Gianni Lupo and how she betrayed ThorGate. I asked to see you because I think she knew the asteroid was going to destroy the research station and I think she sent Gianni there on that day to be killed. I also think – in fact, I know – she was behind the discovery of microbes in the aquifer where ThorGate was supposed to build Noctis City."

Julie balked at the allegations. Perhaps he was crazy after all. "Why would she sabotage ThorGate's own projects?"

"Because Ecoline promised her enough money to buy out her contract and return to Earth."

Julie shook her head. "Those are some serious accusations. Do you have proof?"

Luka looked down his hands clutching the top of the bedsheet. "I *had* proof, but I transferred the messages from Ecoline to Anita to my personal account and I've been locked out of that. I imagine Erik has already seen to it that they are deleted. Permanently."

"Erik?"

"A man I thought was a friend," said Luka. "He's probably gone through my room and destroyed Gianni's diaries too."

"Then..." Julie thought about what she was going to say. "What you have brought me is a series of – forgive me – rather farfetched allegations with no evidence. Spoken by a man who – and don't take this the wrong way – recently suffered hypoxia, admits that he might have brain damage, and has been having visions of his dead family."

What little color was left in Luka's face drained away. "But you believe me, don't you?"

Despite everything, Julie was starting to think that

she did. With everything she had discovered during her investigation into the asteroid disaster, she could believe a lot of terrible things about a lot of people in power. Sometimes the simplest answer wasn't always the right one. "It doesn't matter whether I believe you, it's what I can do with the information. Without evidence, there's nothing I can do."

"You said when we met at the construction habitat that you didn't think the asteroid crash was an accident."

"I said too much when we met at the construction habitat. I'd had somewhat of a bad day."

"But it wasn't an accident?" Luka pressed her.

"No," said Julie. Even though she knew she shouldn't be telling a virtual stranger after the threat that Rufus had made to her.

"Then we have to do something!" said Luka.

"Do what?"

"I don't know… *something*. I didn't drive across Mars and nearly die to let this go."

"OK," said Julie, taking a seat. "Convince me."

CHAPTER THIRTY-FOUR

Days later, Julie sat in her office and cradled the full sized Tab onto which she had copied her report into the asteroid disaster. She couldn't prove any of the things Luka had told her about Anita, but he had convinced her that the truth needed to be aired. Otherwise, other corporations would feel free to crash asteroids into rival projects when they didn't like them and bribe whoever they wanted to carry out their nefarious schemes.

Her only opportunity was the Terraforming Committee funding review. Rufus had banned her from holding a press conference to reveal the conclusions of her asteroid disaster investigation, so she would turn Rufus's own committee meeting into the platform she needed. All the other corporation heads would be there and ICN cameras would be transmitting live. Anything she said would be broadcast across the planet – across the solar system – and everyone would know the truth.

It pleased her to know that Bard Hunter would be there. Still on crutches from his encounter with an upside-down rover, she wanted to watch him as she revealed what she knew. None of the evidence she had, or the evidence Luka had uncovered implicated him directly, but everything that had happened was very convenient for CrediCor and that made her suspicious. Just when ThorGate had their research station destroyed and their construction project halted, Bard arrived on the planet and promised to spend his corporation's own money on making everything right again. The aftermath of the disaster seemed to be going very well for Bard, and not even Rufus seemed to care that an asteroid had crashed where it shouldn't.

Luka had agreed with her concerns remarkably quickly. The very mention of the name Bard Hunter had caused a ripple of emotion to flicker across his face. He, even more than her, wanted to put questions to Bard under the gaze of multiple news cameras and in front of the other corporation leaders and political parties. What Julie knew, and no one else did, was that Bard had come to Mars to secure CrediCor's future beyond the crashing of asteroids. She hated to use the confession of a man who thought he was going to die against him, but she was going to go out in a blaze of glory anyway and his admission as he lay under the rover was the ace up her sleeve.

She had decided not to tell Kareem about her plan. He was a good and loyal colleague, and he didn't deserve to get caught up in whatever the consequences would be for her.

Her WristTab bleeped and told her it was time to leave for the Terraforming Committee. She took a breath, gathered her thoughts, waited to see if the part of her with doubts would talk her out of it, then stood up to leave. At the last minute, she checked her reflection in the surface of the turned off window and deemed that she looked suitably professional for her big moment.

Outside, in the office communal area, Kareem came to join her. "Ready?" he said.

"As I'll ever be," she replied.

They walked to the stairs together.

"Good luck, Julie!" shouted Alejandro from his desk.

"Good luck! Good luck! Good luck!" shouted the others.

Julie blushed. She was embarrassed, not because she was the center of attention, but because they thought she was going to the Committee to ask for money to fund the projects they were working on.

It was a relief when she was able to enter the stairwell and close the door to the communal office behind her.

"So, you're clear about our greenhouse gas proposals?" said Kareem, following her down.

"Yes, Kareem."

"We're to increase production of perfluorocarbons – except, remember to call them 'super greenhouse gases' for the people who only pretend they can understand the science. Emphasize that we need to build more GHG factories to produce it. At the same time, we need to ramp up carbonate processing to produce more carbon dioxide..."

"Kareem, you don't need to tell me all this, I am fully aware of what we're proposing."

"It's just that I've been working really hard on this, and I want to make sure we get the MegaCredits we deserve."

"I know," said Julie. She wished he would stop talking so she didn't feel so guilty.

"You've got all the charts that show the progress we've made over the past year and how we can build upon that next year?"

Julie stopped on the landing at the bottom of the first flight of stairs and looked directly at Kareem's worried face. She hated lying to him, but it was for his own good. "I've got it, I'm prepared, everything's ready to go, it'll be fine."

"Sorry," said Kareem. "I get nervous about this sort of thing. It's like being back at school and sitting an exam. Is there such a thing as exam nerves by proxy?"

"I don't know, but I'm sure you can find a scientist on Mars willing to study it if you really want. But, for now, can you try to be a bit calmer? You're supposed to be backing me up, not making me feel more nervous."

"Right, boss. Got it. Sorry."

They descended the second flight to the ground without any more talking.

When they stepped out into the street, they found two security officials in black uniforms waiting for them.

"Julie Outerbridge?" said one. A large, bald man with an impressively deep voice.

"Yes," she said, warily. For once, they didn't seem to recognize her from the news.

"We represent the Terraforming Committee and are under strict orders to detain you." He grabbed her arm just above the elbow and she stared at the touch and then to Kareem in disbelief.

"There has to be some mistake!" said Kareem. "This is *Julie Outerbridge*, the head of UNMI."

Julie tried to pull her arm free, but the security official

held her tight. "You can't do this. You aren't a police force. You have no rights."

"We're under orders from the Terraforming Committee. In the absence of any recognized police force, we can detain you," the security official repeated.

Panicking, wondering how the hell the Committee could know what she was about to say, she reached out her free arm to hand the Tab to Kareem. "Do my presentation for me."

Kareem went to take it, but the other official snatched it instead. "I'll have that."

"It's OK," said Kareem, trying to reassure her. "I know our proposals backwards. I don't need a script."

The first official pulled at her arm to take her away. She struggled and the man's fingers dug deeper into her muscle. Maybe she still had time to tell Kareem what she had been planning to do – that the script in his head was not the script which needed to be delivered – but if he got detained too, she would never forgive herself. The second official grabbed her other arm and, even though she struggled against the reality of defeat, it gripped her tight.

Between them, the officials led her away while an increasing number of shocked onlookers stopped and stared.

Kareem also stared, uncomprehending. "I'll get you a lawyer, Julie," he shouted after her. "I'm sure it's just a misunderstanding and everything will be fine."

But Julie knew that everything wouldn't be fine. Being detained for something she hadn't even done yet was the worst of both worlds.

CHAPTER THIRTY-FIVE

Luka watched the tedious proceedings of the Terraforming Committee annual funding review on the ICN feed from his hospital bed with anticipation. He had never before in his life been so intent on paying attention to corporation representatives spouting their grand plans to spend taxpayers' money. It was an unending wish list of things which he understood, like constructing a magnesium mine, to things which he didn't, like regolith eaters.

None of it mattered. The only thing he wanted to see was Julie Outerbridge take the stand and tell every human being in the solar system that Gianni Lupo had been murdered. So he watched, intently.

Rufus Oladepo looked to the ICN cameras as he stood at the podium to address his audience in the Committee Hall and, via the live feed, every human being who was interested in the future of Mars. "Now we will hear about the progress being made in terraforming by our friends at the United Nations Mars Initiative."

Luka sat up even straighter in bed and leaned forward to be closer to the window on which the feed was playing. He ordered it to turn up the sound.

"They have been leading the way with greenhouse gas production since before the Committee was established," continued Rufus. "To tell us more about what they have achieved in this past year and to outline their plans for the year to come, may I introduce Kareem Saadeh."

Luka went cold as polite applause rippled around the hall, Rufus left the podium, and another man took his place. The clean-shaven man with jet black hair smiled nervously at the waiting attendees and glanced down at the full-sized Tab he was holding. Once the applause had died down, he lifted his head again to look out at the audience.

"I know many of you would have been expecting Julie Outerbridge to be here today..."

"Yes!" Luka yelled at the screen. "Where is Julie?"

"...but as you may have heard, she is currently indisposed. So, as I make this presentation, I want you to imagine that it is as slick, as considered and as professional as I know Julie would have made it if she were here."

Luka barely breathed as he listened out for what Kareem had to say. He remembered the Englishman from when he and some of the other ThorGate migrants helped Julie to retrieve a sample of the asteroid from the crash site. At the time, he had seemed to be a close colleague of hers who was involved in the investigation. Maybe Julie had believed the information they had planned to reveal would be better coming from him.

The microphones in the hall picked up some nervous

laughter from the other attendees, as Kareem cleared his throat, glanced down at his Tab again and touched something on the screen. On a display window behind him appeared a line graph which showed greenhouse gas targets and emissions from across the past year.

"UNMI believes the key to raising the temperature on Mars lies in the amount of greenhouses gases we can release into the atmosphere. Carbon dioxide is important, of course, but..."

"Greenhouse gases!" Luka was so angry, he threw out his arms and knocked over the jug that sat by his bed. It clattered to the ground and spilled water underneath the visitor's chair where Julie had sat and talked to him only a couple of days before. "What happened to the truth? What happened to exposing the lies and the corruption? Where's Julie? What have you done with Julie?"

He was so furious, his mind stopped finding English words for him to shout at the screen and returned to his native language as he shouted the foulest string of swear words German could provide.

A nurse rushed in and was suddenly at his side, holding onto his arm and trying to persuade him to calm down. "It's OK, it's OK," she said in English.

"It's not!" he replied, pointing a finger at the window. "It's supposed to be Julie Outerbridge. What happened to Julie?"

"You haven't seen the news?" she said, surprised.

Luka found it within himself to quieten enough to listen. "What news? I've been watching the Terraforming Committee."

"Julie Outerbridge was detained," she said. "There's a chance she'll be removed from her position."

"What for?"

The woman shrugged. "Something to do with a conspiracy against the Committee. I wasn't paying very much attention."

He swore again and collapsed back onto the pillow which was propped up against the headboard. He didn't understand how it could have happened. Unless she had confided in someone about what she was going to do, and they had leaked it to the authorities. But the decision to reveal everything at the Committee session had been something they had decided on together and agreed to keep secret.

"The head of UNMI is a friend of yours, isn't she?" said the nurse, matter-of-factly.

"I wouldn't say 'friend' exactly," said Luka, gazing up at the ceiling and wondering what he was going to do now.

"From what I understand," continued the nurse. "She talked to you for quite some time while she was here the other day. One of the staff told me he could hear your voices down the corridor."

The horror of that statement caused Luka to sit bolt upright. Julie hadn't told anyone, and he realized they must have been spied upon. How foolish he had been to believe that the same hospital staff who had brought him back from near death would have respected his privacy.

If the authorities had come for Julie, it was entirely possible they would come for him next. With Anita demanding he be extradited back to Thor Town, they wouldn't need much of an excuse.

He jumped out of bed and the sudden exertion caused his legs to buckle. He grabbed hold of the back of the visitor's chair until he steadied himself and then turned to the locker beside the bed where the clothes he'd been wearing under the rad-suit had been laundered and put away. He grabbed them and threw them on the bed.

"What are you doing?" said the nurse.

"Leaving."

Luka threw off his hospital gown, not caring that he was suddenly standing naked in front of the woman, and started getting dressed.

"You can't leave, you're not fully recovered."

"I can't stay."

He searched in the bedside locker for the WristTab he had been wearing when he left Thor Town. It wasn't set up properly, it only had the information on it that Erik had provided, but it was something. He found it in the top drawer of the locker and began strapping it to his wrist, only to stop halfway. WristTabs could be tracked. Even if he didn't load his personal profile onto it, there was no telling what Erik might have secretly installed. Erik had a competent technical mind and if he had hidden some kind of tracking program on there it could take Luka a long time to find and delete it. He couldn't take the chance. He unstrapped the WristTab again and threw it on the bed.

"Wait!" said the nurse, as Luka walked round the bed and headed for the door. "You can't go without seeing the doctor."

"No!" Luka turned back, afraid that she was going to tell one of the people who might have informed on him. "Please don't tell the doctor."

"You might need medication, you might need to come back for an appointment."

Her concern for his health was commendable, but she didn't understand what else was at stake. He glanced up at the window where Kareem was still talking about emission targets. "Don't tell anyone I've left. I need a head start. Can you do that for me?"

"Absolutely not! You need to get back into bed."

"Then… find the doctor if you must, but please take your time."

She scurried off with the haste of someone intending to do the complete opposite of taking her time, and Luka was forced to let her go. He couldn't waste precious time on the nurse, he had to get out and he had to get to the Terraforming Committee offices. He dashed out into the corridor, followed the signs to the exit, and left the hospital behind him to enter the main street of the city.

With no WristTab, no friends in Tharsis City other than Julie and no idea where anything was, Luka was completely lost.

He walked aimlessly for a few minutes along the unfamiliar street in the unfamiliar place, looking at the faces of unfamiliar people who passed by. He hoped, in among them, to find someone who looked friendly and helpful. He selected an old man who didn't seem to be in a hurry, although when he asked him for directions the man looked as if he had requested that he perform an aria from his favorite opera. In enclosed cities where everyone had a WristTab, no one ever asked for directions.

When the man realized Luka was serious, he obliged by

telling him how to find the Terraforming Committee office building. Then added, as an afterthought, "If you get lost, just follow the boring people."

Luka memorized the directions without difficulty and made his way to the corporate quarter where he found two rows of almost identical buildings facing each other across a pedestrian walkway. Each declared who they belonged to with the corporation name and logo above the front door, but Luka didn't need to read them all because a gathering of people outside one of the buildings told him where he needed to be. As he closed in, he saw the sign which confirmed it was the headquarters of the Terraforming Committee.

The gathering consisted of one ICN news team, very few security personnel in uniform and a few hangers on in civilian clothes. It was impossible to tell by looking whether any of them were boring or not.

Luka stopped about a hundred meters away, ducked into a doorway and considered his next move. He breathed deep and savored the sensation of twenty-one percent oxygen while he went through everything he knew, everything that had to be done and tried to think how he was going to do it.

Julie had a privileged position and was able to walk into the hall where everyone would take notice of what she said, whereas Luka was a nobody. His only notoriety was as the man who had collapsed outside the Oasis and nearly died. No one would listen to him unless he forced them to. So, he knew he couldn't replicate the plan the two of them had devised together. He had to think on his feet.

First, however, he needed to get inside. With so many people between him and the building, he had no chance of sneaking in, and so decided to go for the brazen and confident approach.

Secondly, whoever was in charge of security for the building clearly wasn't expecting any trouble. Why should they? Nothing terrible had happened at these events before. Well, Luka reflected, that was their problem. Or rather, it soon would be.

Luka smoothed down his shirt and ran his fingers through his hair. He stepped from the doorway, pulled his body up tall and made assertive strides to where, once again, he sought a friendly face. He chose a short woman with her hair tied back neatly in a bun who was leaning against a wall while watching the Committee proceedings on her WristTab.

"Excuse me," he said.

She lifted her eyes. "Yes?"

"I'm with the UNMI delegation. I've got some last-minute information for the man who's giving the presentation. It's rather important. After all the fuss about Ms Outerbridge, they sent me and I'm not sure where to go."

She glanced at her WristTab again where the small image of Kareem speaking to the hall was playing on the screen. "He's nearly finished! You better get a move on."

She ushered him into the hall and directed him to a corporate green room. The route turned out to be the corridor that led straight to the Committee Hall. He felt a flutter of nerves as he saw the two security officials standing either side of its elegant, double door entrance along with three ICN HoverCams which floated outside. The cameras were there to presumably catch the delegates' reactions as they left the meeting. For one, rash moment, Luka considered breaking through the doors and telling everyone what he knew about Anita, Gianni, and the asteroid crash. But he realized he would barely get far enough to utter a sentence before he would be stopped and almost certainly arrested. He needed to stick to the plan he had hastily concocted in the doorway in the street. If being confident and brazen had worked to get him into the building, there was a good chance it would work to get him past the security officials and down the corridor.

He lifted his chin and resumed his self-assured walk, choosing a path which took him around the back of the hovering cameras and away from their prying lenses. He even gave one of the officials a pleasant smile as he passed, to make it appear he had every right to be there. She didn't so much as register his presence, let alone return his smile, and continued to stare straight ahead in a world of her own.

A round of applause drifted from inside the hall and the HoverCams adjusted their positions to get ready for a possible exit of delegates. Luka had nearly passed by when the final camera backup and nearly collided with him. He was about to walk round it when he realized this was an excellent opportunity. With the security officials turned towards the doors, also expecting a stream of people to come out at any minute, Luka grabbed the HoverCam and put his hand over its one seeing eye. The camera protested, its hover fans whirring to pull it free, but they were only meant to levitate and direct it, not provide enough power to evade capture.

He muffled its struggle against his shirt and carried it away totally unseen by the man and woman on guard.

On the opposite side of the corridor to the hall were a series of rooms with signs on their doors indicating the various corporations. He read them as he passed: Helion, Inventrix, Phobolog. The fourth one was the one he was looking for: UNMI. He let himself in.

There was, to his relief, no one inside. Just a waiting room with three comfortable chairs set on one side of a short oval table laid out with refreshments and facing a window placed into the wall. The window was showing the live feed from the hall where it appeared that Kareem had just finished his presentation and was shaking hands with some of the other delegates in the front row. The volume, although turned down low, was loud enough for him to hear the voice of an ICN commentator recapping the main points of his speech.

Luka sat in one of the chairs and put the protesting HoverCam in his lap, making sure that its lens was facing down on his leg. He found the off switch and the camera stopped struggling, its fans slowed to a halt, and it became inert. Luka placed it on the table next to a plate of half-eaten canapés. He wasn't sure what the orange and white things were on the top of the toasted pieces of bread, but he ventured to try one. The tiny piece of food contained a burst of flavor which broke free on his first bite. Salty and crunchy on the outside while, at the same time, sweet and soft in the center. He couldn't imagine how anyone could have only eaten half of them. Luka gobbled up the rest, poured himself a cup of water from an elegant bottle which had been left on the table and sat back in the chair to wait.

The man talking over the ICN feed said that the Committee were taking a short break and the image on the window cut to the ICN studio where the commentator was sitting alongside a female guest. He turned to her: "So, pretty much what we expected from UNMI, continuing to concentrate on greenhouse gas emissions…"

As the guest in the studio began to agree with him, Luka heard the sound of the door opening. He stood up, brushed his hands free of canapé crumbs and prepared himself for who he hoped would enter.

Kareem, fresh from his presentation, stopped in the doorway on seeing Luka. "Who are you?" he demanded.

"Can you close the door?" said Luka, quietly.

"Not until you tell me who you are and what you're doing here."

"I'm a friend of Julie."

The sound of movement and voices from the delegates in the corridor became louder.

"Please," said Luka. "Can you close the door?"

Warily, Kareem pushed the door shut behind him. "You're not a friend of Julie," he said. "I know all of Julie's friends."

"Friend might be over stating the case, but she knows me. She came to visit me in hospital."

"Ah," said Kareem. "You're the man who collapsed outside the Oasis. What are you doing here?"

"I've come to do what Julie was going to do before she was detained."

A spark of interest flickered behind Kareem's eyes, but also a spark of suspicion. "What do you know about that?"

Luka explained as much as knew about what Julie had been planning to do.

Kareem sat down beside him and listened intently, but as Luka finished he shook his head. "I don't believe you. If she was going to do that, she would have told me."

"Even if she wanted to protect you?"

Kareem was silent for a moment, then admitted, "That sounds like Julie, always taking everything on herself. Would it really have been so bad to fill me in on the plan?" He shook his head like he disapproved. "It all makes sense now. That's why they took her before she could get to the Terraforming Committee. That's why they wouldn't let me see her before I gave the presentation. That's why they took the Tab away from her before she could hand it to me."

"It's not too late to do what she was going to do."

"But it is," said Kareem. "My presentation is over. I won't get the chance to address the hall again."

"Then we have to think of another way," said Luka. "We have to expose the truth about what happened and challenge Bard Hunter over what he did and what he knew. It's something I'm prepared to do myself, but I can't do it alone – I need your help."

CHAPTER THIRTY-SIX

Luka adjusted the strap of the shoulder bag Kareem had lent him, as he stood in the back of the hangar of the rover depot and watched the live ICN feed on a WristTab which Kareem had also agreed he could borrow. Bard Hunter, full of zeal and bravado, was at the podium.

"I propose to bring Deimos down!" he declared to the Committee Hall. "It will be an amazing spectacle that will prove to the entire solar system that we are serious. There may be some who say the very thought of sacrificing one of this world's natural satellites is sacrilege, but I say to them: terraforming Mars is a bold step, and we shouldn't be afraid of being bold to achieve our ambitions."

The audience responded with tentative applause while Bard soaked in their reaction.

The duty dispatcher at the rover depot, a man twice the size and half as pleasant as his female counterpart at Thor Town, interrupted Luka's viewing. "No, sorry," he said glancing down at the full-sized Tab resting on his arm. "The rover you brought from Thor Town ended up at Depot B. There's a big recovery bill attached to it, so you won't be able to take it out again until that's paid off."

"Never mind," said Luka, pretending to be disappointed.

"You could have looked all this up on the network, you know."

"I realize that, but I thought if it wasn't here, I could take out one of these other rovers."

He craned his neck to see past the man where approximately twelve rovers were parked nose to tail. It was a lie, of course. He wasn't intending to go anywhere, but it was a good excuse for him to be there.

"If you pay off that bill, I don't think it'll be a problem," said the dispatcher. "But you'll need to book it for another day because it's getting dark out there. All the controllers have gone home and I'm about to do my last round of checks before closing up. You can let yourself out."

"Thanks for your help," said Luka.

The man shrugged like it didn't matter to him one way or the other whether he was helpful or not, and disappeared off down the first row of rovers, making sure each hatch was locked as he went.

Luka approached the airlock which led to the admin area and the way outside. He peered through the porthole in the reinforced door to check it was still empty and touched the pad beside it. It triggered a loud, but brief warning buzzer and uncoupled the locks which released with a series of clicks. Luka glanced behind him as the airlock door opened on automatic arms and saw that the dispatcher was hidden from view by the rovers. Luka grinned to himself, knowing the dispatcher would believe he had left, and hit the control a second time. The door closed again as he doubled back into the hangar to hide behind a rover which had already been checked. It was at that moment he realized the ICN feed was still burbling away on the WristTab. He heard the commentator say that proceedings at the Committee funding review were ending for the day just before he muted it.

Remaining as still and as quiet as he could, Luka waited for the dispatcher to leave. It wasn't long before the warning buzzer of the inner airlock door sounded again to indicate he was alone. A few minutes later, the dimming of the lights around him confirmed it.

Luka sat on the hangar floor and took the stolen ICN HoverCam out of the shoulder bag. He had already severed it from ICN control and set in place a new program to highjack their broadcast so the feed from the camera would be sent directly to every window and every Tab on Mars which was monitoring ICN. He had to use the power of the ThorGate network to do it, as it was the only system he had access to which allowed him to create a backdoor to bypass the normal authentication required. He hoped it would be enough. If not, he discovered the HoverCam itself had its own recording facility which would operate as a backup. He made the final adjustments to his programming and left it on standby.

Next stop was the control room.

Luka had expected the dispatcher to have locked the airlock door to the control room as part of his final round of checks. Which would have been fine because, with both rooms fully pressurized, Luka would simply have to use the manual override. But it appeared the man had not bothered, and he was able to let himself in by simply touching the control.

The room had a perfect view of the hangar through a view port of toughened glass which took up the majority of the wall separating the two areas. Underneath was a bank of simple controls and a screen giving the status of the hangar: pressurized. Luka threw the empty shoulder bag across to the far side of the room and sat down at the screen to familiarize himself with how everything worked. With relief, he saw that all was required was a simple bit of programming. He accessed the central locking system, unlocked the front entrance which the dispatcher had only recently secured, and sent a message to Kareem to say that he was ready.

He had almost finished his programming when a warning buzzer alerted him that someone was coming through the airlock door at the entrance. Through the view port, he saw Kareem emerge from the opening and into the hangar.

The monitors in the control room relayed his distinctive English accent. "It was one of the first things I did when I came to Mars," he was saying to someone behind him. "If you're really going to bring Deimos down so Mars only has one moon, you should first see how it disappears behind Phobos when their two orbits coincide – it's quite breathtaking."

With a frisson of trepidation, Luka saw a pair of crutches reach through the airlock door, followed by Bard Hunter's injured and bandaged left leg and, finally, Bard Hunter himself in his trademark white cap.

Kareem had done it!

It was Kareem's suggestion to bring Bard to the rover depot. Luka had thought it was too risky and wanted to challenge him at the Terraforming Committee offices as he and Julie had originally planned. Kareem had convinced him that he would be arrested before he got anywhere near Bard Hunter, whereas at the depot, they could be sure of not being disturbed. Luka had liked the plan and added some modifications of his own, but it had all depended on Kareem being able to persuade CrediCor's CEO to fall for the ruse. It seemed his assurances to Luka that he could do it had been well founded.

Luka finished up the program he was working on at the control desk as Bard started to twig that something was wrong.

"Where is everybody?" he said, looking around as he steadied himself on his crutches. "Isn't this supposed to be an organized tour?"

"How strange," said Kareem. "Let me find out what's going on."

Kareem jogged up to the control room, let himself in via the airlock and gave Luka a self-satisfied grin. "This better be worth it," he said to Luka under his breath.

Luka nodded and readied his finger on the control. "I just need to take the HoverCam into the hangar. It's in your shoulder bag at the back – can you get it for me?"

Kareem glanced over to where Luka had earlier thrown the empty bag and went to retrieve it.

With Kareem on the other side of the room and his back to him, Luka hit the control and his program swung into action. The warning buzzer sounded as the airlock door began to close, Luka dashed for the opening and jumped through the gap just before it became too small for his body.

"What are you doing?" he heard Kareem yell behind him.

Luka turned to see Kareem's alarmed face through the door's porthole. Kareem frantically swiped at the control as the realization it wasn't responding spread across his face.

"Luka!" he screamed.

"The airlock has been preprogrammed," said Luka. "You can't stop it."

Kareem grabbed at the edge of the door and pulled. But his strength was not enough to defeat the closing, impenetrable barrier.

"It's better this way," Luka told him through the diminishing gap. "This is my fight, not yours."

At the last moment, Kareem retrieved his fingers and the airlock sealed shut. He mouthed angry words through the porthole, but their sound was cut off by the airtight door. The locks clicked into place and, with Kareem out of the way, Luka knew there was only one other man to deal with.

"What's going on?" said a voice behind him.

Luka turned to see Bard Hunter wavering on his crutches. The mighty CEO of CrediCor looked confused, small, and vulnerable standing all alone with his injured and bandaged leg.

Luka couldn't help but smile as he felt his plan falling into place. He touched the WristTab Kareem had given him and heard the faint, reassuring hum of the HoverCam waking and lifting off the floor. Elation surged through his body as he prepared to enact his revenge.

"You're going to tell me everything," he explained to Bard with calm assurance. "And you're going to do it all on camera."

CHAPTER THIRTY-SEVEN

Red warning lights circled around Luka and Bard, dancing across the static rovers as the air was slowly sucked out of the hangar. There should have been a warning siren too, but Luka had disabled it. He wanted to hear every word that Bard had to say for himself.

"What's going on?" said Bard. "Who are you?"

"I'm the one who has locked you in here," replied Luka, taking a step towards him.

Panicked, Bard looked up at the view port separating the hangar from the control room. "Kareem? Can you hear me?"

"He can hear you," said Luka. "But the airlock door is locked. He can't get to you."

Bard clasped his crutches under his armpits and balanced on his good leg as he operated his WristTab and brought it to his mouth. "This is Bard Hunter! I'm in Rover Depot A in Tharsis City. I need urgent assistance."

"They can't help you either. I've started the depressurization process and the airlock doors can't be opened until it's fully reversed."

"Are you mad?!" he screamed. "You'll kill us!"

"Possibly," admitted Luka. "But not for a little while. I've set the program to take a lot longer than normal, so we have enough air to talk."

Bard stared at Luka, and it was almost possible to see the terrified thoughts racing behind his eyes. An instinct for survival kicked in, he turned and ran, dropping his crutches and limping on his injured leg as he charged towards the sealed airlock door. Luka was prepared to let him go until he saw what Bard must have seen – the emergency button to repressurize the hangar. Luka snatched up one of the crutches and reached Bard just as his hand stretched out for the button.

He jabbed the end of Bard's crutch into the back of Bard's wounded leg, and it collapsed from underneath him. Bard fell sprawling to the floor. His trademark white cap slid off his head and skidded underneath the nearest rover.

Luka heard the whir of the HoverCam coming up behind him to witness it all.

He stood above Bard, with the crutch in his hand like a weapon, and breathed deep. It wasn't yet possible to tell that the air was getting thinner, but it wouldn't be long. Just to make sure, he bashed at the side of the mechanism with the end of the crutch until was knocked free of the wall and hung uselessly from a pair of wires.

"Now," said Luka, turning to Bard with an intimidating stare. "I want you to tell me how CrediCor crashed the asteroid into the ThorGate research station."

"It was an accident!" yelled Bard.

"Financial records prove CrediCor's asteroid controller was paid to do it."

An alarmed realization passed across Bard's face. "You know about that?"

"Course correction data pulled from the guidance system show the station was deliberately targeted."

"Someone bribed her to do it, I don't know who and I don't know why."

Luka was getting frustrated. If Bard countered every allegation he put him, they would run out of air before he ran out of lies.

Luka jabbed the point of the crutch on the floor and rested his hand on the top. "Let me tell you how oxygen deprivation works. First, you get a bit breathless. It's like you're walking up a hill, it feels normal. Then your lungs begin to hurt as they struggle to find enough oxygen. It starts to affect your brain, you get an ever worsening headache, you feel sick and dizzy. You might even start to hallucinate before you collapse, become unconscious and, eventually, suffocate. I can stop all that." He held up his WristTab. "But only after I've heard the truth."

Luka could feel himself getting breathless and he could see that Bard was feeling it too.

"You won't do it," said Bard, defiantly. "You're breathing the same air as me. If I die, you die."

"You've already killed the people I most cared about. Inside, I'm dead already."

"You're crazy." Bard shuffled himself away from Luka and sat himself up to lean against the wheel of the nearest rover. Luka stood over him and watched him squirm.

The HoverCam adjusted its position to get a better look.

"Remember the Rhine Valley Disaster?" said Luka. "The

factory owner took the blame, but the truth is, if CrediCor hadn't withdrawn its loan at a critical time, corners wouldn't have been cut and the chemical release would never have happened. CrediCor was warned about the consequences, but all those warnings were ignored. And *you*, Bard Hunter, signed off on it. You're the reason my family died from breathing in poison. So, yeah, I'm prepared to suffocate alongside of you if that's what it takes."

Fear burned in Bard's eyes. He was gasping now. "I did know about the crash," he admitted. "No one wanted ThorGate to run that research – *no one*. Everyone said it should have been Ecoline. This was a simple way to stop them. I was the one who paid my asteroid controller to organize it. She thought she was being bribed by an outside organization because I knew that was the best way to make sure she told only the essential people the most crucial information. I also made sure no one could trace the payments back to me. But no one was supposed to die. Ecoline was going to make sure that no one was killed – I don't know why that man was there."

"Gianni," said Luka.

"The station should have been empty."

"Ecoline paid Anita Andreassen to make sure all the scientists were evacuated from the building."

"I don't know the details," gasped Bard. "They dealt with all that."

Luka put too much weight on the crutch, it slipped out from under him and he would have fallen if he hadn't reached out for the hull of the rover next to him. He rested his hands there, taking gulps of thinning air. The muscles in his legs wouldn't be able to keep him standing much longer. "Then," he said, "you came along with a ready-made deal to save the day."

"Yeah," Bard whispered.

Luka dropped himself to sitting. His head was beginning to hurt, and thinking was becoming difficult. He might have misjudged how quickly he should deprive them of air. "And the Martian microbes?"

"Restore the air, for Christ's sake!" Bard broke into a wheezing cough, his lungs spasming in the struggle to breathe. He tried to crawl to reach the broken emergency button, even though it hung uselessly from a pair of wires, but he barely shuffled half a meter before he collapsed.

"The Martian microbes," Luka repeated. "I know Ecoline paid Anita to plant them under the Noctis City site."

"Their idea." Bard's words as he lay on the floor were quiet, slow and labored. "Ensure their biology experts controlled the site. Hit ThorGate harder. Take their city too."

Bard's face was blurry. Luka couldn't hear him anymore, just the whistling screeching in his ears. He had miscalculated; he'd thought someone would be there to rescue them by now. He had locked Kareem out of the control room systems, but the ones in the admin area should still be functioning. He had lied when he said he could restore the air using his WristTab. He had tried to link it, but the systems weren't made to talk to each other, and he hadn't had time to work it out.

Luka slumped to the floor and felt its cold, hard surface on his cheek. The pressure on his lungs and the pain in his chest seemed to lessen as he lay still, panting. Perhaps it was his dying brain releasing chemicals to ease his passing. He thought he heard footsteps and people shouting Bard Hunter's name, but it had to be another hallucination.

He was going to meet his wife and children soon. Death was coming and he embraced it gladly, with the satisfaction of knowing he was taking the man who killed his family with him.

CHAPTER THIRTY-EIGHT

Julie answered the door to her apartment to find Rufus Oladepo outside. His tall, lithe body and muscular build made him look as impressive as ever, as he stood in the corridor with the sense of calm authority he always seemed to carry.

"Hello, Julie," he said.

"Rufus! I suppose I should thank you for getting me released. Although, seeing as it was you who had me detained in the first place, I'm not sure that is appropriate."

"Indeed," he said. "Can I come in?"

Julie shrugged. She could hardly see how she could stop him. She left the door open and went into the kitchenette as he followed her in and closed the door behind him.

"Would you like some water?" she said, standing at the dispenser. "But, unfortunately, I only have one glass left because I dropped and smashed the other one. So, on reflection, I think I'll just get one for myself."

Julie filled her last remaining engraved glass and took it

over to the sofa. Rufus stood patiently and waited for her to
sit down before he sat next to her.

"I came to offer an apology," he said.

"You're sorry that you had me detained because, on
reflection, it would have been better for me to have delivered
my evidence before the Terraforming Committee, rather
than have a crazed man extract a confession out of Bard
Hunter and nearly kill him in the process. Am I right?"

He smiled. "I wasn't going to put it exactly like that..."

"Apology accepted," said Julie. "If you promise to do
something for me."

He looked a little taken aback, but maintained his calm
confidence. "Depends what it is."

"Kareem."

"If you're going to ask me to pardon him, I don't think
even I have the power to do that. He lured Bard Hunter to
the rover depot – almost to his death. He can't stay on Mars."

"He didn't know that was what he was doing."

Rufus merely responded with a doubtful look.

Julie took a sip of water to hide her discomfort and
watched the pattern of tiny rainbows on her hand caused by
light refracting in the cut glass. "He thought Luka was just
going to ask him some questions. He didn't know he was
going to suck out the air."

"In an airlock?" said Rufus.

Julie was going to have trouble getting round his use of
logic. "All I'm saying is, he's not the villain of the piece. Don't
treat him like a criminal, Mars needs men like him."

"I'll consider it."

"Thank you."

"If you consider something for me."

"Ah," said Julie. "I knew it couldn't just be an apology you came round for. You're after something."

"I need you to keep quiet about your asteroid investigation."

Julie, who was about to take another drink of water, almost spilled it over herself. "After Bard's confession was broadcast all over ICN? What's the point?"

"I believe they call it plausible deniability."

"You can deny it all you like, but CrediCor doing a secret deal with Ecoline behind everyone's back seems very plausible to me."

"Be that as it may, at the moment we have a confession extracted under duress. Without supporting evidence, Bard can claim that he only said what he said to save his own life."

"But I *have* the supporting evidence. It's in my report."

"Which has been filed with the Terraforming Committee and will be available for general scrutiny when the archives become public."

"In twenty years, Rufus! What good is it going to do after twenty years? We need to act now. Corporations have come to this planet and are running roughshod around the law, the Committee and the people who believe in the terraforming project. Don't let them get away with it, Rufus. Don't become part of it. Just look at what you did to me – detaining me is a slippery slope to individualized police forces per each organization! They're not separate countries with separate laws – we're supposed to be working together."

She couldn't stop. She continued, "Look what they've

done to Earth. Luka may be a 'crazed man', as you put it, but he wasn't wrong about what happened in the Rhine Valley Disaster. I looked it up to remind myself. Corruption doesn't belong on Mars, and you should be making sure it doesn't get a foothold."

"There are more ways to skin a cat, Julie."

"What's that supposed to mean?"

"It means, if I allow – indeed, *encourage* – Bard Hunter to be made the scapegoat for this whole sorry business, what happens then? He steps down from CrediCor and someone takes his place who I have no leverage over. Much better to keep Bard there where I can make sure he dances to my tune. At the moment, he's out there trying to atone for his sins after his dice with death, and that makes him a valuable commodity. Plus, of course, he has a personal fortune which he's currently plowing into his pet terraforming projects and I cannot deny that the Committee finds this rather useful."

"So, because he's rich, he can get away with it. Is that what you're saying?"

Rufus shifted position on Julie's sofa and, for once, seemed to lose his composure. "No, that's not what I'm saying."

It was Julie's turn to respond with a doubtful look.

"The point is, I've decided not to press charges against you and I would like to keep it that way, but on condition that you stay out of this whole asteroid conspiracy mess."

"What if I refuse?"

"You go to back to Earth, and likely to jail. The same for Kareem… it's not a course of action I would recommend."

Julie breathed deep, then drained her glass. It gave her a moment to decide what she was going to do. Not that she really had a choice. Rufus, the sly politician that he was, knew that he had the upper hand. "OK," she said, averting her gaze from him so she didn't have to see the glint of victory in his eyes.

"Excellent!" declared Rufus. He stood up and clapped his hands together like it was mission accomplished.

"I still have my own copy of that report," said Julie. "In a safe place, naturally."

"I don't doubt it," he replied.

"If I think that your alternative way of skinning a cat is bad for Mars, I won't hesitate to go public – and damn the consequences."

Rufus smiled. "Julie, that's what I like about you. You're a woman with integrity."

"I like to think so."

"Then we're agreed."

"So it would seem."

Julie stood and showed Rufus to the door.

"What are you planning to do now?" he asked.

"I was thinking about taking a walk around the Oasis. Enjoy a little taste of freedom after my incarceration."

"I rather meant more long term. Are you going to stay with UNMI and generate more of those fluro-whatsitsnames you're so keen on?"

"Perfluorocarbons," said Julie. "Super greenhouse gases."

"Yes, those things. Why does everything in science have such long and complicated names?"

"To confuse the non-scientists."

He laughed. "You could be right there. But you haven't answered my question."

"I don't know, Rufus." She opened the door and stepped aside to allow him to leave. "I'm going to think it over."

Kareem opened the door to his apartment and a look of astonishment formed on his face. He clearly wasn't expecting company because his shirt was unbuttoned and inside out like he had hastily thrown it on.

"Julie!" he exclaimed.

"Hello, Kareem," she said, calmly.

He stepped into the corridor and flung his arms around her. His masculine scent filled her nostrils as he squeezed her tight for a long and, if she was honest, slightly uncomfortable moment. She had to admit it was good to see him and gave him a hug in return.

They separated and he stepped back again. "I didn't know they'd let you out."

"Last night," she said. "I should have sent you a message before coming over, I'm sorry. I can come back another time."

"You absolutely can't! Come in, come in!" he waved her in and shut the door. "Sorry about the mess."

Julie had seen much messier apartments over the years. Kareem's place, by contrast, looked more lived in than unkept. His accommodation was basically the same design as hers, but crammed into a smaller space and without the kitchenette. The sofa was smaller and the window was smaller, but it was reasonably furnished for a single man and was much more comfortable than some of the places where the newer migrants were being housed.

Kareem went to button up his shirt, realized the problem, and had to take it off and put it on again. But it wasn't the only clothing anomaly in the room. There was also a bundle of clothes on the sofa which were too small to fit him and looked like they belonged to a woman. He bundled them up and dumped them on the table to free up space on the sofa.

"So," said Kareem, as he sat where the clothes had been. "Tell me what happened."

Julie took the seat next to him. "I was housebound for several days where I watched a lot of ICN and read a couple of books. There's not much to tell."

"I meant, why did they let you out?"

"I think they believe I'll be more likely to cooperate that way. But that's not why I'm here."

"Oh?"

The door to Kareem's bathroom opened and they both turned to see a woman emerge. She wore only a long robe cinched tight at the waist. It was the same woman Julie had met briefly at the restaurant. She wore no makeup, had tied her sleek, black hair up into a messy bundle at the back of her head and had the same deep brown, engaging eyes that Julie remembered.

She stopped as still as a statue and gaped when she saw Julie.

"Julie, you remember Areesha?" said Kareem.

"Yes," said Julie, not sure if she was more embarrassed for herself for intruding. "Hello again."

"Areesha, you remember my boss, don't you?" said Kareem.

"Julie Outerbridge, yes." Her face flushed red. "I'm going to, um… I'm going to get dressed."

She avoided Julie's gaze as she hurried into the bedroom.

"You should have said you had company," said Julie, when they were alone again.

"Oh, Areesha doesn't mind."

Julie glanced over to the bedroom door and suspected that she probably minded quite a bit, but decided not to get involved.

"What is it you wanted to talk about?" asked Kareem.

Julie took her time and chose her words carefully. "How would you like to run UNMI in the future?"

"Run UNMI?" Kareem shrugged. He thought. He blinked. "Well, yeah. Who doesn't want a promotion? In the future – sure! What's going to happen to you? Are they going to charge you with something?"

Julie shook her head. "No, nothing like that. I'm thinking about going home."

"Home? Earth home?"

"Yeah. Mom's all alone since Dad died and I have a nephew I haven't seen – plus another on the way. I'm not too old that I can't make another life for myself back there. I think it's time."

"I'd like to say I'd be happy to take over, but I've got this Bard Hunter thing hanging over me," said Kareem.

"I don't think that will be a problem."

"You didn't hear the threats the CrediCor people shouted at me when they came to rescue him. I thought the rover depot would be a quiet, secluded place to question him and I knew I had the perfect excuse to get Bard Hunter there. What I didn't know was what Luka had planned. I feel stupid and embarrassed, but it's true."

"I believe you," said Julie. "As I say, I don't think it will be a problem."

Kareem looked suspiciously at her. "You've done something, haven't you? Don't think you have to put yourself out to protect me. I made my own foolish mistake, I'm prepared to take the consequences."

"Kareem." She leaned over, took his hand and clasped it between her two palms. As she looked into his eyes to convince him she was serious, she remembered this was the same gesture Bard had used with her when they had first met. "The things that I do are up to me. If it means that one of the most talented and enthusiastic men on Mars can lead the United Nations Mars Initiative onto greater things, then that's all that matters."

Kareem slowly pulled his hand away and she let it go. "I don't know what to say."

"Accept the promotion you deserve. It's not strictly up to me, but I still have some sway with the UN on Earth. They'll realize there's no one better. It won't be for a while, anyway. They advise months of preparation before someone who's been on Mars for as long as I have goes back to Earth. My body hasn't had to cope with that gravity level for a long time."

"I'll be sorry to see you go, Julie."

"Me too."

A silence fell between them. One that was broken by the bleep of her WristTab.

"That's one thing I'm not going to miss," she grumbled. "This wretched thing going off all the time."

"I guess that's something I'll have to get used to," said Kareem.

"Yeah." She glanced down to dismiss the notification, but paused with surprise when she saw who it was from. "Bard Hunter has sent me a message."

"What does he want?"

Julie opened the message and read it out to him. "Dear Julie, I'm delighted to say that the Terraforming Committee has approved my plan to bring Deimos down. You were the first person on Mars who I told about what I was planning to do and, I remember, even though you thought it was a bad idea, you still sat with me and held my hand while I was trapped under the rover, and I shall be forever grateful. I would be delighted if you could join me as my personal guest to watch the amazing spectacle on a date to be arranged. Yours most sincerely, Bard."

"Wow," said Kareem. "Do you think he has an ulterior motive?"

"I don't know," said Julie, still looking at the words of the message. "I suppose the only way to find out is to accept his invitation."

CHAPTER THIRTY-NINE

Rufus Oladepo looked across the podium of the Terraforming Committee Hall to where Luka was standing, flanked by two security officials and in front an array of empty seats. If it was Rufus's intention to make Luka feel small and helpless, then he had succeeded. The man was not only impressive in stature, but he was also the ultimate power on Mars and, to emphasize that, he was backed by all the political leaders of the Committee who stood behind him. Luka examined the faces of each and every one of them and saw no emotion as they stared down on him from their exalted position.

Luka, barely out of hospital, and still breathing supplementary oxygen from two prongs inserted into his nostrils from a line to an air tank on the floor at his feet, couldn't stop himself physically trembling as he waited to hear his fate.

"Luka Schäfer," said Rufus, in a booming voice made

more imposing by the acoustics of the room. "You have been found guilty by this committee of the attempted murder of Bard Hunter and shall be sentenced accordingly."

The weight of anxiety pressed down on him. Even though he had admitted everything, even though he had broadcast his own crime to the whole of the planet, he still feared for his future. He was fully prepared to accept whatever sentence they saw fit, but he wasn't sure he had the strength to endure it.

"Before I pass sentence, the Committee would like to acknowledge that your act – even though it was heinous and misguided – highlighted some serious failings at the hierarchy of the corporate structure on Mars. The exposure of these failings is leading to widespread reform as we speak, and many have expressed the view that we should be grateful to you for revealing the corruption and misdeeds which threaten to blight our growing society on this planet. I have also been asked to make allowances for the personal sacrifices you have made to bring these matters to our attention. Nevertheless, attempted murder remains a serious issue that comes with serious penalties."

Luka went cold and staggered sideways. His leg knocked against the oxygen tank and it wobbled until the security official standing next to him caught it and set it straight again.

"However, this is Mars," said Rufus. "We have no prisons here. Not yet. We also have need of people with your skills. It is the view of the Committee, therefore, that your punishment shall be to work for the good of Mars society in any role that we, or any future administration, sees fit. In the light of this, Luka Schäfer, I have decided to pass a *suspended* sentence on you of twenty years."

Confusion clouded Luka's mind as he stared up at Rufus.

Rufus looked directly into Luka's eyes. "Do you understand what I am saying?"

"I..." Luka's mouth was dry. He had to swallow before he could speak. "I don't think so."

"It means you will not go back to Earth. You will not go to jail. The sentence is suspended. But, if you commit another crime within that period, those possibilities could occur."

"So... I'm free?" He barely dared to hope.

"You will be assigned a supervisor at the Terraforming Committee offices who you will report to once a month and you must abide by a nighttime curfew for a year. But, yes, other than working in the roles assigned to you, you are free to go."

Luka's legs gave way from beneath him with the shock and he fell backwards onto the seat in the row behind. He allowed his head to fall into his hands as days of pent up anxiety evaporated, relief caused his muscles to release their tension and emotion flowed out of him in uncontrollable sobs.

Out on the street, once Rufus had pulled away the attention of the waiting ICN crew by offering to make a statement, Luka headed back to his accommodation. After leaving hospital, he had been assigned an apartment where he was put under house arrest and, without anywhere else to go, it made sense to return there.

But he had barely walked a few steps before he saw a tall,

blonde man leaning against the wall of a nearby building and looking back at him. With a sting of recognition, Luka knew it was Erik Bergman and a sudden anger swelled inside of him.

"Luka!" The Swede's face beamed into a smile as he waved an exuberant hello.

Luka pretended not to hear. He clasped his air tank tighter under his arm, averted his gaze and kept walking.

"I came to Tharsis City, especially to see you," said Erik, bounding towards him. "I'm so pleased the Committee let you go."

Luka was forced to stop and look up into the smug face of the man who had betrayed him. "Leave me alone!"

He wanted to ball his hand into a fist and hit him. After that, he wanted to keep hitting him until Erik knew what it was like to feel his life being pulled away. But such an act of violence would breach the terms of his sentence and so he forced himself to hold back.

Erik looked confused. "I thought we could catch up."

"Catch up?" Luka raised his voice so loud that it echoed off the surrounding buildings. Passersby hurried past while pretending not to notice. "You tried to *kill* me!"

Erik's confusion deepened. "What are you talking about?"

"You sent me out to die in a solar flare."

Not so much as a flicker of guilt or remorse passed across Erik's face. Luka couldn't bear to look at him anymore and resumed his walk, feeling the pain in his damaged lungs as he breathed harder and faster.

"I don't know what you think I did, but it wasn't me," insisted Erik.

Luka stilled and thought back to the food which was brought to him when Anita had him locked up. As he went over the events in his head, Luka remembered it had been the security official who had told him the tray had been sent by his "friend". After that, Luka had assumed it had been Erik who had engineered his escape. It hadn't occurred to him that it could have been a false assumption.

Luka stopped again and turned. "You didn't send me a WristTab hidden in a bowl of stew?"

"No! Luka, I have no idea what you're talking about."

"What about the rover? The one that stranded me? The one that was booked out in *your* name?"

"I wouldn't do that to you – I wouldn't do that to anyone. If I did, do you think I would put my name on it?"

Luka hung his head, embarrassed that he had doubted his friend. It was obvious who had tried to kill him. "Anita," he said. She must have used Erik's name because she knew Luka would trust something which appeared to come from him. And she had been right.

"I'm sorry I didn't believe you when you told me about her," said Erik. "That woman has a lot to answer for."

"Yeah." Luka was full of emotion. After all he'd lost on Earth, all he'd thought he'd lost on Mars, it seemed that there was a glimmer of hope for him.

"Why don't we talk over lunch? I'll pay – I've got some news I want to share."

Luka had assumed they would go to one of the mass catering halls in Tharsis City to eat, like they had done so many times back at Thor Town, but Erik had really meant it when he said he was going to pay. He led them to a quiet restaurant which was experimenting with opening in the middle of the day for light meals such as sandwiches and soup. By the look of it, it wasn't a successful experiment as there was only one other table occupied when they arrived.

They were met by the owner, an older man with hollow cheeks and a thin wisp of gray hair who greeted them with enthusiasm. When he recognized Luka, his face brightened even more as he reached out to shake his hand. Which he did vigorously.

"Luka Schäfer!" he exclaimed. "Can I just say, I think it's brilliant what you did. It was about time someone stuck it to those corporation heads. A bunch of crooks, the lot of them."

Embarrassed, but also gratified, Luka let the man pump at his hand until he ran out of steam and let go. The man then composed himself, resumed the manner of a restaurateur and invited them to sit at any of the seven available tables. Luka, wary of being recognized by somebody else, opted for the back corner where he pulled his chair tight into the two meeting walls to huddle away from the rest of the world as much as he could. He placed his air tank on the spare seat next to him and adjusted the tube so it ran over his shoulder and down his back to be out of the way as much as possible.

From his vantage point at the back of the restaurant, he could see how old and tired it had become. In the evening, the owner most likely kept the lights down low to create an intimate atmosphere, but it was brighter during the day which allowed the scuff marks on the walls and the wear marks on the floor to show. Printed posters on ageing paper along one wall proudly detailed the history of the place, with pictures of its grand opening showing the smiling owner, when he was a little younger with a little more hair, presiding over a restaurant packed with diners. It also detailed the man's journey from university on Earth, to being chosen to come to Mars to work on an early construction project, the diagnosis of a heart condition which led to a complete career change and a decision to go into the restaurant business. It was obviously a personal project for the man and Luka felt sorry that he didn't seem to have very many customers.

On the opposite wall, a window showed the live view across the desolate Martian landscape. Luka gazed at it, while Erik spent an inordinate amount of time studying the menu, watching a single rover traverse across the plain with a trail of dust stretching out behind it.

Luka, still dealing with the emotional fallout of being freed by the Terraforming Committee, didn't have much of a stomach for food and ordered soup while Erik eventually went for a very grand-sounding sandwich platter. The owner brought them both a mug of water to drink while they waited for their meals, and they began to talk.

"How are you?" Erik asked.

It was a general question, but the way he glanced over the table suggested he was referring to the oxygen line running into Luka's nostrils. "My lungs are bad," Luka said, "but the doctors say if I improve enough over the next month, I shouldn't have to carry an oxygen tank around with me the whole time."

"What about work? They said at the hearing they were going to give you some kind of job."

"I have an appointment at the Terraforming Committee offices next week to find out. I have a feeling I might be back working on the Noctis City project. Although, I'm in no condition to do any physical labor."

"That's ironic, seeing as that's what you came here to do."

"Yeah," said Luka, who was still waiting for the reality of it to sink in. "What about you? You said you had some news?"

Erik's smile widened. "I got promoted!"

"Congratulations! Promoted to what?"

"Anita's old job: Head of Martian Projects." Erik grinned again and drank from his mug of water as the restaurant owner brought over their soup and sandwiches.

Erik's platter was a triumph of presentation over generosity with four neatly cut sandwich quarters placed equidistant around a small plate with a swirl of brown relish between each one. Luka's soup was vegetable broth with recognizable green and orange pieces of beans and carrots suspended in the thick liquid. It smelled amazing and it made him hungry after all.

"What happened to Anita?" asked Luka. "I heard she'd been detained, but I don't know what happened after that."

"She's denying everything, so there will have to be a trial. I don't think they'll let her off with a suspended sentence, like you. There's already talk about having to build a prison on Mars."

"So, we really are shipping all of human life to the new frontier," reflected Luka.

"Yeah."

Luka scooped up a spoonful of soup from the edge of the

bowl where it was cooler and brought it testily to his mouth. As he crunched down on a piece of green bean, the soup released a salty, wholesome sense of real vegetables which warmed him from the inside. Either the restaurant owner was a marvel in the kitchen, or Luka was learning to enjoy the taste of freedom.

"Why haven't they arrested Bard?" he said.

Erik scoffed at the very suggestion. "A corporation head vital to the terraforming project? No chance! He's busy mending his reputation by launching an all-out war on corruption and vowing to stop unscrupulous practices being brought from Earth."

"Even though he was the one who brought them."

"I heard him say on ICN that he only confessed to all those things because he wanted to save his own life. He denies any of it was true and blames everything on some shady figure at Ecoline."

Luka looked across the table at Erik through the steam rising from his soup. "Surely people don't believe him?"

"He can be very convincing when he wants to be. Which, seeing as it's his future on the line, he *really* wants to be. They say he's actually making a difference in the way business is being done out here. I suppose nothing stops corruption more than being caught in the act."

"You can't be saying it's for the best?"

"I'm saying, if there's nothing you can do about it, you're better off looking on the bright side. You achieved a partial victory – you exposed the truth and you've escaped with your life and your freedom. That's not a bad deal when you think about it."

Luka considered his friend's words as Erik's WristTab interrupted their conversation with a bleep.

"I'm getting these more often now that I've been promoted. Did I mention that I've been promoted?" He grinned at his joke as he glanced down at the device. "Oh, it's a message from Pete."

"Pete?" said Luka, remembering the affable American with a smile. "How is he?"

"His wife gave birth to a baby boy last week, so he's wandering around with the stunned and tired expression of a proud dad."

The thought of Pete becoming a father brought an inner glow which warmed Luka even more than an amazing tasting soup ever could.

"He says I should watch ICN – there's breaking news."

Erik brought up the news channel on his WristTab, but Luka didn't want to watch it on such a small screen. He waved across to the restaurant owner. "Excuse me! Could you change the window to ICN, please?"

"For Luka Schäfer, it will be my pleasure!" said the man.

The view of the Martian landscape disappeared from the window and was replaced by the image of a grave-looking group of people. A banner across the top declared it was *LIVE FROM THE ADVISORY BOARD FOR MARTIAN SCIENCE*.

The man in front spoke in a Russian accent and Luka remembered him as the one who had been interviewed about the discovery of life on Mars on the day it was first announced.

"As you know," he began, glancing down at the Tab he was

holding and then back to the ICN camera. "The discovery of what we believed were Martian microbes during a routine survey at the Noctis City construction site was made public after only initial tests were concluded. This was an unauthorized leak of information that, speaking for myself, I would rather not have happened."

He pierced the camera lens with a steely look which conveyed the loathing he had for the person who had leaked it. "Since that time, as in all science, we have worked to confirm or deny our original analysis – always keeping an open mind and trying not to get caught up in all the excitement which, understandably, was all around us. We conducted many more excavations and studies of the site and we found more living microbes in the aquifer, but only in that one isolated place.

"We believe this is consistent with the suggestion that the microbes had not been living there for centuries, but had been put there within the last few months by human hands."

There was some murmuring behind the camera. The HoverCam itself wobbled a little. The man, and the faces of the people behind him, remained stoic.

"Following the recent allegations that these microbes were not Martian at all, but genetically engineered Earth microbes created by human science, we have extensively studied this possibility. In addition, we received information from a whistleblower at Ecoline which has confirmed our conclusion. The microbes discovered under the Noctis City construction site are native to Earth, genetically altered to suggest they might have come from Mars. In short, this was a cleverly designed hoax to make people believe that life had evolved independently on this planet when, in fact, there is no evidence to suggest that is the case. I am stating categorically to you today that we have not, sadly, found the holy grail of life on Mars. If it exists, or has ever existed, then it still remains out there for us to find."

The Russian turned from the camera and disappeared into the huddle of his grave-faced colleagues while the words, *LIFE ON MARS: HOAX!* appeared at the bottom of the screen.

"Wow," said Erik, as ICN cut to an excited reporter who began babbling a repeat of the information which had just been relayed. "So, Anita really did plant fake microbes under the Noctis City construction site. This means you were right, Luka."

"Do you know what else this means?"

"What?"

"It means that humans – and any other creatures we might have brought with us – are officially the only lifeforms on the planet." Luka held up his mug of water to propose a toast. "To humans on Mars!"

Erik laughed, picked it up his mug and clonked it against Luka's. "To us!" he said.

CHAPTER FORTY

Julie approached the ridge of Noctis Labyrinthus, near to where she had stood all those months ago and looked down at the devastation caused by the crashed asteroid. It had all been swept away with the remaining pieces of the rock removed to salvage the nickel and iron contained within them. In their place was a new and impressively large research station which sprouted various satellite and radio receivers from the top of its roof. In front of the building were the arching transparent domes of greenhouses where some plant experiments would take place. At a distance, they looked to be empty, but she imagined they would soon be full of adapted plants which the scientists hoped would have enough resilience to survive in the harsh climate. Perhaps they would be strong enough to live outside of the greenhouses where the canyon's own natural geography would help protect them from the worst that Mars had to offer.

Julie took a few more steps further down the ridge to get a better look at where Noctis City was gradually emerging out of the bedrock. ThorGate had managed to wrestle back control of the project after the discovery of life on Mars was proved to be a hoax. It had set ThorGate back some considerable time and other corporations had used that to their advantage so there were now many more plans in the pipeline for cities to be built in that region of Mars.

Nevertheless, ThorGate was still determined that Noctis City would be the most impressive of them all and hints of its future grandeur could already be seen in the construction. Struts of a new magnesium-steel alloy rose out of the ground in a skeleton of what would soon be homes and workplaces and recreation facilities. There would even be, in the center, a large park to rival the Oasis. At the far end, where machines and migrant workers in rad-suits busied themselves around the construction, they had begun to fill in some of the walls to form embryonic buildings and streets. It would be, she hoped, for the sake of every human being who would eventually live there, a triumph of engineering and design.

As she stared at it, she realized she had been out there for longer than intended. She needed to get back to Tharsis City because that night – her last night on Mars – was to be the night that Deimos was brought down. If she was to see the impressive sight from the best vantage point possible, she needed to claim her place on Bard's "party bus".

As the sun was getting low in the sky, the vehicle that Bard had specially built for the occasion left Tharsis City and traveled out into the Martian desert where it was to witness the amazing spectacle of bringing Deimos down.

The bus consisted of two decks. The lower one was reserved for the driver and support crew, plus a team of caterers who were in charge of the all-important refreshments. The upper deck was where the privileged guests could mingle under a transparent roof with windshields on all four sides to give them an unhindered view of the stricken moon's fall from grace.

Everyone who was anyone was on Bard's party bus. Rufus was there, as were the leaders of all the other political parties which made up the Terraforming Committee, along with all the heads of the corporations and a select number of CrediCor personnel. All of whom were mingling and chatting as if it were a corporate event on Earth. It was all very surreal. They were even serving real wine, as Julie discovered when she took a sip from the glass of pale yellow liquid passed to her by one of the staff. It must have cost Bard an absolute fortune to bring it out from Earth.

They reached Sinai Planum just as the daylight faded and the sky went dark. Even without the spectacle of a descending moon, it was beautiful. Mars still had no clouds and no pollution to speak of, so the stars were as clear as if Julie were looking through the portal of a spaceship. Thousands of individual pinpricks of light from thousands of suns many light years away gazed down on them while the hazy band which made up the milky way snaked through the middle of the sky. It was an awe-inspiring backdrop to the night's events. Julie gazed up at the wondrous sight, sipped her wine and felt a little dizzy at the enormity of it all.

"Julie!" Bard came up to her holding out his hands to clasp Julie's fingers between his two palms.

"You're looking handsome tonight," she said, admiring the black suit he was wearing which contrasted rather effectively with his white cap.

"Thank you," he smiled. "You also look stunning."

Julie was wearing her one and only dress which she brought out for special occasions. It was deep blue velvet with a slanting line of sparkles which ran in a wave from her left shoulder to her right hip, very much like the stars of the milky way. "It's my last chance to wear it. I have a limited payload for my journey back to Earth and I can't take it with me."

"You're leaving soon?"

"Tomorrow."

"I hope all goes well."

"As things seem to be going well for you," Julie suggested.

"I don't know," said Bard, rubbing his leg where it had been trapped under the rover. "I'm having to have physiotherapy twice a week."

"I was more referring to Luka Schäfer's conviction and Anita Andreassen facing charges of murder. Whereas you are standing on a party bus serving expensive wine to your friends."

"That's because Luka and Anita are criminals, whereas I, as you know, am innocent."

"Of course," said Julie, placating him. She sipped at her wine. "As I say, things seem to be going very well for you."

He chuckled. "You're a very funny woman, Julie. Maybe when I return to Earth, we could meet up somewhere and chat about old times."

"That would be…" Julie considered which word she should choose to end the sentence. "Interesting."

He gave her a knowing smile, then abruptly turned, limping slightly, and walked to the front of the bus where he had spotted the Chair of the Terraforming Committee.

"Rufus!" Bard declared and clasped the politician's hand between his two palms, causing him to break away from the people he had been talking to. "How's it going?"

"I like your bus, Bard," said Rufus. "How much did this wine cost you?"

Julie stopped listening. She had had enough of schmoozing politicians and corporate heads for one lifetime and was glad to be soon leaving it all behind.

"Look! Phobos!" shouted a woman on the left side of the bus. Julie didn't know who she was, and so imagined she must work for CrediCor. As the woman pointed up into the sky, everyone turned to look in the same direction. Julie could just about make out the knobbly celestial body against the black of the night.

"It's so small!" said one of the partygoers.

"I can't see it!" said another.

"Never mind Phobos, where's Deimos?" said a third.

"The moon started its descent three days ago," declared Bard, breaking away from Rufus to address the whole of the bus. "We have been bringing it lower and lower as it lapped the planet ever since. It means Deimos is set on its final journey and there's nothing now that anyone can do to stop it."

A sense of trepidation descended over the bus. Julie wondered how many people were thinking, like she was, about the asteroid disaster than had killed a man and destroyed a research station only months before.

"Before Deimos comes into view, I want to share something with you," Bard looked around the faces of each and every partygoer gathered on the upper deck to ensure he held their full attention. "I've just had official confirmation that the average temperature on Mars at the equator is now minus twenty-seven degrees. That's a whole three degrees warmer than when the Terraforming Committee was formed."

The assembled dignitaries gasped and broke into a round of applause. Even Julie tucked her wine glass under her arm and clapped at the achievement.

"All thanks to the warming actions of CrediCor's asteroid program."

"And UNMI's greenhouse gas emissions!" Julie shouted from the back.

Bard grinned. "As our friend from the United Nations Mars Initiative points out, hurling asteroids at Mars isn't the only way we're warming the planet – but let's face it, it's the main way!"

The assembled guests laughed. It wasn't the funniest joke in the universe, but they were probably slightly drunk.

Julie had to admit to herself, however, that despite her reservations over inviting corporations to take part in the terraforming project, they had achieved far more than UNMI had before the Committee took over and in far shorter a time. It seemed that, for the sake of humanity's future on Mars, it had been the right thing to do.

"I believe it's almost time." Bard turned to face the front

windshield and pointed out into the night sky. "Deimos shall appear soon, coming low over the horizon, just there."

He pointed out through the front windshield and people jostled to get a better view. Julie felt the anticipation quicken her heart as she waited, like everyone around her, for the moment they had all been told was inevitable.

She saw the glow before she saw the moon, looming up over the horizon like the first rays of the morning sun, tantalizing at the edge of the land. The glow turned to fire as Deimos rose above the surface of the planet in a huge, blazing ball of rock hurtling through the atmosphere. Others around her gasped as the fireball became brighter, traveling fast against the black and cutting through the air like a flaming arrow.

The fiery moon swooped to its death directly ahead of them, crashing into the distant plain with the energy of a nuclear missile. It exploded into an immense mushroom cloud which bellowed up into the night and was lit dramatically by the still glowing remnants of Deimos beneath.

Tremors shook the bus and people screamed as some of them staggered sideways and others grabbed onto whatever was to hand to stop them from falling. Several people dropped their wine glasses and the sound of them smashing on the deck were like cymbal crashes in the great orchestral movement that was Bard's grand gesture in terraforming.

The maverick CEO – who had been holding onto a handrail at the side the whole time – whooped at his triumph and began dancing around the bus, hopping on his good leg and engaging everyone who was prepared to look foolish in a victory dance. Taking their cue from him after realizing they weren't going to be killed by the falling moon or the resulting earthquake, the partygoers laughed and clapped along.

Eventually Bard calmed down a bit and returned to the front of the bus where he addressed the assembled, slightly drunk people once again. "I'm glad you were all able to come to celebrate this milestone of Mars terraforming tonight, but I wanted to remind everyone that this is only one step on a very long journey. We have warmed the planet by three degrees, but we still have thirty-five degrees to go before we reach our goal of an average temperature of plus eight. It is, as my grandfather might say, still a bit nippy out there."

He waited for his audience to laugh at his joke, and they obliged.

"The amount of oxygen on Mars remains at near zero, but air pressure has increased and we are making progress. That progress will mean that, one day, forests will grow out on the planet's surface without the need for a greenhouse or a protective dome. The trees and plants will produce oxygen to enrich the atmosphere so we can breathe, and it will be warm enough for water to exist as liquid on the surface for long periods. These amazing things will not happen in our lifetimes, but they will happen if we persevere. In the future, our descendants will walk on Mars without the need for rad-suits and they will do so within a self-sustaining ecosystem that flourishes with oceans and fish and mammals and birds.

"But we can only do this," he continued. "If we cooperate. I know to some of you corporate heads, this may seem like a fanciful notion. We are rivals in a competitive world, after all. But if I have learnt anything from my short time on this planet, it is that the global warming I am able to achieve today is the global warming that will benefit you tomorrow. The oxygen that you produce tomorrow will be the oxygen that people working for all corporations will breathe the day after. We all have our individual goals and our individual projects, and it is right that we pursue them. But, in doing so, we must remember that we are sharing the same planet and working towards the same, ultimate end."

He paused and glanced down to gather his thoughts. His captivated audience remained quiet in anticipation. "I debated with myself whether to share something else with you, tonight. Something personal. After due consideration, witnessing the amazing thing we have just seen and drinking two glasses of wine, I have decided that I will.

"I remember that when I was trapped under a rover out on the Martian surface all those months ago, it was the head of a rival corporation – UNMI – who sent out a distress call while she sat next to me in a dust storm and told me not to give up hope. It was workers from a rival corporation – ThorGate – who heard that distress call and came to save my life. Without my rivals, I wouldn't be standing here speaking to you today. So, I ask you to think about the benefits of cooperation when you plan your various schemes to harness the resources of this planet and be grateful that you don't have to have the painful experience of a rover falling on top of you to learn this very valuable lesson."

He waited for his message to be absorbed by every single person in front of him.

"Now," he said, taking hold of the brim of his white cap. "Let's party!"

He threw his cap spinning into the air and it came down on a tray of wine glasses being carried by an unsuspecting member of staff who was so startled he nearly dropped the tray. The moment broke the tension, everyone laughed and the party began again.

It was a rousing speech and Julie couldn't help being moved by it. Bard was an expert at playing a crowd and he wouldn't let a little thing like truth stand in the way of making a good impression. But, on this occasion, she believed he was being sincere.

It affected her more because, in the morning, when the sun rose again on the dusty Martian plain to reveal a huge crater with the remains of a crashed moon in the middle of it, the bus would return to Tharsis City and she would make her way to the spaceship that was due to carry her home. She would leave Mars behind her forever, but the work would continue. It would take many generations, much hard work and many scientific endeavors, but one day she was certain they would succeed in their goal of terraforming Mars.